"I don't get involved with the subjects of my stories," Melissa informed him heatedly. "A reporter has to stay objective."

"I see," Robert returned, gravely mocking. He slipped one arm around her waist, then tilted her chin up with his other hand. "Then you won't want me to do this to you while you're here," he murmured softly, just before he dipped his head and took her mouth in a kiss.

Melissa stood in frozen shock while he caressed her mouth with his own, gently exploring and probing with his tongue, arousing her to the point where she began to cling to Robert as though he offered the only security in a suddenly shaken world....

Dear Reader,

We're so proud to bring you Harlequin Intrigue. These books blend adventure and excitement with the compelling love stories you've come to associate with Harlequin.

This series is unique; it combines contemporary themes with the fast-paced action of a good old-fashioned page turner. You'll identify with these realistic heroines and their daring spirit as they seek the answers, flirting with both danger and passion along the way.

We hope you'll enjoy these new books, and look forward to your comments and suggestions.

The Editors
Harlequin Intrigue
919 Third Avenue
New York, N.Y. 10022

SECRETS OF THE HEART

JACQUELINE ASHLEY

Harlequin Books

TORONTO • NEW YORK • LONDON
AMSTERDAM • PARIS • SYDNEY • HAMBURG
STOCKHOLM • ATHENS • TOKYO • MILAN

Harlequin Intrigue edition published August 1984

ISBN 0-373-22004-9

Chapter One

At dawn on the morning of her twenty-eighth birthday, the peace and quiet Melissa McKee had come back to her hometown of Rockport, Maryland, to find was shattered as usual by the triumphant crowing of her Grandma Kate's star rooster, Algernon.

Normally Algernon's announcement that he was anticipating his day's work with a great deal of enthusiasm didn't bother Melissa in the slightest. Upon her return two months ago she had found it a welcome change from the rumblings of traffic and the screams of police sirens she'd grown used to during her years in Washington, D.C., and as time passed, she had found it a welcome reminder that she was out of the rat race now. She no longer had to arise from her bed to the prospect of yet another assignment to investigate such charming phenomena on the American scene as child pornography rings, arms smuggling, or the ways some of the powerful political elite of the country found to amuse themselves, such as with cocaine orgies.

This particular morning, however, Melissa had a slight hangover, a result of having overindulged her taste for her grandmother's dandelion wine the night before in anticipation of her birthday, and she was in no mood to listen to Algernon's anticipatory crowings.

"Oh, God, Algie, can it, will you?" she muttered as she fumbled for the pillow on the other side of the bed to pull over her head.

Fortunately Algernon's fervent dedication to duty meant that his cacophonous early morning greetings didn't last long, and before the last crow had died away, Melissa was asleep again, the pillow still over her head. Unfortunately that fact meant that she slept through her alarm for a good half hour before her inner clock succeeded in prompting her to wake up and try to make it to work on time.

Being on time shouldn't have mattered too much, since she didn't have any hot deadlines to meet. In fact, the summer season news was so slow as to be practically nonexistent. However, her editor, Malcolm Keller, an unsentimental relic from the days of the sweatshop, would have a few choice words to say if she wandered into the office so much as five minutes late, and though he was as likely to shove a broom as a typewriter at her when she did get in, he considered the *Rockport News* a candle lighted to curse the darkness crawling through the streets of its namesake, and he required a similar attitude from his star reporter.

Therefore, with much groaning and head clutching, Melissa shut off the alarm and dragged herself out of bed, muttering to herself that as birthdays went, this one was starting out a real bummer.

Her mood improved slightly after a shower, and as she peered into the mirror while she brushed the even white teeth that had cost her father a pretty penny to have straightened during her teen years, she searched hopefully for a tiny crow's-foot, a wrinkle, a line... anything that would impart a modicum of maturity to the face that stared back at her.

It was not that there was anything *wrong* with her looks. She was not a stunner, but she was put together pleasingly enough not to give her any major worries. It was just that she still looked every bit as sweetly innocent as she had at seventeen—a fact that had both helped and hindered her over the years—and she would have preferred something more exciting in the way of a face to being stuck with big blue eyes, bouncy blond hair, and a tender, vulnerable mouth that, in Melissa's opinion, would have looked more appropriate on a toddler.

She found no evidence of the hoped-for "mature" look, however, and she sighed as she bent to spit the toothpaste out of her mouth. After drying her mouth and hands on a towel, she left the bathroom through its other door to cross to the closet in her bedroom and extract a blue-denim skirt and a yellow T-shirt, which would serve as her sophisticated attire for the day.

As she dressed she reflected that so far her decision to return to her hometown and the "quiet" life had been the right one. She had been approaching a classic case of burnout for quite a while before the incident involving her fiancé, Bill Warren, had occurred, which was what had precipitated her decision to leave Bill and her job as an investigative reporter on the large Washington, D.C., paper behind her.

Remembering that incident brought a wry smile to Melissa's mouth as she reflected that while it might not have been one of the high points of her life, walking in on Bill, a legislative assistant to a powerful congressman, in a cozy little hideaway where he, his congressman, various other notable figures, and some of the highest-priced call girls in the city were all stark naked and high as a kite on cocaine had certainly proved to be a turning point. And for the time being she didn't regret one whit leaving behind everything she'd worked for in order to savor a more normal, and certainly more peaceful, existence away from the sordid aspects of modern life she had been immersed in for several years.

While putting on a light coating of makeup, she grinned, remembering that her editor at the time, Thurman Wilcox hadn't seen things her way. For two weeks he had hidden every resignation letter she'd sent in to him, until at last she'd stormed into his office and demanded that he accept the letter she had thrust under his nose. He had been forced to take her decision seriously after that, but even then he had chosen to regard her defection as temporary, and as far as Melissa knew, he was still holding her job open for her, though for the present she had no intention of returning to the sort of work that had soured her outlook on life—at last her very soul had cried out for relief from association with the dregs of humanity.

Now, ensconced in her grandmother's garage apartment behind Kate's hundred-year-old house, employed at a job where her most exciting assignment in the last two months had been covering a fire in a vacant house set by two overenthusiastic boys anticipating the Fourth of July, her days passed with a pleasant, soothing calmness. She felt relaxed, cheerful, and for the first time in ten years, free of the drive to excel and to prove that her face was not representative of her inner qualities. There was none of the hectic, demanding mayhem she had endured during both her university days and her newspaper days in the nation's capital, and she was surrounded by people who were reasonably normal for a change.

And that's just fine and dandy with me, Melissa thought contentedly as she snatched up her shoulder bag and headed for the door leading to the peaceful outside world she had come home to find. *Thurm Wilcox, eat your heart out,* she thought with a grin as she shut the door of her garage apartment behind her, donned a pair of sunglasses to shut out the sun's glare, which accentuated her headache, and started to skip down the stairs.

She was heading for her 1964 Dodge Dart, a relic from her high school days that her father had, for some inexplicable reason, refrained from disposing of, when the stern, upper-class, authoritarian tones of her grandmother halted her.

"Have you forgotten how to say good morning, Melissa?"

Melissa swung on her heel to peer at her grandmother, a smile of pleasure decorating her childlike face. "Sorry, Gran," she caroled cheerfully. "I didn't see you."

But as she said the words she was thinking fondly that Grandma Kate would be hard to miss. Though the straight posture, the lined, dignified face, the sparkling intelligent blue eyes, and the indefinable air of breeding were imposing, that impression was belied somewhat by the elderly woman's costume. Dressed to feed her "darlings," which was a somewhat euphemistic designation for the cluttering, pecking, multicolored hens gathered at her feet, Kate had on a disreputable pair of baggy jeans, a man's blue-denim shirt that was decorously buttoned at the wrists and that reached to her knees, and a broad-brimmed Mexican sombrero she had picked up on one of her travels in her earlier days.

"How are you feeling this morning, Granddaughter?" Kate McKee asked in a bland voice that didn't acknowledge the twinkle in her eye. "No aftereffects from my dandelion wine?"

Melissa gave a rueful grimace. "No more than I deserve, Gran," she confessed. "I should have listened to you and left those last two glasses alone. My head has grown a size or two since last night."

"Ah, well." Kate sniffed unconcernedly. "Youth always overdoes." As she spoke she continued to dispense chicken feed with regal dignity to the cluster of hens at her feet. "Perhaps if you told Malcolm you weren't feeling well today, he'd remember he has a heart and let you off for your birthday?"

"Ha!" Melissa said, disputing this. "More likely he'd have me down on my hands and knees scrubbing that disreputable floor in the print room. A lack of sensitivity must be a prerequisite for newspaper editors. At least

I've never met one yet who wouldn't have made Simon Legree look like a kindergarten teacher.''

"Well, then, you'd better be on your way," Kate said with mock sympathy, "because you're running a little late, and if I know Malcolm Keller—and I do," she added wryly, "he'll keep you overtime to make it up, and I want you home on schedule tonight. Delia's making your favorite dinner for your birthday, and she'll have a screaming, hissy fit if you let it get cold."

Delia was Kate's daily help, who occasionally consented to dispense culinary magic in her employer's kitchen, and Melissa's mouth watered at the prospect of dining on one of Delia's superb meals.

"Great!" Melissa agreed happily. "I'll scoot then, because I don't want to miss Delia's fried chicken." She started to turn away, then turned back, an anticipatory light in her blue eyes. "Is she making me a coconut cake, too?" she inquired hopefully.

"Don't ask silly questions," Kate scoffed. "When has she ever failed to bake your favorite cake on your birthday?"

"Never," Melissa returned with complacent satisfaction. "See you later, Gran," she called as she made her way to the Dodge Dart.

Settling herself comfortably on the pillow in the driver's seat, which served the dual purpose of covering the hole in the upholstery that had been carved by too many years of use and of providing a buffer against the hot vinyl that still remained around the hole, Melissa gunned the ever-dependable motor and backed out the long driveway past the house her grandmother adored and maintained with scrupulous care.

Since her grandmother's fondness for her aged house and her multitudinous chickens necessitated that she live outside the city limits of Rockport, Melissa had to drive three miles before she came to the tree-shaded, dignified streets of her hometown. As she came to a stop at the corner of Main and Forsyth, she sucked in her breath as a redheaded teenager driving a jeep ignored the one-way sign, turned into Melissa's street headlong, and then had to swerve drastically in order to avoid crushing the one intact fender left on the Dodge.

Under the circumstances Melissa temporarily forgot to curb her penchant for foul language—a defense mechanism she had adopted in her latter teen years against people's tendency to view her as a small blond child who had inexplicably developed the bosom of an adult—and yelled a few choice words out the window, finishing up with the obligatory, "Why don't you look where you're going!"

Her reward was the usual comical look of disbelief that such words could issue from such a sweet face, and then the satisfaction of seeing the redhead nearly lose control of his jeep and come close to climbing the curb and demolishing Mrs. Dahler's carefully nurtured peony bushes.

The incident lightened Melissa's mood considerably, and she was smiling as she drove on. It had felt good to let loose like that for a change, though she had dispensed with this childish defensive reaction some time ago, except for a few mild expletives here and there, or even some stronger ones when a situation called for it, and there had been a lot of situations like that in her years on the Washington, D.C., newspaper.

Feeling both relieved that such situations were behind her and pleased with the degree of creativity she'd exercised on the redhead, Melissa's slight headache was abating by the time she walked into the hole in the wall that boasted on its one grimy window that it housed the offices of the *Rockport News*. She was grateful to hear voices coming from Malcolm Keller's cubbyhole, because she was, despite her best efforts, definitely late, and she hoped her editor's visitor would keep him from noticing.

However, his visitor had also prevented Mr. Keller from making the morning coffee, as he usually did, and Melissa, feeling the need for a strong cup and two aspirins to dissolve the last of her headache, picked up the empty pot and headed toward the minuscule bathroom to fill it with water. As she passed Mr. Keller's door the content of what was being said inside his office made her pause.

"Malcolm, you've got to do something, I tell you!" shouted the female side of the conversation, and Melissa recognized the peculiar tugboat shrillness of Mrs. Muller-Smyth, her editor's cousin, one of the leading social lights of Rockport, and a woman for whom the name *harridan* might have been invented.

"You can't just sit there and let that monster get away with what he's done to my poor Delilah!" the shrill tones continued. "And what about the other youngsters he has in his clutches?" Mrs. Muller-Smyth's voice contained overtones of dire tragedy now. "How can you live with your conscience if anything happens to one of them?"

Melissa heard the subdued, calming murmur of her boss answering, but she couldn't distinguish the words. Mr. Keller always got quieter when anyone shouted at him, which, admittedly, didn't happen too often.

"What can *you* do?" yelled Mrs. M-S, a nickname Melissa had long since devised for the unpleasant woman. "How do *I* know what you can do? You're the newspaper editor! *You* think of something! That's your job!"

At that point Melissa shifted her weight, causing the ancient flooring to give an audible protesting groan, and an instant later her editor called out to her with all the relief in his voice of a twenty-pound poodle looking for rescue from a slavering, 250-pound mastiff.

"Melissa, is that you? Come in here!" The tone meant now, and it meant without equivocation, and giving a silent sigh for her bad luck, Melissa obeyed.

"Yes, sir?" she murmured respectfully, eyeing Mrs. M-S's red face and wildly tufted gray hair with interest. Mrs. M-S might be the hysterical type, but she was normally a *neat* hysterical type. But where her daughter, Delilah, was concerned, Melissa remembered, the women was not only deaf, dumb, and blind, but inclined toward dementia besides, and since Melissa had heard that the much put-upon *Mr.* Muller-Smyth had finally done something about his daughter's proclivity for older men looking for a hot time in the old town any night—sent her away to a correction facility or something—Melissa suspected that Mrs. M-S had a good reason for her present distracted state. Obviously Delilah, the delectable nymph, was back.

"I may have an assignment for you," was Malcolm Keller's grim reply to Melissa's circumspect greeting, and Melissa could tell by the degree to which the habitually unlighted cigar in Mr. Keller's mouth had been shredded that he had about reached the limit of his never very abundant patience. However, before he could explain what he meant, Mrs. M-S cut in with a shrieking objection.

"*An assignment?* Malcolm, we're talking about family matters here," she cried. "Can't you forget about your stupid newspaper for two minutes and deal with what's really important?"

Wincing a little, Melissa waited for the explosion that should have burst from her boss at hearing his newspaper described as "stupid" and "unimportant." The paper was his pride and joy, and in all fairness, while Melissa thought it might deserve other unflattering terms, "stupid" was not one of them. Mr. Keller occasionally wrote very pithy editorials on matters of national interest and made quite a lot of sense out of them.

No explosion was forthcoming, however, though Mr. Keller's flinty eyes grew a shade more desperate at having to suppress one.

"If you will be patient, Martha," he murmured, his voice dropping to barely audible tones, "this *does* have to do with family matters. It also has to do with my... newspaper." The pained inflection on the last word expressed Mr. Keller's injured feelings clearly. "I think perhaps Melissa can help us with this."

"Melissa?" Mrs. M-S's bulging gray eyes glared at Melissa. "What can *she* do?" Having expressed by her tone her contempt for Melissa's abilities, the woman suddenly turned from belligerent to nervous. "Besides, Malcolm," she said cautiously, "this is a *private* matter."

While Mrs. M-S looked at Melissa as though she suspected the younger woman of harboring a desire to parade down Main Street toting a sign detailing whatever indiscretion Delilah had committed most recently, Melissa gave Mrs. M-S a sweet, disarming smile, though privately she found the prospect of embarrassing the woman singularly appealing. But she would let Mr. Keller demolish his cousin while she silently cheered him on.

"Melissa can be relied upon to be discreet," Mr. Keller said, coming through with the expected defense, looking as though *he* would like to paint and tote a sign. "Why don't you tell her all about it, and then we'll all put our heads together and try to come up with a plan of action."

Mr. Keller leaned back in his chair and gazed up at the ceiling then, but Melissa knew from his tone of voice that once Mrs. M-S had left his office, Melissa had better find some excuse to get lost for a while herself. The fallout, once Malcolm Keller was free to express the feelings obviously consuming him, was going to be ferocious.

Mrs. M-S looked doubtful for a moment longer, but when she turned her gimlet eyes on Melissa again, Melissa promptly gave her another sweet smile, hastily set down the coffeepot she was still holding, and seated herself in the only remaining free chair in the room, a ladder-backed antique that, while it seemed to punch holes in an occupant's derriere, was nevertheless sturdy and supportive. Her action encouraged Mrs. M-S to accept her presence, but Melissa had the feeling the explanation was going to take some time. Mrs. M-S had a pathological aversion to saying anything derogatory about her only daughter, and Melissa soon found herself substituting mental clarity for verbal duplicity.

"You know Delilah," Mrs. M-S stated to Melissa in a tone that was confident that everyone in the town of Rockport did. Melissa nodded, smiling sweetly until her jaws ached, while she reflected that indeed, while she hadn't seen the now eighteen-year-old Delilah in five years, she remembered very well the luscious thirteen-year-old the girl had been, as perhaps did half the male population in the whole county.

"You know how...ah...friendly she is," Mrs. M-S understated feebly, her blotched face growing redder. Melissa nodded encouragingly, trying to keep her knowledge of just how friendly Delilah was out of her expression, while she began to feel a faint sympathy for Mrs. M-S. The humiliation must be killing the woman, and while Melissa never had and never expected to like Mrs. M-S, she did feel sorry for her.

"Well, her father"— a grim note in Mrs. M-S's voice boded ill for the unfortunate Mr. M-S—"her father decided Delilah wasn't getting the help she...ah... needed from a...ah...psychiatrist she was seeing, and he thought she might do better somewhere else."

Melissa conjured up a suitably sympathetic look and again nodded encouragingly. "Girls that age do sometimes have...problems," she submitted helpfully, thinking that Delilah probably had more problems than her mother could ever begin to realize, much less understand.

Mrs. M-S seemed to take heart from Melissa's apparent sympathy. "We...*he*..." the woman corrected herself quickly as she went on, "sent her to a ranch in Montana for delin—ah, for young people who have problems and need help," Mrs. M-S plodded gallantly on. "She was there several weeks, but a few days ago she called me to beg me to get her out of there, and yesterday, when she got home, she was in such a state!"

Mrs. M-S surprised Melissa then by dragging out a voluminous white handkerchief to mop her wet gray eyes. "Oh, she was in terrible shape," the woman moaned pitifully. "She had bruises...scrapes..." Mrs. M-S blew her nose resoundingly in the handkerchief before she could continue. "She *said* it was from working on the ranch, but I know it wasn't. I can tell by the look in her eyes. My little girl is terrified! I've never seen her like that in my life!" she declared with a shudder.

Melissa, though she thought it quite likely Delilah might have been terrified at coming into close contact with work for the first time in her life, murmured quietly, "Did she admit being terrified?"

"No!" Mrs. M-S blew her nose strenuously again. "She pretended she wasn't. But I know my little girl, and she was, and what's more, she still is!" She turned to where Mr. Keller sat with closed eyes, leaning on his elbow as though exhausted by the proceedings taking place in his office. "And I want Malcolm to find out why!" Mrs. M-S stated determinedly. "There's obviously something awful going on out at that ranch, and I want to know what it is and put that terrible man who runs the place behind bars before he hurts some of the other kids the way he did Delilah!"

Mr. Keller opened weary eyes. "Martha doesn't want to go to the police with this until we know something definite, Melissa," he explained before Melissa could ask the obvious question. "She wants a quiet investigation."

The word *investigation* jarred sourly in Melissa's ears. She didn't think there was really anything going on at that Montana ranch worthy of such a designation since she considered Delilah's life-style and character probably made her a target for a great many things her mother couldn't be expected to understand, but just the suggestion of embarking on such a job raised her defenses. She was through with that sort of thing, and Malcolm Keller knew it, damn him!

But Malcolm Keller didn't look as though he knew any such thing. Instead, he looked like a man who was ready and willing to pass the buck.

"Why don't you go talk to Delilah before we make any decisions, though, hmmm?" he said to Melissa as he rose from his chair, obviously eager to bring the session to an end. Mrs. M-S forestalled him.

"Malcolm, you can't be serious!" she cried, looking at Melissa as if placing the matter in her hands was the equivalent of sending a toddler into a den of child molesters. "She's...she's..."

"I think Melissa can handle herself better than you suppose, Martha," he said with dry humor, avoiding Melissa's angry eyes. "She may look like an innocent, but she had to have learned something during her years as an investigative reporter in Washington, D.C." And while Melissa was silently fuming over his less than complimentary way of phrasing her qualifications, he continued blandly, "Besides, if we do have to send her out to Montana to look things over, her looks will be an advantage. Who would think her capable of conducting a serious investigation?"

While Melissa glared at him, both for his insult and for his underhandedness in shoving Mrs. M-S's problems onto her unwilling shoulders, he smoothly ushered Mrs. M-S out the door while he returned Melissa's glare and nonverbally ordered her to follow them.

"Is Delilah home now?" he was inquiring of his

cousin as Melissa reluctantly got to her feet and trailed the two of them out of the office.

"Yes, she's home in bed," Mrs. M-S answered grudgingly. She peered at Melissa, obviously still unsure that this sweet-looking, petite female could accomplish anything other than looking like an angelic featherbrain. "I suppose Melissa could come home with me and talk to her," she admitted with as much reluctance to have her as Melissa was feeling about going.

Melissa, suddenly remembering that talking to Delilah couldn't be much worse than staying in the office and witnessing the explosion that would be forthcoming from Malcolm Keller, pasted a wan smile on her face and nodded.

"All right," she gave in, ignoring the gleam of triumph in her editor's unsympathetic eyes. She started to offer Mrs. M-S a ride in her Dodge since she hadn't seen the woman's Cadillac outside the office, then thought better of it. Mrs. M-S would probably throw up at being faced with the prospect of riding in the corroded, twisted hunk of metal Melissa used for transportation. And since, in any case, the Muller-Smyth household was only a couple of blocks away, and Mrs. M-S looked as though she could use the exercise, Melissa kept quiet and with assumed meekness followed the woman out of the office and down the street.

"When did Delilah get back?" she questioned tentatively after the first block had been traversed in utter silence except for the thud of the woman's sensible shoes on the pavement.

"Last night," Mrs. M-S answered shortly, making it clear that she was not at all pleased that her cousin had ducked what she saw as his duty and landed her with Melissa instead. But then the white handkerchief came out again as Mrs. M-S dabbed at her eyes. "I couldn't believe my eyes when I saw her." She sniffed, her genuine distress apparent even to Melissa's doubting ears. "That poor child looked as though she'd been in hell!"

In spite of Melissa's initial skepticism, she was beginning to feel uneasy that there really might be something to investigate on that Montana ranch. And the prospect alarmed her, since she knew who would get stuck with the job of proceeding with that investigation if it was decided that one should be carried out. Damn it, she didn't want to leave her peaceful routine for another round of dabbling in the dirt. She'd had enough of that to last her for a lifetime! she thought grimly as she accompanied Mrs. M-S up the steps of a house as old as Grandma Kate's, but not nearly as charming.

Mrs. M-S escorted her into a hideously decorated living room as the woman got herself under control again. "I'll get Delilah," she said stoically. "Please wait in here."

Melissa did, shuddering at the dark oppressive furniture and feeling a reluctant pang of sympathy for the unfortunate Delilah. No wonder she had "gone wrong," being brought up in this mausoleum under the tutelage of such a mama. Mr. M-S seemed all right in a vague, ineffectual way, as best as Melissa could remember, but she was certain he wouldn't have had much say in his daughter's upbringing. She was surprised he had prevailed in having Delilah sent to a correctional environment at all. The girl must have pulled a beaut to initiate such action on his part, Melissa thought.

She was inspecting a cabinet filled with assorted distasteful knickknacks when she heard a sound behind her and straightened up to turn and face Delilah Muller-Smyth. The girl was standing in the entranceway to the living room dressed in a man's shirt—which, judging by the tousled disarray of her blond hair, was obviously serving as her nightgown, indicating that she'd just gotten out of bed—and her pose would have done credit to any high-priced model.

Standing with one languid hand placed on an out-thrust hip, Delilah looked, to Melissa's jaundiced eye, sexier than hell. Her legs were long and perfectly shaped, her bosom was a Hollywood starlet's dream, she had red, pouting lips, and she was staring at Melissa out of sleepily seductive blue eyes that contained not a trace of friendliness. Melissa instantly developed an equally firm dislike for Delilah that she freely admitted to herself was based in sheer jealousy. Delilah had every attribute most women longed for, and obviously knew what to do with them.

"Hello, Delilah," Melissa greeted the girl, managing to keep her envy out of her voice and, she hoped, out of her eyes. Delilah was a man's woman, and her disparaging look at Melissa spelled out her disregard for her own sex without any attempt to conceal it.

"I remember you," Delilah said dismissingly as she glided into the room in a sexy walk that made Melissa want to trip her. "You were one of those smart kids," she added with further dismissal as she picked up a pack of cigarettes from the living room coffee table, lit one, and blew the smoke from her nostrils with practiced effect. She then collapsed languidly onto the couch behind the coffee table. "What are you doing here?" she asked in a rude tone.

Melissa counted to ten and used the time to seat herself beside Delilah on the couch. As she surreptitiously inspected her for the alleged bruises Mrs. M-S had been so upset about, she was surprised to see that they were actually there! There were dark blotches on Delilah's wrists, as though someone had held her in a brutal grip, and there were also dark circles under the girl's beautiful blue eyes, as well as a certain haunted look in those eyes that elicited a feeling of pity on Melissa's part.

"Your mother didn't tell you?" Melissa stalled as she continued her inspection. The nightshirt covered Delilah's upper body, but her legs had an abundance of scrapes and bruises, and there was an ugly knot by her temple.

Delilah, noting the inspection and putting two and two together in light of Melissa's question, began to see the light.

"Has my mother been talking to you about me?" she demanded in almost a snarl as the fear of a caged animal sprang up in her eyes, jolting Melissa.

"She was talking to your cousin Malcolm Keller," Melissa admitted cautiously. "I work for him."

Delilah's reaction was startling. She jumped to her feet and crushed out her cigarette in an ashtray with a vicious motion. "You leave me alone!" she snapped shakily. "My mother had no right to talk to anybody about me! Get out and don't come back!"

She swung on her heel and was halfway out of the room before Melissa could jump up and intercept her. "Delilah, wait!" she demanded hastily. "We only want to help you!"

Delilah gave an ugly little laugh that was close to being hysterical. "Help me?" she said contemptuously. "Then leave me alone! That's how you can help me!"

She was almost to the door before Melissa could reach out and grab her arm. "Wait, Delilah!" she coaxed. "Can't you tell me what's the matter? What happened to you out on that ranch?"

Delilah winced at Melissa's grip on her arm, and Melissa realized she'd inadvertently grabbed the girl on one of her bruises. She loosened her grip a fraction, but she didn't let go, feeling this was no time to be delicate. Something definitely *had* happened to Delilah, and Melissa meant to find out what it was.

"Let me go!" Delilah said viciously, showing surprising strength as she used her other hand to try to dislodge Melissa's grip.

"Not until you explain some things," Melissa answered firmly as she held on, but then she injected sym-

pathetic patience into her voice. "You're better off talking to me than to your mother, Delilah, and you know
she won't let up until she's gotten the story out of you."

Fear returned to displace the pain and anger in
Delilah's blue eyes. "I'm not telling anybody anything!" she raged with a determination that was convincing. "I'm not talking to anyone about that place!
He said if I did, he'd—"

She stopped abruptly, and before Melissa could encourage her to say more, Delilah yelled, "Let me go!"
and with a vicious jerk pulled her wrist out of Melissa's
grip and ran upstairs.

Melissa was tempted to go pound on Delilah's bedroom door until the girl had to let her in, but from the
note in Delilah's voice when she'd said she wouldn't talk,
Melissa was forced to conclude that the girl had meant
what she'd said. And as Melissa hesitated, then shrugged
and went to find Mrs. M-S to tell the woman that her efforts to get Delilah to talk had been fruitless, she found to
her chagrin that her interest had been aroused. And in
spite of the fact that she didn't want to get involved in an
investigation of what had happened to Delilah, the question of who had beaten the girl and in the process had
frightened her so badly she was terrified to talk about it,
revolved in her head unrelentingly.

Chapter Two

Two weeks later, as Melissa sat staring glumly out of the filthy window of the dilapidated van that was bumping and jostling its way toward the Rocking R Ranch near Missoula, Montana, she decided that, just as advertised, Montana really was Big Sky Country. The wheat fields stretched for miles, but they weren't flat and uninteresting. They rolled in undulating hills, the grain swaying and dancing in the wind. From the golden color she knew it wouldn't be long before it was time to harvest, but meanwhile the sight was there in all its glory for the appreciation of any chance traveler who happened by.

Melissa was not traveling by chance, however. She had a definite purpose in mind. But despite the whirl of preparations that had taken place to make her presence here possible, she still had trouble believing she was actually in Montana...and on an investigative reporting assignment at that. Just thinking about it made her stifle a resentful groan and clench her teeth in exasperation. *Damn all newspaper editors to hell!* she thought with a hostility that had grown over the preceding two weeks and was nowhere near to abating.

Delilah had kept her promise not to talk in spite of everything—her mother's incessant prodding, any inducements Melissa could think up as bribes, and even Malcolm Keller's brand of intimidation. That in itself was enough to convince everyone that there was something going on at the ranch in Montana that deserved investigating.

But Melissa hadn't planned on doing the investigating herself, and she had protested the assignment strenuously from the time she'd arrived back at the newspaper office after her interview with Delilah right up until the moment she'd arrived at Dulles Airport to board the plane that had brought her to the wide open spaces of Montana.

Her protests that the Montana authorities should be the ones to investigate whatever was going on at the Rocking R Ranch had availed her nothing; Malcolm Keller had proceeded in his slow, plodding way to gather material about the ranch and its owner, one Robert Redding, a man who admittedly had a spotless reputation, but who was nevertheless Martha Muller-Smyth's, Malcolm Keller's, and even Melissa's chief suspect as the villain behind Delilah's beating. After all, he ran the place, and Melissa, at least, had seen many people with spotless reputations who were engaged in exploiting and actively harming young people. For her part, she was convinced that this Robert Redding was probably using his young charges as slave labor, and possibly exploiting young females like Delilah to boot.

A sinking feeling of inevitability had begun to grip Melissa when the Muller-Smyths had offered to fund the investigation and as Malcolm Keller had grown more and more caught up in his research on the place where Delilah had met her downfall. Mr. Keller had pored over references the Muller-Smyths had gotten from the Montana Department of Social Welfare extolling the program at the Rocking R, as well as the correspondence between the Muller-Smyths and Robert Redding when they'd made inquiries about sending Delilah there, and he had ordered Melissa to do the same.

The results of the research had been predictable, in

Melissa's opinion. Though Robert Redding had no professional qualifications and made no bones that he had started the program at the ranch five years ago more from the necessity of obtaining funds to keep his land than from a highly developed social conscience, he had ostensibly made a huge success of the project, turning semi-delinquent young people with emotional problems around toward the straight and narrow before the law had to take a hand in their rehabilitation.

Despite her suspicions of anyone who had no professional qualifications, Melissa had to admit that, in principle, she agreed with his deceptively simple formula. He simply worked the kids' butts off on his ranch, supposedly treating them with respect but with firm authority as well, and built their confidence in themselves up to a point where they began to function from a position of faith in themselves and others rather than from paranoia and self-centeredness, which were often found in anyone who had no real sense of self-worth.

Accordingly, grateful relatives and authorities had kept him in business, though opinion was divided over whether Robert Redding's success ratio was due to the fact that the kids actually liked back-breaking physical labor in the great outdoors in the company of other young people in the same boat as they themselves, or whether Robert Redding had some sort of charismatic personality that elicited a positive response from his young charges. Melissa held the private opinion that the latter explanation was the case, only she substituted fear for charisma as her explanation for why the man had never had a whisper raised against him. She had seen that sort of thing before, both in her investigations of sexual abuse against youngsters, who were usually too afraid to talk about it, and in her investigations of other so-called charismatic personalities who managed to accumulate followings of young people to exploit.

Melissa might have continued to resist the Muller-

Smyths and her employer if her ex-fiancé, Bill Warren, hadn't had the nerve to call her with the information that the incident she had witnessed had been hushed up, and with the suggestion that they get together again. Bill, in his suave, charming, debonair way, had talked over Melissa's vehement refusal and indicated he would be paying her a visit in the near future.

So now, as Melissa sat disconsolately in the creaking, filthy van on her way to the Rocking R Ranch, she had to admit to herself that she was here not only because the pressure to make her come had been unbelievable, but because she was afraid that if Bill Warren did come to see her, she would kill him and spend the rest of her days in prison.

In her customary way, however, when faced with a job that was inevitable, she was determined to give it her best shot, and now she sat in the bouncing van, clad—as an act of rebellion as much as to perpetuate the idea that she was a silly, fluttering female journalist bent on extolling the virtues of one Robert Redding, and as an afterthought, his successful program—in a resplendent Stetson hat, plaid shirt, blue jeans and an elaborately stenciled pair of Western boots. Grimly she decided that she would soon find out whether Mr. Redding had any virtue to extol or whether he was just another guru bent on making a fast buck out of the hides of a bunch of pathetic youngsters. Though he had not officially agreed to allow Melissa to do an article, insisting that he had to meet her first, she was confident he would fall for the flattery she intended to lather over him and would be eating out of her hand before long.

And with that task in mind, she turned to attempt conversation once again with her escort, an elderly but spry version of a stereotypical Western man who had so far proved the old adage about the "silent" cowboy true. A laconic "Yep" or "Nope" was as much as Melissa had been able to get out of him since he'd picked her up at the Missoula airport.

Her view out the flyspecked, dirt-runneled window of the van had disclosed that the wheat fields were giving way to pastureland now, with beef usurping the place of bread on the menu of the landscape, and Melissa used that fact to launch a discussion.

"Does Mr. Redding have many cattle?" she posed in what she hoped was a suitable tone of demure feminine interest.

"Some," was the brief answer, given just as the old cowboy made an abrupt turn into a rutted lane leading toward some distant hills.

After rescuing herself from almost certain collision with the dashboard, Melissa took a deep breath and tried again.

"Is it far now to the ranch?" she asked, and despite her best efforts, she realized her tone had deteriorated somewhat from breezy femininity to a sort of strained politeness.

"Nope."

Communication personified, Melissa thought grimly, but she was far from giving up the struggle.

"Ah...could you be more specific?" she persevered. "Such as telling me how many more miles it is?"

"'Bout ten."

That reply gave Melissa hope. It was still a brief reply, but for the first time it contained two words instead of one and was actually informative.

"Is there a town nearby?" she asked hopefully, thinking it would be just as well to establish an escape route since she didn't have any transportation and it was barely possible that Robert Redding might turn nasty if he discovered she was more interested in splashing his sins across the front page of a newspaper than his good deeds.

"Nope."

Melissa sighed audibly at being back to a monosyl-
labic reply and stifled the pungent, explicit expletive
she'd been about to utter. On second thought, however,
she uttered it anyway, hoping her escort was the type to
respond more verbosely to a female he didn't view as a
"lady." She had heard that cowboys put women either
on a pedestal or in the back room of a bar, and in her
mood she was inclined toward the latter location at the
moment.

She did get a reaction, but it wasn't the one she'd expected. Fixing her with a pitying, disapproving look
from his faded brown eyes, her driver informed her that
if she spoke like that at the ranch, she was likely to get
her mouth washed out with soap.

Torn between laughter and indignation, Melissa elected to try nonchalance instead. "Ha!" she scoffed good-
naturedly. "Not likely."

Her companion merely shook his head with tired disgust, and Melissa had the impression he had heard
worse and lived to see the utterer eat his or her words.
Well, no matter, she thought with breezy unconcern.
She was no Delilah Muller-Smyth, and if this Robert
Redding tried any rough stuff with her, she knew a trick
or two to make him change his mind.

Back to practical matters, she tried for information
again. "Just how far *is* the ranch from a town?" she
asked, thinking that despite her inner bravado, an
escape route was still a handy thing to have.

"'Bout fifty miles," came the disconcerting reply,
leaving Melissa with the disappointing realization that
fifty miles was rather a far piece to hike if she ever did
need that escape route. But with her customary shrugging away of problems, she decided there was no doubt
some form of transportation at the ranch she could beg,
borrow or steal if the need arose. And surely the ranch
had a telephone, even if it would take quite a while for
rescue to arrive.

Her companion then surprised her by launching into what was, for him, a lengthy lecture, the content of which puzzled Melissa.

"You won't be worryin' about no town after a day or two at the ranch, missy," he predicted with what struck Melissa as anticipatory sadism. "You won't want nothin' more than a place to lay down and die, and maybe you'll be scared you *won't* die at that!"

The chuckle that accompanied his words made Melissa a little uneasy. True, as far as Robert Redding knew, she was just a featherbrained reporter who had gushed all over him on the telephone after Malcolm Keller had completed the preliminary arrangements for the supposed interview she was traveling all this way to conduct. But what if he found out differently? she wondered with wry caution. Delilah had been worked over pretty thoroughly, and you only had to mention the ranch to put her into a panic. The possibility of walking into danger made Melissa's senses sharpen in the way they always did when faced with an assignment of this sort.

A short while later the arched entrance to the ranch, emblazoned with a leaning double R that looked more drunken than rocking, came into view. It was still a good three miles from the entrance to the large, multistory wooden ranch house and the outbuildings and corrals that surrounded it, but they were visible, and as she studied them, Melissa wondered where she would be housed. . . in the main house? Or did they perhaps have separate facilities for guests? Or would she be expected to dorm with the female "inmates" of this isolated semi-prison?

Parker, her companion of the pithy conversation, settled the matter by driving up to the main house. "Hop out, missy," he ordered briskly, "and take your bags with you."

Aha, Melissa thought with gloomy comprehension.

Apparently reporters were not on the favored guest list. At least, it was obvious that not only were bellboys unavailable to scamper to her bidding, Mr. Parker was not even going to offer the minimal courtesy of carrying her bags in.

Deciding against voicing the sweetly sarcastic comment that hovered on her lips, Melissa climbed down from the van, hoisted her two large suitcases out of it, and proceeded to heft them one at a time up the six steps to the veranda of the old-fashioned house. By the time she had them beside her at the front door, she was glumly pessimistic, certain that this ancient house was going to have three floors and her accommodations would be at the top of them . . . and, of course, no one would offer to carry her bags up those steps either.

So far the place looked as empty as a tomb. No one had ventured out to extend whatever passed as a welcome in this outpost in the wilderness, and Parker had driven off the instant she'd had her bags out of the van. With a shrug, Melissa lifted a hand to pound on the screen door she faced, hoping whoever answered her knock would be more forthcoming than her erstwhile driver had been.

It took several knocks before a small, apron-clad virago of a woman came and thrust the screen door open with a vigorous shove.

"Well, come on in, why don't you?" she demanded impatiently as Melissa made no attempt to move inside. "I've got pies in the oven! I can't stand here waiting for you all day!"

A dry "Thanks" was all Melissa could manage in the face of such a greeting. But despite her tone, the woman's little black eyes, which were set in a prunish-looking face topped by a gray topknot of tightly bound hair, didn't give an inch. Melissa reached down for one of her bags and was then disconcerted when her welcomer gave an impatient cluck of her tongue and stepped outside to grab up the other one, which Melissa knew was quite heavy, as easily as she would lift a hamper of underwear. Obviously what there was of the woman—which wasn't much; she was shorter than Melissa—was all muscle.

Melissa followed her hostess into the house and found that they were in a long hallway culminating in a steep flight of stairs to the upper stories. The hall was decorated with antlered deer heads, old-fashioned mirrors, and other antique-looking furnishings that were as Western-looking as anyone who'd ever seen a cowboy movie could expect.

At least the setting is authentic, she thought with dry appreciation as she hurried after the little woman who was now climbing the steep stairs with a step as light as the wind.

Melissa shortly found she'd been right about the three stories, as well as about the prediction that she would be lodged on the third one. Her room was at the very top of the house, in an airless attic furnished with one single bed topped with a patchwork quilt, one four-drawer dresser, and a cubbyhole with a curtain over it, which Melissa supposed was an excuse for a closet.

But the place was clean, and as she collapsed, panting, onto the bed, thoroughly convinced by now that not only were reporters not considered "special" guests, but were actively discriminated against, she was willing to make the best of things... until her hostess informed her in the tone of an order that Melissa was expected to keep the room clean.

"You're to make your own bed and sweep in here every day," the woman instructed, and much to Melissa's disgust, the woman wasn't even breathing hard from their climb. "Breakfast is at six, lunch is at twelve, and dinner is at six, and if you're late, you don't get any! Mr. Redding will talk to you after dinner tonight. Until then, you just get settled in and wait till it's time to eat!"

With that the woman swung on her heel and was gone

before Melissa could get her breath sufficiently to protest that while she hadn't expected the Ritz, she damned well hadn't expected to be treated like a servant either, and furthermore, she hoped the lady's pies burnt all to hell!

With a scowl Melissa stretched out on the bed to contemplate her surprising introduction to the place she'd come to investigate. It was clear that manners weren't high on the list of priorities here, and Melissa found herself wondering how the permanent residents were treated if a guest was viewed as fair game for the hired help.

A few moments later, however, taking her hostess's admonitions about mealtimes to heart, Melissa glanced at her watch, and discovering that she only had an hour to unpack and bathe before dinner, she dragged herself off the bed and disposed of her belongings in short order. Then she went looking for a bathroom.

There was none on her floor, naturally. She grabbed clean underwear, a clean blouse and skirt, and a pair of sandals and descended to the second floor, which was deserted. There were several closed doors, but Melissa wasn't up to any surreptitious peeking for the moment, and the only one she opened was at the end of the hall. As she had suspected, the room was a bathroom, and inside the old-fashioned cavern was a claw-toed bathtub—no shower, of course, she thought mournfully—a dilapidated sink, and a cupboard filled with towels astonishingly bereft of nap.

Since there was no one to hear her, Melissa gave vent to her feelings with a heartfelt active verb or two before she began to run water in the tub. Once clean, she felt much better and cleaned up behind herself before she left the room.

As she came out of the bathroom she realized that there were now occupants behind the closed doors she'd passed earlier. She could hear female voices as she passed by on her way to return her soiled clothing to her room, but she continued past the doors without attempting to make contact, thinking she would prefer to meet the "inmates" when she was in a better mood.

After dumping her things in a wooden box in her room she arbitrarily decided was a clothes hamper, Melissa retraced her steps downstairs, thinking she would explore a little before dinner.

The downstairs seemed deserted, and she wandered into what she supposed was a living room-parlor. It contained faded red velvet sofas, sloping chairs that were certain to give an occupant a permanent case of backache, and lacy white curtains at the window. Melissa backed out without exploring thoroughly and crossed the hall to a room that she considered must serve as a den. At any rate, there were tables set up with various games, a record player, and a piano, and lots of fashion magazines and books scattered around.

Melissa seated herself on one of the chairs in the den and was idly leafing through a magazine when the first of the "inmates" came into the room. At least Melissa assumed it was an inmate, though the young woman who sidled into the room looked about as far from any preconceived idea of a youngster in trouble as Melissa could possibly have imagined.

Tall, blond, and liberally stacked, the girl opened her mouth in surprise before voicing a greeting. And when she did so, she even had a sultry voice to go with the rest of her attributes.

"Well, hullo," she said. "Who are you?"

There wasn't a great deal of friendliness in her voice, but she wasn't hostile, either—just vaguely disinterested. Another Delilah, in fact, Melissa decided before answering.

"Hi, I'm Mel McKee," Melissa said, unthinkingly using the name her co-workers in Washington had always used, perhaps because she was back on that type of assignment.

The girl's winged eyebrows lifted somewhat disdainfully, but before she could introduce herself, four more visions of loveliness drifted into the room one by one while Melissa could only stare in astonishment at the quality of "delinquent" the Rocking R attracted. She was especially unnerved by the knowledge that, aside from the fact that a girl apparently had to pass a Hollywood screen test in order to gain entry to Robert Redding's harem, not one of these beauties was over eighteen years old, yet each and every one of them could have passed for her older sister without an eyebrow being raised in protest. Therefore, Melissa's feminine ego was dragging around her ankles when Mrs. Price, the gray-haired dynamo who had shown Melissa to her room, called everyone in to dinner.

Melissa elected to remain silent during the meal, which turned out to be a wise decision, since none of the girls, nor Mrs. Price, paid the slightest bit of attention to her. It was as though she were invisible, and Melissa, too tired from her long plane trip and the drive to the ranch to begin any delving into what had brought such a prime group into the pathways of sin and degradation, decided she would wait until morning when she was rested, before she initiated any questions. Besides, she had to check in with the "guardian" of these girls, who was conspicuously absent at the moment, before she had any right to begin her job here.

Meanwhile, she had a delicious meal to get through, complete with lemon pie—which despite Melissa's earlier hopes had turned out perfectly rather than burned—and Melissa did full justice to the meal.

Afterward two of the girls helped Mrs. Price clear the table and do the dishes while Melissa and the other three removed themselves to the den. Again Melissa was ignored, and though she could barely keep her eyes open, she picked up a fashion magazine to try to keep from going to sleep on the spot while she awaited her interview with the mysterious Mr. Redding.

At last Mrs. Price appeared at the doorway to the den, caught Melissa's weary eyes, and wiggled her fingers in a come-hither gesture, indicating Melissa should join her. Melissa came out of her stupor immediately at the prospect of at last meeting the man whom she was convinced was the villain of this piece. She had visions of being ushered into the presence of a seven foot, 350-pound Goliath who couldn't get a woman any other way than under the guise of "reforming" them and who was addicted to beating up his paramours after sampling their charms.

As it turned out, Melissa couldn't have been more wrong. Upon entering a room furnished as a study-library for the master of the Rocking R, she saw that in the first place, the man was a mere six feet, with a physique—from what she could tell of his back, since he was standing at a window facing the view outside—designed to instill an extra heartbeat in the breast of any female over twelve.

He had wide shoulders that tapered to a slim waist; long, blue-jean clad legs that looked as though they could cover a lot of ground and manage to look graceful in the process; and booted feet. At the top of all this male magnificence lay a thick mane of tousled blondish hair that fairly ached for a woman's fingers to scamper through. Melissa could only assume that when Mr. Robert Redding turned around, he would have crossed eyes, a hooked beak of a nose, and rotten teeth, which could explain why he had to resort to turning his ranch into a home for delinquents rather than finding his women in the normal way.

Wrong again! As the man slowly, gracefully pivoted to face her, Melissa almost gasped out loud as she got first the perfect profile, and then the full impact of a man who could have graced any movie screen in the world and made a fortune on his looks alone.

Chapter Three

Faced with an image that robbed her of breath, left her mouth hanging open in stunned astonishment, and had her blue eyes opened to their farthest limit the better to enjoy the sheer male beauty she faced, Melissa lost all sense of her mission here and reacted like a starstruck teenager.

Had she only known it, she looked exactly the way she felt. The man surveyed every inch of her, from her childishly tousled blond hair to her wide blue eyes, straight little nose, and vulnerable mouth, then went on to investigate the trim, petite body right down to the painted pink toenails peeking out of her sandals, hiding a smile that this reporter, whom he'd expected to look as ridiculous as she'd sounded over the phone, instead looked younger and less sophisticated, yet somehow prettier and sexier, than his teenage inmates.

"Miss McKee, I presume," he said, finally breaking the spell Melissa was under, and the mocking intonation he employed, along with the amused look in his eyes, woke her up with a start.

Melissa tore her eyes from the thick blondish-brown hair, those incredibly sexy eyes, the thick mustache, square chin, and perfect white teeth of her host and focused her gaze just above one of his wide shoulders, which she would have given a lot to feel bare under her palms.

"Yes, Mr. Redding," she said, struggling for her fluttery female voice, which didn't come out quite the way she'd intended. Oh, it was fluttery all right, but the quality was breathless in a fashion she couldn't afford to let him hear.

"Have a seat, Miss McKee," Robert invited in a lazy drawl. He extended a strong, tanned hand toward a chair across from his desk as he spoke, and Melissa's eyes fastened on that hand as though it were a magnet and her whole body the piece of metal it should glue itself to.

Without trying to speak, Melissa did as he'd suggested, sinking into the leather chair he'd indicated. Then she watched as he moved toward her, and a helpless little moan almost escaped her mouth as she saw the power and grace of his movements. He wore his jeans low on his hips, where they rode with clinging affection to what they covered—the slight bulge of his maleness, the trim male derriere Melissa had noticed when he'd had his back to her, and the muscular tautness of thighs she thought had probably been carved from a Greek statue's and transplanted onto his frame to make women like her have heart attacks when he walked.

Her agitation increased when instead of seating himself behind his desk, he moved to the front of it and leaned one perfect thigh on its edge. He stroked a long, slender finger over his mustache as he stared hard at her.

"What the hell are you doing here?" he then asked in a mild, questioning voice that nevertheless had the sting of a whip on Melissa's incredibly sensitized nerves.

She jumped at the question, which was, of course, an entirely inappropriate reaction coming from a trained investigative reporter. She had to clear her throat before she could speak, and again her planned image lost credibility when she stumbled over the words.

"Why...ah...I told you over the phone, Mr.—Mr.

Redding,'' she fumbled along. "I...that is, my editor...thought what you are doing here would make a good...ah...story. So uplifting...so admirable...."

The flattery she had planned to use to wrap this man around her little finger died right on the vine as one of his arched brows rose in an expression of cynical mockery. *Okay,* Melissa told herself while she took a deep breath to try to restore her equilibrium. *Scratch flattery from the game plan. Apparently he's been overdosed on it, probably since infanthood, and it looks like it leaves a bad taste in his mouth.*

"Do tell," he murmured in a tone that verged on being insulting.

"Yes." She spoke more calmly now and managed a bland smile as well. And then, concentrating all her efforts into observing his reaction, she launched her first trap. "One of your former...ah...pupils...recently came back home, and we were all so impressed with what you'd accomplished with her." At the inquiring lift of his brows, Melissa spoke the name she hoped would provoke some revealing reaction from him. "Delilah Muller-Smyth," she clarified, watching him intently. "You remember her of course?"

Melissa didn't know whether to be disappointed or relieved when Robert Redding's reaction was a look of puzzled surprise. "You consider her one of my successes?" he asked with mild incredulity.

Melissa could have kicked herself when she felt the skin of her face heating up. "Don't you?" she hedged, trying to sound innocent.

He snorted with gently mockery. "Hardly," he drawled. "I'm not sure there's any cure for what ails her other than a continuous stream of men to satisfy her appetites. She should never have been sent here in the first place."

Curious and surprised by his admission, Melissa forgot to conceal her reaction. "Then why did you take her in?" she inquired.

He shrugged his shoulders. "Let's just say her parents weren't entirely honest with me about what her problem was." He dismissed the matter without any discernable hostility toward Delilah's parents that Melissa could detect, an emotion that would have been understandable, since he must be proud of his record here and Delilah had thrown a clinker in his statistics.

She shortly learned that Robert Redding was far more interested in why *she* was really here than in why Delilah had left so abruptly.

"So I wouldn't have considered Delilah's ah...*rehabilitation*," he mocked, "sufficient reason to have you scurrying out here to do an article on my success at helping young people," he went on thoughtfully, holding Melissa's gaze with his own and displaying a considerable force of will as he did so. "So why did you come here, Miss McKee?" he probed with soft—and dangerous—curiosity.

Melissa hastily gathered her composure, finding it easier to do so once she was able to break contact with those blue eyes of his.

"Oh, well, ah...we checked up on you," she said with what she hoped was casual understatement. "And we learned that Delilah was the exception rather than the rule. We thought the world would be interested in what you're accomplishing out here." She hesitated, wondering if she was pushing her luck just a little too far by adding another sentence to her explanation, but under the propulsion of a growing sense of irritation with this man who could knock her off balance so easily, she said it anyway. "After arriving here today, I'm more fascinated by the subject than ever. I met some of your...girls...this evening, and I confess, I find it hard to believe they ever did anything more delinquent than stand too long in front of a makeup mirror.''

The slight smile that curved his gorgeous mouth in re-action to her statement made her irritation with him change into full-blown hostility for an instant. Damn him; he looked as though he *knew* Melissa was feeling somewhat inadequate.

"They are attractive, aren't they?" he murmured mockingly, provoking a slightly sulky pout on Melissa's part, which she was disconcerted to find drew his atten-tion to her mouth with disturbing intensity.

God! she thought on another intake of breath. *The man is a walking seducer of the first order! He probably never even has to ask. He just looks at a woman and she comes crawling on her hands and knees to offer him anything he wants!*

Deciding that it was time she got control of her own reactions to this man, she bravely lifted her gaze to his and gave him a polite smile she hoped offered no hint of what she was thinking.

"Am I passing inspection? Will I be allowed to mingle with your kids, Mr. Redding?" she asked with bland innocence. "I really do want to do this story, and I assure you, I'll do it in the best possible light, both for you and for the youngsters."

Robert Redding straightened slightly and folded his muscular arms over his chest. "No yellow journalism?" he inquired with polite mockery. "No attempt to sensa-tionalize what's going on out here?"

Melissa's pride in her craft came to the fore then, and she frowned at the handsome man staring intently at her as though trying to strip away an outer layer and bare her soul to him.

"I've never been guilty of yellow journalism in my life!" she snapped irritably. "I just report the facts."

His gaze narrowed, and Melissa thought she detected skepticism in his eyes. "Ah, but that brings up an interesting question, Miss McKee,'' he said very softly. ''I wouldn't have thought you'd have much opportunity to practice journalism in the larger sense at all, working on as small a paper as the *Rockport News*. And I find myself wondering how such a small paper can afford to send someone like you all the way out here to Montana to do a story like this. Is that the only paper you work for?''

The quiet note of challenge in his voice alerted Melissa to the fact that she may have underestimated the sophistication of a man who spent his time out on a ranch in the wilds of Montana. Surely he didn't take the paper where she'd made her name and didn't know about her background? He had a point about the financing of this venture as well, but Melissa was prepared to slip by that question, as he couldn't possibly know that the Muller-Smyths were the backers rather than the *Rockport News*.

Covering, she smiled and shrugged. ''Well, occasionally, if a story's good enough, it will be picked up by the larger papers,'' she said in the tone of a shy admission. ''And I confess, I hope this one will be good enough to help me go on to bigger and better things.''

There, she thought in a cynical vein. *Maybe if he thinks I'm an ambitious career woman hoping to make the big time, that will be a good enough explanation for why I'm here...unless he has other reasons for being suspicious.*

At this reminder that despite his sex appeal the man facing her might be guilty of abusing the kids put in his care, Melissa began to find her objectivity returning and she was exceedingly grateful to have it so. For a while there she had been behaving like a sappy little awestruck kid herself, and she determined that it wouldn't happen again. Robert Redding might be extremely likely material for a few nighttime fantasies, but until Melissa proved that his character was as appealing as the rest of him, she intended to resist that appeal firmly.

"Ah, I see," he murmured thoughtfully, still watching her. "You want to use me and the kids to make a name for yourself."

The flat censure in his tone made Melissa bristle, and she unconsciously sprang to her feet and took a step forward, bringing her within a few inches of the magnetism of the man, a mistake she was too wrought up to appreciate having made until it was too late to do anything about it.

"And a name for the admirable work you're doing as well!" she challenged him tautly. "Did it ever occur to you that since your method of dealing with these kids has been so successful, others might use it to help kids in other parts of the country? Or would you rather keep it a deep, dark secret?"

An instant after the words had left her mouth, Melissa could have kicked herself for possibly antagonizing the man who was the key she needed to employ to find out the truth behind what had happened to Delilah. *Damn it,* she thought frustratedly, *he could kick me off this ranch in a second, and there wouldn't be a thing I could do about it!*

Hastily attempting to undo any damage to her cause, she backtracked quickly. "I'm sorry, Mr. Redding," she apologized with all the sincerity she could project, though she could detect no overt hostility on his part as a result of her accusation. "That was uncalled for. I . . . you just . . . seem to . . . ah . . ."

"Rub you the wrong way?" he inquired mildly. Melissa squirmed, conscious of the amusement at her expense visible in his eyes and of the slightly suggestive tone in his voice that told her he was well aware he affected her on a primitive level, which made her wish she was a robot instead of a living, breathing human female.

And then she almost melted at his next words. "Maybe it's because I'd like to rub you, Miss McKee," he uttered in a soft drawl that was curiously tender. "And not in any way I consider wrong at all."

He held her eyes for a bare moment while Melissa stared helplessly back at him, before he got lazily to his feet, which brought him towering over her and much too close for Melissa's peace of mind. Then he side-stepped around her and went to a sideboard where there was a drinks tray set up.

He poured two snifters of brandy and turned to hold one out to her. Since by that time Melissa felt she needed some Dutch courage, she stepped to his side and took it from him, jerking at the touch of one of his long, slender fingers on hers. Lifting her startled blue eyes to his, she was surprised to find him smiling down at her in an almost gentle, and certainly tolerant, fashion.

"If I let you stay, we're going to have to do something about this chemistry between us, Miss McKee," he drawled softly, mocking the way her eyes suddenly dropped. "Is it against your journalistic principles to become involved with the subject of one of your stories?"

Melissa had lifted her brandy to her mouth to take a restoring sip, but she choked on it at his blunt proposal. She heard his soft chuckle and then felt his hand slapping her on the back with gentle force.

"I'm all right!" she choked out, unable to bear the warmth of that fiery palm against her back. "You don't have to beat me to death!"

Blessing the unconscious words that brought her back to the job at hand, Melissa finished her coughing and then looked up at him belligerently, scowling at the complacent grin on his handsome face.

"No, I *don't* get involved with the subjects of my stories," she informed him heatedly. "A reporter has to stay objective."

"I see," he returned, gravely mocking. He reached out, took the brandy glass from Melissa's hand, and set them both down, and while she was looking down and frowning at his action, he moved to slip his other arm around her waist, then tilted her chin up with a gentle hand. "Then you won't want me to do this to you while you're here," he murmured softly, just before he dipped his head and took her mouth in a kiss.

The kiss went on and on and on, eliciting from Melissa sensations she had never felt so intensely and wasn't sure she *wanted* to feel this intensely. At first she just stood in frozen shock while he caressed her mouth with his own, gently exploring and probing with his tongue the tender curves of her vulnerable lips. Then, as she helplessly let her mouth open under the pressure of his to allow him the access he sought, she was treated to a full-fledged assault that thrilled her, frightened her, and aroused her to the point where she began to cling to him as though he offered the only security in a suddenly shaken world.

He drew back very slightly until his breath wafted over her open mouth and his eyes glittered with a primitive need.

"You're going to get involved with this subject, Melissa McKee," he grated with soft control. "You're going to get involved all the way during every second we can spare together while you're here. You're as hungry for me as I am for you."

It was only the truth, but Melissa was immediately aware that she was breaking every rule of her profession in allowing this to happen, as well as breaking her personal rule against casual affairs. But Robert Redding didn't give her time to voice her thoughts as his mouth swept over hers again and she felt him start to lift her in his arms.

"No!" she cried with a pant. "I can't. It's too soon.... it's not right," she practically wailed, her eyes huge and unconsciously begging him to understand.

"Why do you try to resist me?" he asked, cupping her face in his large hand and tilting it up so that Melissa had to look at him. "Why do you feel there's something wrong with what's happening between us?" He insistently held her gaze until she felt she might drown in his eyes.

"I. . . ." She struggled to answer in a way that was not dishonest. "I guess it's. . . nothing like this has ever happened to me before. I've never reacted to a man this quickly or this. . . strongly."

Rob's pleased smile made her relax somewhat. "I'm glad to hear that," he teased, "because I'm in the same boat. Makes life interesting, doesn't it?" he asked in a light tone before he dipped his head to kiss her briefly.

"I'll take the time to court you if that's what you want, Melissa," he agreed. "But not much time. In the first place, whatever is between us won't be denied. This sort of chemistry doesn't come along every day, and I'm damned if I'm going to let it slip away without exploring it fully."

Melissa echoed his assessment wholeheartedly, but she also had to contend with her doubts that he was the honorable, upright man he seemed to be. And chemistry or not, she wasn't going to bed with a man who might be guilty of physical brutality against young people placed in his care. . . not if she could help it, that was, she admitted.

"Thank you," she said quietly, obviously shaken. She turned away to shut out the look of arousal still gleaming in his blue eyes. "I. . . I guess this means you're going to let me stay?" she asked weakly.

She heard his snort of disbelief at her question. "You must be joking," he drawled without humor. "The way I feel right now I'd chase you to Mars if you tried to leave here."

A shiver of combined apprehension and excitement traced Melissa's spine and she knew she had to get out of this room.

"I'd like. . . ah, to go upstairs now," she said hesitantly, still trying to avert his gaze. "Please, Mr. Redding...." she started, then stopped as she heard how ridiculous she sounded addressing this man by his formal name when she'd just been kissed by him.

His soft chuckle told her he had reached the same conclusion. "I think you'd better call me Rob, don't you?" he teased mockingly. "Even the kids grant me that informality, and you certainly aren't a kid, are you, Melissa? Even though you look like one," he added on a thoughtful note. "I'll let you go to bed and to your dreams in a minute, Melissa," he then added in a lighter, teasing tone. "But first we have to decide on what cover you're going to use while you're here."

"Cover?" Melissa asked uneasily, the word evoking distinct guilty feelings and an equally strong fear of exposure in her.

"Yes, cover," Rob affirmed as he lifted his drink to his mouth and downed a heavy draft. "I'm not going to have you upsetting the kids, or provoking dramatic tendencies in some of them, by coming on to them like a reporter." He set his now empty glass down with a thump and hooked his thumbs in his back pockets while he surveyed her critically, without a trace of the sensuous interest he had displayed only moments before.

"Hell, you look younger than most of them yourself," he said thoughtfully. "So it seems to me like the best course of action would be to pretend you *are* one of the kids who's been sent here to be straightened out. No one but I knows who you really are, Melissa—" He stopped, and in crisper, more businesslike tones, asked, "Unless you told someone after you got here...?"

Melissa thought back to her conversations with Parker and Mrs. Price and the girls. "No," she said slowly. "It just didn't come up. I assumed they knew who I was, so I didn't say anything. But come to think of it," she added with a wry frown, "I think they must already think I'm one of the inmates, judging by the way they've treated me since I arrived."

"You mean you didn't get star treatment?" Rob drawled teasingly.

"Well, let's just say I was beginning to think reporters were regarded with about as much politeness as a visiting rattlesnake," Melissa snorted.

Rob laughed, and his look was tenderly affectionate. "Yes, Parker and Mrs. Price don't believe in coddling," he admitted without apology. "But that doesn't mean they don't have hearts," he added, as though he suspected Melissa of being critical of his employees. "You'll find that out before you've been here much longer." He gave her a direct look of speculation then, tempered with respect and something that made Melissa's heart beat faster. "Something tells me you're going to find out a lot of things before you've been here much longer, Melissa," he said with soft meaning. "I have the feeling you haven't found out yet what it can be like when the chemistry is this strong. For that matter, neither have I," he added with a grin.

Melissa didn't answer that. She *couldn't* answer that without precipitating exactly the sort of exploration that had almost gotten out of hand earlier.

"Don't let it worry you, honey," he drawled softly against her ear. "Just play it like you're one of them, babe," he instructed her softly. "We'll make out that you're a tough little number. You have a natural rebelliousness in you that should go along with that image nicely, even if it doesn't fit with your face."

He stepped back and took her shoulders in his strong, warm hands. "Fight me all you want, honey. It will look convincing to the others and it will make you feel better about what's going to happen between us."

Melissa gasped in indignation at his bluntness, but Rob merely chuckled. He ignored Melissa's glare as he escorted her to the door, took her into his arms, and proceeded to kiss the glare away and replace it with an expression of full submission she was helpless to combat.

He drew back slightly and traced the delicate curve of Melissa's cheek with a gentle finger. "The only thing that worries me about you," he whispered then, "is that I'm afraid you could get to be a habit, and that's a hard thing for an old bachelor like myself to accept at this late date."

Pleased and alarmed by his confession, Melissa reacted instinctively. "You aren't old," she whispered back. "You're just right."

"Am I?" he growled, a gleam of appreciation in his blue eyes. "For you, you mean?"

Melissa nodded. "For me," she admitted, helpless under his spell.

"I'd better be, hadn't I?" he mused on a deep note of satisfaction, "since it's going to happen anyway."

He opened the door then and gently pushed Melissa through it. "Go to bed now, sweetheart," he murmured smilingly. "For the time being I guess you and I are just going to have to dream away what's troubling us."

And with that, he shut the door, leaving Melissa feeling incredulous at how differently the interview had turned out from what she'd expected.

Chapter Four

At 4:30 the next morning Melissa was aroused by the delicate chirping of her Japanese travel alarm which, for lack of a bedside table, she had put on the floor beside her bed. She fumbled with a hand until she located the clock, slammed off the button that would shut off the alarm, then flopped onto her back to stare up at the darkened bedroom ceiling with a bleary glare that spelled out her mood.

"The oldest trick in the book," she muttered groggily. Rob Redding had caught her with one of the oldest tricks in the book—seducing the enemy—and she had fallen for it hook, line, and sinker! God, he was smooth!

She shook her head as she remembered how he hadn't turned a hair when she'd mentioned Delilah's name. Of course, he'd known that Rockport was Delilah's hometown, and he must have wondered about the connection when the arrangements had been made for Melissa to come out here, but he hadn't mentioned Delilah—nor her precipitous departure from the ranch—over the telephone, and he hadn't mentioned the circumstances under which Delilah had left during his and Melissa's discussion last night either.

So why didn't you ask him about it instead of trying to trap him by referring to Delilah as one of his successes, Miss Hot Shot Reporter? Melissa asked herself grumpily as she got up from the bed. But she knew the answer to that. She hadn't wanted to put him too much on guard. Rob had covered all the bases regarding Delilah by calling the girl's parents when Delilah had disappear from one of the shopping trips to Missoula the kids were allowed occasionally. He had seemed grimly concerned at first—had even contacted the sheriff to look for her. And when he had learned that Delilah had returned home with her mother's permission, he had quietly dropped the matter without even mentioning Delilah's condition when she'd left. Mrs. Muller-Smyth had said that he had seemed genuinely puzzled when she had screamed something hysterical over the phone at him about it; she had been so distraught at the time that she had slammed the phone down without accusing him directly or questioning him in detail.

The only logical conclusion to draw then was that either Rob hadn't known that Delilah had been beaten, which Melissa considered unlikely, or else he was going to pretend that he didn't know.

And as Melissa went about her preparations to begin the day, the only thing she knew for certain was that she wanted to get this investigation over with as quickly as possible and go back home to the peace and quiet of Rockport, where she could forget all about a certain blond Don Juan who was turning out to be a lot cleverer than she had expected him to be.

Of course, she decided in an attempt to maintain scrupulous fairness in the matter, Rob Redding might not be the guilty party in Delilah's beating and might not even have known about it, in which case, before she departed for the peace and quiet of Rockport, she would have to give some serious thought to whether she dared embark upon an affair with a man who had been capable of wiping out her years of training in one short hour.

And of course, she thought rather bleakly as she donned an old pair of jeans and a faded denim shirt, if he was guilty, she would have another misjudgment about men to chalk up on her private scoreboard of the heart. The thing to do meanwhile, was to view him as she should have done at meeting him last night—as just another human being who might, or might not, have secrets that for the sake of those kids in his care needed to be brought out into the light of day.

After visiting the bathroom and completing her some-what unglamorous toilet for the day, Melissa went back to her room, did her cleaning chores in keeping with her role as a delinquent inmate of this place, then made her way back downstairs for breakfast.

As she seated herself at the table she began playing the role Rob had assigned her by remarking in a grumbling tone that 4:30 in the morning was a hell of a time to start the day. That remark gained her a sharp rebuke from Mrs. Price and some mildly respectful glances of interest from her fellow inmates.

"What's the routine around here anyway?" she continued in the same grumbling tone, ignoring Mrs. Price's glare. "Are we expected to do slave labor or something? Is the great Mr. Robert Redding going to try to break my spirit and turn me into a good little girl?"

"That'll be enough," came the remembered tones of the man in question from behind Melissa, but the tones didn't contain a trace of the velvet seduction he'd employed on her the night before. Instead, they were quietly inflexible, and when Melissa swung around to view the man who, despite her expectations, had managed to surprise her by speaking to her like that, she saw that his expression was intimidating.

Rob's blue eyes were coolly assessing as he stood in the doorway with his hands on his hips, and Melissa had to grant him the charisma in the area of exerting authority that she had only speculated about before she'd met him. For an instant she actually felt like a delinquent kid all wrapped up in a shell of blustering hostility to hide the vulnerable interior of a scared youngster.

"Your spirit won't be broken here," he went on in that same authoritative voice, "but it sure as hell had better bend, or you're in for a long haul of sheer drudgery. You don't leave here until I'm satisfied that you've earned the right, and the faster you learn to cooperate, the faster you're going to be that much closer to going home."

Melissa felt slightly disconcerted that she couldn't detect a trace of a double meaning in his voice. Obviously—considering what had happened between the two of them last night—Rob Redding was a master actor, which only made Melissa more uneasy, as behind his facade could hide a character which, despite her earlier determination to remain objective, she didn't really want to find out was sinister.

"I can *work*, tough guy," Melissa replied, immediately falling into the role he was prescribing for her, "but if you think you're going to lord it over me just because you're in the driver's seat, you've got another think coming. I can take anything you can dish out."

Melissa cast a defiant little glance around the table to see how the rest of the girls were taking her performance, and was pleased to discover that they were viewing her with something like respectful awe. But overlying the awe was a sort of collective pity for her foolishness that gave her a little sinking sensation, for if Rob was determined to carry this farce to its limits, she just might regret entering into her role quite so wholeheartedly. After all, he would have to exert his authority to the full now, wouldn't he?

"So?" An anticipatory, slightly nasty smile curved his lips as Rob set about doing just that. "And how about clean living and good manners?" The voice was softly challenging. "Do you have any experience at practicing either of those?"

Melissa shrugged and tossed her hair back with a languid hand. "I take a bath occasionally," she replied in a flippant tone. "And I know what 'please' and 'thank you' mean, but I don't strain myself."

She was in the midst of congratulating herself on her acting talents when Rob paced to within a foot of her and bent from the waist to fix her with a look that brought a quick end to her self-congratulation.

"Then we shouldn't have any trouble, should we?" he said softly, giving her a cynical smile. "We'll test your capacity for work by assigning you to muck out the stables this morning, and when you're through doing that, I think I can guarantee that you'll be ready for one of your 'occasional' baths."

At the look of chagrined alarm that sprang up in Melissa's eyes, the smile became nastily benevolent. "You might even find that your manners improve when it means the difference between being assigned to the stables and learning how to rope and ride," he went on silkily. "Meanwhile, I want to hear you practice some manners right now." His silky tones disappeared abruptly then, and his eyes held Melissa's and displayed a force of will that made her distinctly uncomfortable. "Apologize to Mrs. Price for your attitude this morning, Melissa!" he rapped out in a tone of command.

Melissa had to admire his forcefulness, since she felt a compulsion to do as he ordered in spite of the fact that she wasn't one of his charges. For an instant she debated what her reaction would be if she were one, however, and decided that she would let him win this one, both from the standpoint that she wasn't here to create a focal point for active rebellion for the other inmates and because she sensed Rob might devise something even more unpleasant for her than cleaning out the stables if she defied him too strenuously.

Nevertheless, she gave her apology in a begrudging tone. "I'm sorry, Mrs. Price," she muttered, flashing the older woman a look that said she was acting under duress. Mrs. Price nodded regally, and Melissa was amazed to discover that the woman's little black eyes seemed to contain a hint of laughter Melissa would have sworn was out of character for such a dour-faced creature.

Rob straightened up and nodded then. "Good girl," he murmured with a look that confounded Melissa by making her want to squirm with pleasure that he was praising her! God, she thought dazedly, talk about charisma! This man was a model for the quality!

He looked at the rest of the girls then, who afforded him a much more convincing degree of respectful admiration than they'd given Melissa for defying him, and it was unadulterated by any such tame emotion as pity, either, Melissa noted somewhat sourly. It was plain that Rob Redding had these girls in the palm of his oh, so masculine hand.

"You girls know your assignments for today, don't you?" he inquired mildly, seemingly unaffected by the looks of adoration he was receiving.

There was a chorus of "Yes, Rob" that, to Melissa's sensitive ears, had overtones of something more closely resembling a reply such as, "Yes, master." Mentally she shook her head in a combination of admiration and disbelief at Rob's control over his "guests."

"All right, then, I'll see you later," he said with a smile that made even Melissa catch her breath, it was so magnificent. Perhaps because she was irritated that he could elicit such a response from her, she indulged in an act that was partly an extension of the character she was playing, partly a heartfelt rebellion against his charisma. She stuck out her tongue at Rob Redding behind his back.

There was a collective gasp around the table as Rob

turned his head slightly at that very instant and caught her in the act.

"Temper, temper," he drawled, as though unconcerned by her act of mutiny. "For a moment I was wondering if your face showed your true nature, but it seems as though it's a facade, and you haven't joined us under false pretenses after all."

Melissa wanted to laugh at his inadvertent bull's-eye, but his remark made her too uneasy to gather up the courage to do so. She *wished* he wouldn't say things like that to add to her already ambiguous feelings about deceiving him as well as the kids he was working with.

"Take care, Melissa," he added a soft warning, tempered with a self-confident smile. "I'm a patient man, but I'm not a saint."

Having voiced that soft-voiced warning, in which Melissa definitely heard a double meaning, he stepped out of the room and disappeared from sight, and Melissa was too distracted for a few moments by a combination of anticipation and alarm at having him act on his warning to notice that the indifference with which she'd been viewed previously had disappeared now.

Suddenly the other girls were bombarding her with questions about her qualifications for joining their select group, and Melissa's creative faculties were tested considerably as she spontaneously made up a history of shoplifting and troublemaking for herself that she hoped sounded convincing. Mrs. Price was the only one who didn't seem suitably impressed by her propensity for crime, but Melissa considered that a natural reaction and one she would have displayed herself if she had been in the housekeeper's shoes instead of her own.

When breakfast was over, the girls escorted Melissa to the stables, and on the way she spotted several boys issuing from a bunkhouse nearby, which satisfied her curiosity about where the rest of the Rocking R's contingent of delinquents resided. But after the girls had shown her what she was expected to do before departing for their own chores out on the range, her mood experienced a sudden downturn, and it was no trouble at all to work up a good anger toward Robert Redding for his distorted sense of humor.

The stables seemed to cover an acre of ground, and it seemed to Melissa that every available inch of the acre had been liberally sprinkled with ample evidence that the horses on the Rocking R were well-fed. As she got her first whiff of the pungent aroma that went along with such abundance, she decided grimly that Satan himself couldn't have devised a more fitting punishment for her sins, chief of which was being guilty of sassing the owner of all this outdoor sanitation. She could picture Rob laughing himself silly over assigning her this chore when she'd come here to write a story, but she was unable to appreciate the joke.

By noon she was barely able to crawl to the house for lunch, and her appetite was nonexistent as a result of a morning spent in the midst of that pungent aroma. However, she forced herself to drag her aching body up the stairs to make such repairs as seemed necessary to her appearance and to attempt to regain her own personal odor, but by the time she showed up at the dining room table, it was evident that she was not faring too well on her first day at the ranch.

The other girls gave Melissa amused, half-sympathetic looks when she crept into the dining room, and they pointedly ignored the fact that she pushed more food around on her plate than she ate. And then, all too soon, it was time to report back to the stables for duty again and commence the second half of her sentence to a horsy purgatory.

Melissa staggered back to the stables, cursing Rob Redding all the way, and along about 3:30 in the afternoon, when she had just about decided dying was in all ways preferable to living under such barbaric circumstances, she heard Rob's voice at the wide-open doors that led into the stables, speaking to one of the boys.

Where she got the strength, she would never afterward know, but the mere sound of Rob's by now loathsome masculine tones galvanized her into straightening up her crippled back, unbending the locked stance of her trembling knees, and pasting a cheerful smile on her hitherto scowling lips. She even managed a dry whistle when she sensed that he had come within earshot, and she was forever grateful that the leather gloves she wore concealed the swollen blisters on her palms. She would have died rather than give way to the permanent wince that wanted to take control of her mouth, and by the time Rob stood outside the stall she was working in, she hoped she was giving a convincing imitation of remaining unbowed under a burden she considered might have broken a veteran weight lifter.

When Rob finally spoke to her, she even managed to give a convincing start of surprise that he had deigned to appear on the scene.

"Melissa," he said, dryly amused, "you are a trouper, I'll give you that."

Melissa clutched her pitchfork harder at that tone lest she give in to the temptation to spear him on the spot. Instead, she turned her sweetest smile on him and blinked at him with innocent question. "I beg your pardon?" she inquired abstractedly. "Did you say something?"

A crooked smile appeared to curve Rob's sensuous mouth, and Melissa thought she saw a trace of admiration gleaming at her from those beautiful blue eyes of his, but she was in no mood to accept anything from him by that time, whether positive or negative.

"Come off it, honey," he said with quiet assurance that she was putting on a front for his benefit. Which she was, of course, but Melissa resisted the urge to glare her dislike of his knowing that. "You must be reeling by now," he continued with only a bare trace of sympathy. "You can take a break if you want to."

If she *wanted* to? God, such a word didn't begin to describe what Melissa desired in every cell, every nerve-ending, every muscle of her body! She considered opting for martyrdom and ignoring his offer, but she rejected the idea immediately. She was proud, but she was no fool.

"Well, if you really think so...." She shrugged a shoulder in a manner that was meant to be nonchalant, but which caused her an exquisite sensation of pain to accomplish. The world swayed around her for a moment in reaction to that pain, while a shimmering mist obscured the wretched invincibility of Rob's face from her tormented eyes, but she recovered quickly. Her smile was only marginally fainter as she dropped the pitchfork from her stiffened fingers and let herself slide down the wooden stall divider as gracefully as she could with her legs threatening to collapse beneath her weight.

"Cigarette?" Rob came into the stall, squatted down in front of her, and offered a package, but since Melissa didn't smoke, she had a good excuse for refusing that covered the fact that she couldn't have raised her hand to take the damned package if she'd wanted to.

"No, thank you," she managed to get out through lips stiff with the effort of maintaining her smile. "I don't smoke."

"Good for you," he murmured as he tucked the cigarette package back into his pocket. But his eyes never left her face, and Melissa could only hope that he wasn't detecting the bone-killing fatigue that gripped her whole body. She was damned if she was going to give him the satisfaction of savoring his loathsome joke!

He wasn't fooled, however, and Melissa bristled when he murmured, "I'm sorry, honey, I should have known you weren't up to this."

"I'm doing it, aren't I?" she snapped in a way that

revealed her true mood, and Melissa could have kicked herself when she saw his expression soften into a smile.

"You sure are, babe," he said so quietly she could barely hear him. "You're also doing a good job of making me feel like a heel."

That startled her, and the quick look she gave him disclosed that fact. "Did you think I did this on purpose?" he asked with wry puzzlement. "Don't you know how protective I feel toward you?"

Of course, Melissa hadn't known that he felt that way toward her, and she wasn't sure it was safe to believe him now, as a matter of fact. Still, it was hard to doubt the warm sincerity in his eyes, and it was even harder to resist the warmth that flooded her when he pulled off one of his gloves and stroked her cheek with his fingers.

"Poor little city girl," he murmured, watching intently as Melissa's mouth parted on an intake of breath at his action. "You make me want to take you in my lap and cuddle away your troubles." He smiled with rueful self-knowledge then and added, "Though I don't think I'd stick to cuddling for very long. There are a lot more interesting activities we could explore with you on my lap than cuddling."

Mesmerized by his voice and his touch every bit as much as she had been the night before, despite the warning bells going off full strength in her head, Melissa sat frozen into immobility as Rob bent forward and brushed his mouth lingeringly across hers. And when she made no effort to respond to the kiss other than to accept it, Rob drew back slightly and gave her a commanding, sensuous look that melted the fatigue right out of her bones.

"If you can't put your arms around me because you're too tired, at least kiss me back," he whispered encouragingly. "I've been starving for it since I let you go last night. Have a little pity for a man's famine, will you, sweetheart?"

Giving a resigned little moan, Melissa somehow found the energy to wrap her arms around Rob's neck and meet his descending mouth with all the fervor he could wish for.

For a few seconds Melissa forgot her fatigue, her assignment, and everything else except the exquisite sensations of pleasure Rob's hands and mouth imparted wherever they touched. She didn't even hear the sounds that made him release her abruptly and stand up, and her eyes were huge and soft with the remnants of her passion before the expression in them turned confused at the cool blankness in his as he put distance between them.

"When you're through with this stall, you can knock off for the day, Melissa," he said in a tone that immediately kindled her anger. "After dinner I want to talk to you," Rob went on without the slightest trace of the passion he had been displaying vividly only seconds before. "Report to my study as soon as you've eaten."

"For what?" Melissa retorted hostilely. "Are you a qualified psychiatrist, Mr. Redding? Want to make me lie down on your couch so you can delve into my psyche?" Her glare impaled him as she hoped he took her double meaning and realized the extent of her present disinclination to ever lie on that couch of his again, for any reason.

She saw Rob's jaw tense, and though his look was cold, she also sensed that he was suffering from an underlying frustration, which pleased her in her present state.

"Why don't you work on one of the other girls?" she asked in a flat tone of censure. "I'm sure they're all happy to lie on your couch any time you tell them to, but I'm not quite that gullible!"

Melissa regretted her accusation the instant it left her lips, and it was too late to call it back. She regretted it because she suspected she'd made it in the first place as a defense against the attraction she felt for Rob, which was an unworthy method of self-protection. And she regretted it because it had brought a narrow-eyed, furious reaction from him that made her heart sink with the thought that he might send her away before she'd had a chance to do what she'd come here for...or before she'd proved his innocence and could act on that attraction between them.

Rob's hands were clenched into fists, and Melissa involuntarily shrank against the wood supporting her back as she wondered if he was actually contemplating hitting her.

"Get back to work!" he snarled as he abruptly turned on his booted heel and strode away, every taut line of his body proclaiming his desire for retaliation and the effort it took to control that desire.

Melissa collapsed against the stall, boneless with regret that she had provoked Rob into demonstrating that he had a violent temper. And it was then that she realized that she didn't want Rob Redding to be guilty of anything. She wanted him to live up to his magnificent appearance and be strong and warm and caring to match the lovableness of his exterior.

But that was a trap, she realized wearily as she dragged her body upright. Exteriors were very often masks that hid violent human emotions, and wishing it wasn't so wouldn't change a thing. She would have to remember that when dealing with Rob in the future...especially when she was feeling most vulnerable toward him, as she was right now.

It was only after she'd gotten to her feet that she realized why Rob's attitude had changed so quickly after he'd been kissing her, which made her feel even worse at how she had reacted. They had had an audience during their argument. Two young men astride horses were in the long passage outside the stalls and were staring at her with widely varying expressions. One of them was a skinny, elfish-looking fellow whose dappled gray horse looked, to Melissa's inexperienced eye, as though it would like nothing more than to shake its rider off into the dirt, stomp on him a few times, and then get down to the serious business of guzzling hay. The horse's rider, however, was looking her up and down with an eager, lustful eye.

To escape that look, Melissa turned to the other young man, who was middling tall, stocky, had nondescript brown hair and a pair of frighteningly intelligent, yet curiously dead, pale gray eyes, and who was looking at her in a manner that made a shiver go down Melissa's spine. His manner was above reproach as he nodded politely to her, but for some reason, Melissa felt crawly inside, as though she were being viewed as a potential victim for a large, predatory insect.

Melissa preferred lust to such sensations, so she turned back to the first young man. "Hi," she ventured, mistakenly thinking that perhaps such a mundane greeting would break the fellow's concentration on whatever appeal her body had for him. It did, but only marginally.

"Hi," he returned the greeting abstractedly as he continued to peruse her charms with dedicated zeal. "What's your name?"

"Mel," she replied as she placed a hand gingerly on her aching back and eyed the young man with wary caution. "Mel McKee. What's yours?"

"Lester Smith," the young man murmured after another intent inspection that made Melissa give an inward sigh of resignation. She couldn't fathom why the fellow was so obviously enamored by her when he had obviously been around the ranch long enough to have been exposed to her feminine competition, but she reflected that perhaps the other girls were simply too much for this young man to handle, and he figured she was easier game.

She didn't want to hurt his feelings, but in her present mood his leer was making her want to haul him down off his horse and slap him silly. She turned back to the other young man.

"I'm Micah Gilroy," he said, introducing himself in a soft, uninflected tone that made Melissa feel as uneasy as she had under the gaze of his unexpressive pale gray eyes. Then her attention was abruptly jerked back to Lester Smith, as he voiced a question that put her on the spot.

"Will you go to the barn dance with me Saturday night?" Lester asked with an eager aggressiveness that made Melissa back up a step in alarm.

"Ah...barn dance?" she stalled, knowing there was no way she was going to a dance with this young lecher on Saturday or any other night, but unwilling to damage his perhaps fragile ego with a flat no.

"Yeah," he answered eagerly as he kicked his heels out of his stirrups and slid off his horse. "We have one almost every Saturday night."

Mistakenly Melissa backed up as Lester came toward her, until she felt the stall divider at her back and realized she had trapped herself. Irritation made her straighten her shoulders and stand firm when Lester came to a stop mere inches from her.

"We all go," Lester continued as his avid gaze ran over her body eagerly. "And it's okay to pair off, as long as we don't disappear into the bushes. We do anyway, though, if we get the chance."

"Ah...do what?" Melissa replied as she slid unobtrusively away from the trap she'd gotten herself into and eased out into the long aisle running the length of the barn. She wasn't sure why she was so wary of Lester. He wasn't that much taller than she was and he was skinny to boot, but perhaps the look of a half-starved sex maniac in his darting brown eyes was making her afraid that his libido could make up for his stature.

"Take off for the bushes, of course," Lester said with surprised impatience. "It's the only fun we get around here." Then he was back to the attack. "Will you go with me?"

Melissa hedged. "I...ah...don't think I'd better make any commitments just yet," she said hesitantly. "I mean, I'm new here," she explained gently. "And who knows? I might do something between now and then to make Mr. Redding take away my privileges."

Melissa sensed an alertness from the other young man, Micah Gilroy, at the mention of Rob's name, but Lester's reaction distracted her.

"Rob?" Lester inquired, looking startled and amused. "Oh, he won't do that. He's an okay guy when you get to know him. You don't want to cross him, but he's not a bastard or anything."

A silly, totally uncalled for warmth spread through Melissa at hearing Lester's evaluation of Rob, and she struggled to maintain her objectivity. Lester was waiting to see if his words had made a difference, and Melissa felt a rush of friendly sympathy for him.

"Still," she said with a grin to take away the sting of rejection, "I'd better get the lay of the land before I...ah...head for any bushes."

Lester, although obviously disappointed, seemed to react to Melissa's friendliness positively, and he then elected for prudence in his pursuit.

"Well, okay," he said reluctantly. "But if you change your mind, you'll let me know, won't you?"

He now looked like a puppy waiting to be petted, and Melissa relaxed completely. "Sure," she agreed. "I just need to find my feet around here for a while."

That statement reminded her that Lester might be a fount of information if she handled him right, and as Micah climbed from his horse and led it to a stall farther down the row, Melissa picked up her pitchfork again.

"How do you like it here, Lester?" she inquired

casually as she forced her aching body to resume working. "Is it pretty bad?"

Lester had gone back to his horse and was leading it into the clean stall next to the one Melissa still had to finish. "Bad?" He considered the question thoughtfully. "No," he decided, giving Melissa a rueful grin over his horse's back as he began to unsaddle. "Not that it's a country club, mind you. But Rob is fair and easy to talk to, you know?"

Melissa did know, but she wasn't about to admit it. "Is he?" she answered coldly, and immediately sensed a quality of alertness from Micah as he unsaddled his own horse within hearing distance. He was silent, but Melissa had the impression he was listening to the conversation between her and Lester with intense interest. "You couldn't prove it by me," she went on as she wondered why Micah seemed to come to attention every time Rob's name was mentioned. "He doesn't seem to want to *talk* to me," Melissa continued in a complaining tone. "All he wants to do is issue orders where I'm concerned."

Lester chuckled sympathetically. "Oh, you'll get the dirty jobs for a while," he informed her easily, "and he'll watch you real close and won't tolerate any backtalk, but you'll like him after you've been here a while, and he'll ease up on you."

But Melissa had the impression that where she was concerned, Rob Redding not only didn't plan to ease up, he was determined to push her to her limits. She couldn't say that to Lester, however, so she merely gave a disbelieving snort and bent to her work, convinced that if she didn't arrange her body just right when she went to sleep that night, she'd never be able to straighten it out again in the morning.

"I'll help you as soon as I'm done here," Lester offered as he began to rub down his horse with a blanket, "but Rob won't tolerate us neglecting our horses, so I have to finish this first."

"That's okay, Lester," Melissa said, declining his of-fer. "I'm almost done, and I doubt if Mr. Redding would approve of my accepting your help. He probably likes his pound of flesh to come off of one cow at a time."

A little of the bitterness she was feeling at Rob's sub-jecting her to the sort of slave labor she'd been doing all day crept into her tone, and then she wished she hadn't let it when she heard a nasty chuckle that signaled Rob had returned and had heard every word she'd said.

"You're quite right, Miss McKee," he said in the dulcet tones of a man who knew he had the upper hand. Melissa jerked upright, and as she experienced the pain of that misguided action, she couldn't hide the wince that expressed that pain. She saw that Rob had noted her wince and was evidently feeling immensely satisfied at being the cause of it.

"I'm glad you've picked up on my requirements so quickly," he drawled with smooth silkiness. "I want you to go clean up for dinner now, Miss McKee," he went on smoothly. "And I hope this is going to be one of the infrequent occasions when you choose to bathe before eating?"

Melissa wished she could have stood the thought of coming to the table in clothes she'd worked in all day, smelling like a stable, just to get back at him, but she knew she wasn't up to it. The thought of a long, hot bath was all that was enabling her to stand upright at the moment.

"I'll *think* about it," she snapped.

"I suggest you think hard," he responded in a tone of warning that made Melissa glare her resentment at him.

He challenged her with a blue-eyed stare that even-tually made Melissa drop her eyes, though such capitu-lation made her grit her teeth and wish she didn't have to keep remembering that it wasn't her intention to chal-lenge his authority successfully since, if he really was doing these young people some good, that challenge might interfere with the process of rehabilitation going on here.

"Good." He accepted her nonverbal surrender in a soft tone of approval that, despite her good resolutions, feathered her spine unbearably. "I'll see you later," he then said in a tone of promise that brought a wave of unwelcome warmth to Melissa's loins.

When he had gone, Lester appeared at the opening to the stall where Melissa was furiously working, and his face was alight with curiosity. "What's going on with you and Rob?" he asked. "Nobody else dares talk to him like that."

"Well, I do!" Melissa snapped before she remembered she didn't want to interfere with the respect the young people afforded Rob—at least not until she'd determined whether he deserved that respect. She muted her tone to one of youthful, somewhat helpless, complaint and added, "Who does he think he is, anyway?"

"He's the boss," Lester said in a tone of complete acceptance.

Melissa took a deep breath and dampened down her pride. "Well, I guess he is," she admitted grudgingly, "but I don't happen to like being bossed."

"Who does?" Lester shrugged. "But the way Rob does it is better than most people. He lets you keep your pride."

Melissa straightened at that statement, realizing that from what she'd seen so far, Lester's evaluation was correct—in everyone's case but her own, that is. And as she straightened, her gaze collided with Micah's, where he was staring at her from two stalls away. His pale eyes were showing more animation than she'd seen in him yet, and Melissa had the curious sensation that he was experiencing pride himself, but whether in himself or in Rob, she wasn't certain.

For some reason that uncertainty made her feel uneasy, though she didn't show that uneasiness as she shrugged and went back to work, concentrating now on finishing her task so that she could climb into a hot tub of water and blissfully wash away the dirt and fatigue of the day.

But as she worked, despite her preoccupation with a bath, she couldn't damp down the underlying feeling of anticipation she was experiencing at seeing Rob alone again after dinner. And anticipation was the last thing she should have been feeling about any meeting with a man who might possibly be using the sexual attraction he knew he inspired in her to conceal other, more dangerous, emotions he used against others.

Chapter Five

The bath helped, but Melissa was still so tired after she'd crawled back up to her third-floor warren to dress that she couldn't resist the lure of the pristine little bed. She thought if she could only stretch out for half an hour and experience the bliss of absolute nonmovement, she might be capable of pulling on her clothes and reporting for dinner.

The next thing she knew, someone was whopping her bottom with a hand that seemed composed of equal parts tough leather and concrete.

"Whaa—!" She jerked over onto her back, frantically blinking away the mists of sleep. The precipitate movement awakened sensations resembling the fires of hell in her overused muscles and a strangled "Aargh!" left her lips in a tone of agony.

"Get up, Melissa!" The firm tones were loathsomely familiar, and through the blurriness of agonized tears Melissa made out the towering form of the man she least wanted to see her crying.

"You hit me!" Rage was her only defense against blubbering in emotional reaction to the fatigue, pain, and humiliation she was feeling.

Rob hesitated, his expression denoting regret, but Melissa was in no mood for an apology.

"You damned Neanderthal!" she spat, almost incoherent in her anger, certain that if she let her rage die for an instant, she would cry and humiliate herself further.

"Oh, come on, honey, it was just a little pat on the rear," Rob started to say, although he looked uncomfortable as he spoke, as though he would rather be apologizing if Melissa hadn't reacted so heatedly.

"A little pat!" Melissa yelled. She was forcing her body to obey her in her efforts to sit up, but she wasn't in the least grateful when Rob reached down and took her shoulders in his hands, lifting her to her feet as though she were as light as a child. He subdued her weak struggling easily, his physical mastery aided by the fact that Melissa could barely move her muscles at all, much less in a strong defense.

"Hush, now," Rob demanded quietly as he pulled her against his body, and there was a tinge of amusement in his tone that didn't sit well with Melissa. "Neanderthals hit their women over the head with clubs. They didn't use civilized persuasion like this...."

His tone changed to a silken purr as his head came down, and then his lips and the subtle teasing of his mustache were dispensing the "civilized persuasion" he had mentioned with a great deal more effect than Melissa found herself capable of resisting. The kiss was firm, warm, and comforting, and it was all Melissa could do to keep from winding herself around Rob like ivy clinging to a tree. As it was, she was unable to keep her mouth from softening, then opening under Rob's so that he could deepen the kiss, while she kept her hands clenched into fists against his chest.

When he finally lifted his head, she was physically limp, but there still remained enough gumption in her to protest the pleased, contented expression in his eyes that smacked dangerously of self-satisfaction at having subdued her anger so easily.

"You're not supposed to kiss your inmates," she muttered, the sulkiness in her tone too muted to cause Rob much discomfort.

"Or delve into their psyches on my couch?" he drawled in a voice like rough silk.

Startled by his reminder of her earlier accusation, Melissa looked up at him apologetically. "I'm sorry I said that, Rob," she whispered miserably. "I was just so mad at you...."

"I know," he whispered back, his lips like warm brands as he slid them over the skin of her neck. "I figured that out after I got over being mad myself." And then he chuckled deeply. "Thank God you're not an inmate," he growled as he moved one hand restlessly over her bottom. "If you were, I think you might have cause to question my ethics."

His comment sparked a faint remembrance in Melissa that she was here to do a job, not to conduct an affair of the heart. "I don't see how you resist what I accused you of, Rob," she sighed, striving for a tone of innocence and accomplishing it because she couldn't keep her growing arousal out of her voice rather than through her talent for acting. "The girls here are so beautiful. Is it just because you're responsible for them that you've picked me to seduce instead of one of them?"

Rob drew his head back and frowned at her. "You're joking, aren't you? They're kids, Melissa!" he stated, as though that fact should have been self-evident, though Melissa had never seen females who looked less like kids than the ones who inhabited Rob's ranch. "And yes, they're under my care," he went on, looking at her sternly. "I'd defeat everything I'm working toward if I touched one of them."

"I was only kidding, Rob," Melissa hastily assured him, pleased and relieved by his reaction while feeling guilty about her subterfuge.

At that, he smiled down into Melissa's bemused eyes, and that charisma of his was exerted full force. "Even if they were available," he said huskily, "I'd rather have you. You pack quite a punch of your own when it comes to feminine attraction. I wanted you the instant I saw you.''

"You did?" Melissa asked shakily, feeling so pleased that Rob was attracted to her and so much under his spell that once again she forgot why she was at his ranch and became fully caught up in the interaction between the two of them.

"You know I did," Rob grated, his eyes focusing hungrily on Melissa's sleep-softened mouth. "And I do," he breathed just before he covered her lips with his own again and drained away the last of her resistance.

This time the kiss threatened to get out of hand before Rob at last drew back and took Melissa's shoulders in his hands to push her away. "This will have to wait until after dinner," he said, pleasing Melissa with the shaken quality in his voice. "We're late," he said more firmly, turning Melissa and pointing her toward where her clothes were laid out on the end of the bed. "Get dressed and come down," he urged her as he started moving toward the door of her bedroom. "I've got to go cool off before I show myself downstairs and shock the stuffing out of Mrs. Price."

Melissa smiled at that, but as the door closed behind Rob the smile faded, to be replaced by a look of bewildered unhappiness at her inability to keep her mind on the job she was here to do. Rob and his damned sex appeal kept getting in the way, and at the rate things were heating up between them, her objectivity would be totally compromised before she found one solid piece of evidence to convict or absolve him of hurting Delilah.

As she dressed, Melissa resolved once again to get a grip on her emotions and concentrate on her journalistic ethics, but as she slowly descended the stairs a few minutes later, she was not at all sure she was going to be able to stay on a story where she had already proved herself to be lamentably prejudiced toward the chief suspect.

"I apologize for being late," she murmured to Mrs. Price rather than to Rob when she was at last seated at the dinner table.

To her surprise, the usual ungiving expression was missing from Mrs. Price's black eyes. The woman didn't smile with her lips, but Melissa could have sworn there was one lurking in that ebony darkness, and when Mrs. Price nodded her head in acceptance of Melissa's apology, the rest of the girls began chattering and eating in a normal manner, thus distracting Melissa from thinking about a reason for Mrs. Price's softening toward her.

It wasn't until dessert that Melissa found the courage to dart a look at Rob, and when she did, it was to find him looking right back at her with a disconcerting intentness that shook her to her toes. His look contained a message that brought a warm flush of desire to her skin, as well as a burgeoning sense of panic as she realized what he had in mind for later that evening.

Realizing that she had to delay any such intimacy until she knew for sure that Rob was innocent of harming Delilah, and unable to depend upon her own willpower to provide that delay, she turned her anxious gaze back to Mrs. Price.

"Mrs. Price," she said, burying her instinctive wish to avoid exposing her pride in the way she was about to, "I can barely move. Do you have any liniment you could put on me after dinner?"

Out of the corner of her eyes she saw a frown developing on Rob's face and hoped he wasn't going to make any objection to her plan to avoid seeing him after dinner. And then she realized that he was feeling guilty at having caused her aches and pains, and she found herself wanting to erase that guilty look from his darling face. But she couldn't.

"Why, yes, I do, Melissa," Mrs. Price answered, and Melissa felt a twinge of guilt of her own at the note of concern in the woman's voice, even though it was true that Melissa needed a massage from her hostess rather than her host at this particular point. "The girls can do the cleaning up after dinner," Mrs. Price went on, fixing two of the other girls at the table with a stern eye, "and I'll come upstairs with you to rub you down."

Mrs. Price then gave Rob an exasperated look that condemned him in a mild fashion for inflicting such pain on a young woman in his charge. Melissa felt even guiltier at seeing that look, though a certain part of her felt it was no more than Rob deserved.

Besides, she reflected a few minutes later as she and Mrs. Price climbed three precipitous flights of stairs with Melissa's muscles protesting every step of the way. *It's probably about time Rob Redding had to wait for a woman to cave in to his brand of sex appeal for a change.*

But an hour later, as Melissa lay in her narrow bed nursing aches and pains that had been only partially relieved by Mrs. Price's vigorous rubdown with an evil-smelling liniment, she felt a hollow sense of empty victory at having eluded Rob that was accentuated by the call of a coyote echoing mournfully from a distant hillside, sounding as lonely as she felt.

The next morning, however, Melissa was feeling more optimistic, and when Mrs. Price took her under her protective wing, setting Melissa to lighter household tasks instead of allowing her to be sent to the stables again, Melissa was grateful that she had hit upon the only person on the ranch who might be an effective ally in diverting Rob from his intentions.

Melissa spent the morning in Mrs. Price's kitchen, first peeling potatoes and then rolling out pie dough under the older woman's watchful eye. When it became evident that Melissa knew what she was about, Melissa felt Mrs. Price's attitude relax, encouraging Melissa to begin some discreet inquiries.

"How come all the girls are so pretty?" she asked in what she hoped was a casual manner.

Mrs. Price was at the sink cleaning vegetables, and when she heard the woman's chuckle, Melissa looked up. Mrs. Price was looking at her over her shoulder, amused sympathy in her black eyes. "You're not jealous, are you?" Mrs. Price chided her. "You're attractive yourself."

Melissa shrugged. "I just never pictured delinquents as looking like those girls do."

Mrs. Price snorted her amazement. "And do you think *you* look like a delinquent?" she scoffed. "I can assure you you don't!"

Upon reflection, Melissa thought Mrs. Price had a point. She had spent too many years having to show her ID card at adult entertainment establishments and facing patent looks of disbelief when she was able to produce proof that she was over twenty-one, to be unaware that she looked like an innocent instead of a criminal.

"Besides," Mrs. Price then went on, "those girls—and the boys, too—mostly come from affluent homes. They're more victims than true delinquents. If they were really bad, they'd be in reform schools instead of out here."

"What do you mean?" Melissa asked, delighted that Mrs. Price was proving to be so informative, and hoping the woman wouldn't suddenly remember that she wasn't talking to another adult.

Perhaps it was because Mrs. Price was stuck out on the ranch without an opportunity to speak to other adult women very often, or perhaps it was because she was unconsciously picking up indications that Melissa was a great deal more mature than her image conveyed, but the woman got into her subject vigorously then, astonishing Melissa with her loquacity.

"There's nothing wrong with these kids that a lot less money and a lot more attention from their parents

wouldn't have cured a long time ago,'' Mrs. Price snorted. ''They get into trouble because they're starved to
death for attention, and being bad is the only way they
can get it.''

She shrugged, and her voice took on a disgusted tone.
''Oh, sure, their moms and dads give them everything
money can buy. Instead of spending an hour a day talking
to their children, they buy them something to keep them
occupied and out of their hair, so the daddies can spend
every second piling up more money and power and the
mommies can spend hours at the beauty parlor or tennis
lessons or long lunches with their sophisticated friends.''

Melissa had by now given up on rolling pie dough in
order to listen intently to Mrs. Price's diatribe, but the
woman swung around and waved a finger imperiously
at the mound of dough, telling Melissa nonverbally to
get back to work. Reluctantly Melissa did so, but as she
did she prodded Mrs. Price to go on.

''But if the kids have had every advantage,'' she said
in a speculative tone, ''I don't see how they ended up
here.''

''Advantage!'' Mrs. Price snapped. ''It all depends
on what you think a real advantage is, doesn't it?'' she
asked huffily, and before Melissa could answer, she
went on. ''The advantages a kid needs are attention,
love, discipline, and encouragement. It doesn't matter if
you look like a movie star or are as smart as Einstein if
you feel worthless inside, and most of these kids do feel
that way. After all, if your own parents won't pay any
attention to you, and let you get away with murder for
years, it must mean you're not worth paying attention
to, mustn't it?''

Melissa looked up thoughtfully at Mrs. Price, and
when the woman saw that look, she flushed a little, obviously thinking that Melissa might have had just such
an upbringing. Melissa hastened to reassure her that
such was not the case.

"I guess I was lucky," she said, adopting a noncommittal tone. "I not only had parents who paid attention to me, but an extraordinary grandmother as well. They all still like to know what I'm up to." And then Melissa abruptly shut up, realizing she had said far too much while caught up in Mrs. Price's theories about what had brought about the troubles of the ranch's inmates.

Mrs. Price frowned, first in puzzlement, and then with stern censorship at Melissa. "Then you have no excuse for running wild, do you, missy?" she reproved tartly.

Melissa decided discretion was the better part of valor at this point, and shook her head. "No, Mrs. Price, I don't," she said quite truthfully.

Mrs. Price hesitated, obviously taken aback by Melissa's candor. Then she said, "Hmph! Then maybe there's hope for you yet, if you can learn to control that nasty tongue of yours and your temper."

"I wouldn't be surprised," Melissa murmured, turning her head away to hide a smile. Mrs. Price might not know it, but even though Melissa wasn't what she seemed to be, the accusations of having a "nasty tongue" and a "temper" were all too accurate descriptions of Melissa's shortcomings, and Melissa knew it. However, she considered her main shortcoming at this particular time a regrettable lustiness every single time she came near a certain Montana rancher, and she was quite happy to remain under Mrs. Price's protection when she knew she would most likely do something unethical, if not immoral, under the circumstances, if she were left without that protection.

"So you think the kids are starved for real affection and loving discipline?" she said to direct attention away from herself, seeking to get back to the sort of information she'd come here to get.

"Absolutely," Mrs. Price stated with certainty. "And Rob and the rest of us give them what they need."

Modesty seemed to get the better of her then, and she backtracked a little. "Well, Rob does most of it," she admitted, and the tone of affection in her voice spelled out her admiration and respect for Rob. "He has a way with kids. They sense he genuinely likes them and that he won't put up with any nonsense from them. After one of those poor yet materially-pampered little darlings, starved of love and discipline, is here for a while, they start to develop some self-respect."

"How does he do it?" Melissa inquired mildly.

"Why, he teaches them how to work, for one thing!" Mrs. Price bristled. "And he gives each of them individual, respectful attention. It gives them self-confidence to earn their own way, so to speak, and it makes them feel worth something when a man like him acts like they count." Mrs. Price paused for a second, and then fixed Melissa with a stern eye. "Of course, *some* kids don't like his discipline at first, and they get a little sassy with him, but he knows how to deal with that!"

He certainly does, Melissa thought silently with dry ruefulness, *but I wonder if Mrs. Price would approve the way he exerts his "discipline" where I'm concerned?*

Still, to be fair, Melissa had to admit that Rob had a natural authority about him that enabled him to dispense discipline in a normal way as well as through his sexual dominance. And since he did, she wondered thoughtfully, he wouldn't need to resort to physical violence to bring a young person in line.

Of course, she decided with an inward sigh, she was already far too prejudiced where he was concerned and was more than willing to give him the benefit of the doubt, which was not good journalism. But still, there was something about him that made it almost impossible for her to believe he had hurt Delilah, even though he had certainly been in a temper yesterday when Melissa had half-accused him of taking sexual advantage of the female contingent of his household on his studio couch.

Well, wouldn't it make you mad if someone accused you of something like that? Melissa reasoned. And the answer was disturbingly murky, since she couldn't remember ever wanting to hurt someone physically. Yelling was one thing. Hitting was quite another.

Mrs. Price bustled off to do some dusting and sweeping then, ending their discussion with an admonition to Melissa to finish what she was doing, then go out back and hoe the vegetable garden that provided a good deal of the delicious food that appeared on the dinner table every day.

Melissa changed to a pair of shorts and a halter top before she departed the house, thinking that if she was going to have to grub around outside anyway, she could at least get some extra benefit out of the chore by enhancing her tan at the same time.

She was involved in gently coaxing weeds from between neat rows of turnips when she had the prickly sensation of being watched and looked up to find Rob nearby. He was seated astride a really stunning black stallion, and to Melissa's bemused eyes, he looked like every hero she had ever seen in a Western movie.

He didn't speak to her, and indeed, when she caught his eyes, he gave a flick of the reins and a kick of his heels and disappeared in a gallop, earning Melissa's admiration for the grace with which he rode. But then he hadn't had to speak to her in words. His look had been as eloquently communicative of his feelings as any speech he could have made, and it took a long time before the tremors of aroused feminine response to the promise in his eyes disappeared so that Melissa could think straight again.

At dinner that night she didn't know whether to be relieved or put out that it was Rob's turn to eat with the boys that night, but later, alone in her bed, which she had sought out immediately following the meal, as she was still a physical wreck from her sojourn in the stables, she had to admit that it was best in every way that Rob hadn't had an opportunity to exert his influence over her the way he was so capable of doing.

The next morning Parker appeared after breakfast, just when Melissa was plotting how she could get around to talking confidentially to one or more of the girls. He allowed no protest as he escorted Melissa to the corral attached to the stables, and when Melissa learned that she was going to be introduced to the art of horseback riding, she had to gather all her courage in her hands, since horses had always seemed to her to be much too big, and much too arrogant, for someone her size to fool around with.

Parker left her standing at the corral railing eyeing the powerful muscles and prancing, feisty steps of her next challenge with a wary eye while he went inside the stable to collect a saddle.

When he reappeared, she glanced at the saddle doubtfully. "Are you really going to insist that I ride one of these animals, Parker?" she inquired dolefully. "I really don't think I want to."

Parker cackled, and the look in his faded brown eyes told Melissa he was not inclined to be merciful. "You ain't gonna ride today, missy," he informed her with all the kindness of a snake charmer informing an innocent victim that she wasn't going to get bitten that day. "You're gonna learn how to saddle, how to talk to a horse, and how to take care of one after you've been on its back all day."

Melissa would have sighed with relief, but she didn't think she was going to like the peripheral arrangements of horseback riding any better than she was going to like the actual riding. Of course, she had ridden meek riding-stable horses a couple of times, but even those mild-mannered creatures had quickly discovered they could intimidate her and had then proceeded to do just that. And the horses milling in the corral were a far cry from the breed she had become marginally acquainted with in her school days. These animals all looked as though they were prepared not only to intimidate, but to get downright hostile about who was going to be boss.

Quelling her nervousness as best she could, Melissa nevertheless paid strict attention to Parker's instructions and even managed to carry them out with a creditable degree of success. When that part of the instruction was over, she was about to make her escape when Parker apparently decided—mistakenly, of course—that she deserved a reward.

"Let's put you on old Milly for a few minutes," he suggested in what Melissa privately decided was an expression of his innate sadism.

"Oh, I don't think. . ." she started to say, but Parker wasn't listening.

"Come on, missy," he said impatiently when Melissa hung back away from the side of the huge horse she had managed to saddle a few moments earlier. "Milly wouldn't hurt a fly. She's too old to be cantankerous."

Closing her eyes in despair, Melissa cursed fate and journalism careers and unfeeling editors who sent reporters to do their dirty work, but she moved closer while she was doing so. And just as she reached Milly's side, the horse swung her huge head around and gave Melissa an almost maternal look of gentle affection that eased Melissa's fears considerably.

Fortunately for Melissa's peace of mind, Parker hadn't lied about Milly's gentleness, and after Melissa got over the strangeness of sitting far too high in the air astride an animal who outweighed her by a thousand pounds, Melissa actually began to enjoy the experience. She was feeling pretty confident by the time the lesson was over and was even feeling grateful that it had been Parker rather than Rob who had seen what a little coward she'd been at first. Too, Parker seemed pleased with her, and she began to think he wasn't nearly as sadistic as she'd thought he was.

Her sense of self-satisfaction lasted right up until dinner when, though it was Rob's usual night to eat with the girls, he failed to appear. Mrs. Price volunteered the information that he'd had to go into town—wherever the hell the town was; Melissa still didn't know—and her mood immediately deteriorated as she speculated about whether his visit was business or social. After all, he was a man in his thirties, and more than just attractive to women.

Preoccupied with her speculation as to the reason for his absence, Melissa failed to take advantage of her opportunities to talk to the girls, as they gathered together in the den for an hour's recreation after dinner, and it was only later as she lay in bed trying to sleep that she cursed herself for letting her preoccupation with Rob distract her from her job once again.

Damn it, you've been here three and a half days already, Melissa McKee, she lectured herself sternly as she tossed and turned, *and you haven't learned a thing!*

But she was still unable to concentrate on her reason for being at the Rocking R, and when she fell asleep at last, she did so tormented by images of Rob making love to some Montana beauty who wouldn't make excuses to avoid his amorous attentions but would welcome him with open arms any time he chose.

The next day Parker came for her again, and after an hour or so of riding on Milly's broad, gentle back, he decreed she was ready for something a little more spirited, and that was how Melissa met Fred.

Fred was several hundred pounds of ugly brown walleyed, energetic, supposedly well-trained, and decidedly hostile horse. As Melissa eyed him warily she couldn't decide if his hostility was directed at her personally or the world in general, but since she was the one who was going to come to his particular attention, it didn't matter what his attitude was toward the rest of humanity.

"He's all yours, missy," Parker informed her with a gleeful chuckle that aroused all her suspicions about his sadistic tendencies again.

"Thank you, but I prefer Milly," Melissa stated unequivocally.

"Tough," Parker stated just as unequivocally. "Milly's too old to work the range. It's Fred or nothing."

"I'll take nothing."

"You'll take Fred."

Realizing her arguments would avail nothing against Parker's stubbornness, Melissa gritted her teeth and stomped to Fred's side to mount the monster, certain she was going to die within the hour and hoping Parker would be charged with homicide.

But Fred, it seemed, did not wish to be mounted. Each time Melissa tried to place her booted foot in the stirrup, Fred sidled away, with the result that Melissa repeatedly courted the danger of falling in the dirt.

Parker let this go on for a few minutes before he gave a disgusted little noise through his teeth and grabbed Fred's head to keep him still while Melissa climbed onto the horse's huge back.

When Melissa at last had gained the dubious sanctuary of the saddle, had her feet firmly planted in the stirrups and the reins in her hands, Parker let go of Fred's head, and Fred promptly gave one magnificent, well-timed buck and let Melissa go—right into the dirt of the corral.

Melissa had almost gotten over all the aches and pains of her day in the stable. Fred was reinitiating them with a vengeance. Three times she mounted him and three times he threw her. And as she lay in the dirt after the last throw, every vestige of air sucked out of her lungs, she began to get mad.

When she was at last able to get to her feet, Melissa

rose up, cursing as fluently as she had ever managed in her life, stomped to where Fred stood, apparently smirking in vile satisfaction at having bested her, planted her feet firmly, reared back, and socked Fred right in the jaw, putting every ounce of muscle she had into the blow.

Melissa was unamused to find that her action had convulsed Parker. He was bent from the waist, cackling dementedly and making no effort to hide the fact that Melissa's battle with Fred was the best entertainment he'd had in years.

She got up into the saddle again, uncaring that Fred had an expression in his eye that would have suited an enraged bull and that he appeared to be foaming at the mouth. Melissa was also uncaring that she now had an audience of appreciative kibitzers who had gathered to watch the fun. All she really cared about was showing one oversize, ill-tempered refugee from the range that she was his match.

From the cheers and yells that vaguely reached her ears as Melissa hung on to Fred's pitching, bucking back, it appeared that her audience was having the time of their lives. Melissa was not, however. She was merely determined that Fred would not succeed in bucking her off into the dirt of the corral again, because she had a good idea that if he did, he would stomp her into mincemeat. Sheer rage had pumped her adrenaline to the point where she felt she could have lifted an automobile with her bare hands, if necessary, and she wasn't about to let a mere horse thwart her.

Fred bucked and twisted, reared and whirled, and tried to scrape Melissa off onto the corral fence. He reared back his head and hit her in the nose, making stars whirl before her eyes, but still Melissa managed to hang on. He galloped around and around the corral and generally did his level best to unseat her, but Melissa was as mad as he was, and somehow she managed to stick in the saddle until at last Fred came to a stop in the middle of the corral and stood trembling and snorting and cursing Melissa in horse language.

Melissa sat, trembling and frozen in the saddle, cursing Fred in English, and totally unable to get down. It was as though every one of her muscles had frozen into place. Her legs were locked around Fred's huge stomach, her hands clenched the reins in a death grip, and her back was as rigid as a telephone pole.

If Rob hadn't jumped the corral fence, strode up to where Melissa and Fred remained in an impasse, and pried her fingers and legs loose, then lifted her off Fred's back, she didn't know how or when she would ever have gotten down. After she saw the hard glitter of anger in Rob's clear blue eyes, the grim line of his mouth, and the dangerously taut way he held his jaw, however, she began to wish she was back in the saddle.

Fortunately Rob didn't let go of Melissa after she was on the ground. If he had, she would have collapsed in a heap at his feet. But in defiance of the hostility she saw in Rob's expression, which she took to be directed at her, Melissa did manage to conquer the tears of reaction glistening in her eyes and mutter a shaken defense.

"I won!" she declared with weak bravado just before her knees folded beneath her, forcing Rob to swing her up into his arms.

He carried her toward the house to the accompaniment of cheers and clapping from the other onlookers, but he was ominously silent. Melissa was incapable of speech, and she simply closed her eyes and endured as Rob carried her inside, then up all three flights of stairs to her bedroom, where he placed her on her bed, then stayed positioned over her, supporting himself with both hands on either side of her body.

Melissa opened her eyes, then quickly closed them again when it became evident from Rob's expression that he was not only unsympathetic, he was on the verge of an explosion.

"Don't you *ever, ever,* go near that horse again!" he bit out violently.

Melissa was in no state to argue, but she was definitely feeling abused by Rob's attitude, and she stubbornly refused to answer him.

"Do you hear me?" he then said in a tone Melissa had never heard from him before and that convinced her that Rob in this mood made Fred appear to be a mouse to his lion. Wisely she decided to capitulate, and nodded her head.

Melissa's surrender didn't seem to mollify Rob much. Glaring at her as though she were his worst enemy, he then bent his head and kissed Melissa so hard, she was afraid he was going to split her lip.

The violent kiss didn't last long, much to Melissa's relief, and when it was over, Rob raised himself, turned his back on her, and strode out of the room with every muscle of his back screaming the fact that he was suppressing emotions that would have done credit to a homicidal maniac.

Trembling with reaction, Melissa stared at the door that had closed behind Rob, and her last coherent thought before she fell into a deep sleep that was half faint, half therapy for shock, was that she hoped Parker had sense enough to run for his life before Rob split his lip too.

Chapter Six

Sometime in the early evening Mrs. Price came into the bedroom carrying a tray of soup, crackers, and milk. Melissa couldn't seem to come fully awake and wondered fuzzily if one of the cracks on the head she'd suffered in her battle with Fred had done more damage than she'd realized.

Mrs. Price didn't seem unduly concerned, however, though she did coddle Melissa by spooning the soup down her and forcing her to drink a few sips of milk. Then she stripped off Melissa's dirty jeans and shirt, pulled a nightgown over her head, and left her to go back to sleep.

It was midnight the next time Melissa woke up, and the house was as quiet as a tomb. She was wide awake now, unable to go back to sleep, and surprised to find that her body actually obeyed her with little protest when she got up to go to the bathroom.

Back in her room she felt restless, and as she went to the small latticed window to peer out, she was aware of feeling resentment about the promise Rob had extracted from her to stay away from Fred. She felt she had earned the right not only to go near Fred, but to ride him again. Now that she had time to reflect upon their battle, she was aware of a feeling of exhilaration at having bested the horse, and since she considered she had won fair and square, she didn't see why Fred should reap the reward of never having her on his back again.

Without really thinking about what she was doing, Melissa dressed and slipped downstairs to walk off her restlessness, still feeling resentful that Rob had high-handedly decided she wasn't going to be allowed to follow up her victory over Fred.

It was a gorgeous night outside, the stars bathing the ranch and surrounding countryside in lovely shivers of silvery light. The air was deliciously fresh and cooling, and Melissa felt her spirits lighten and respond to the atmosphere with heady abandonment. She felt capable of taking on the world at that moment—or at the very least, Fred.

She cast a speculative eye toward the stables. She knew where Fred's stall was—hadn't she cleaned it only a few days ago? But would Fred's ugly temper get even nastier at being disturbed in his off hours by the very person who had bested him earlier in the day?

Chuckling silently to herself, Melissa started toward the stables, deciding it was just too bad if Fred was still in an ugly mood. And there was always the possibility he preferred the night and would be more mellow now.

It was very dark in the stables, but Melissa left the doors wide open and thus was able to see where she was going. Too, Fred's stall was near the doors, and as Melissa approached it, she could just make out the solid bulk of his rear.

Melissa considered the problem of getting Fred out of his stall. She had a healthy respect for his hindquarters and for the rest of him as well, and she wasn't about to give him the opportunity to kick her head in or squash her against the side of his stall.

She automatically started murmuring soothing nonsense to the horse, which made him shift slightly and turn his head back to look at her. He didn't seem particularly hostile now, Melissa decided, but it might still be wise to remain cautious, so she finally elected to swing herself up on the wooden stall divider so that she could perhaps get onto Fred's back in the manner of rodeo riders who mounted bucking horses in that way.

There were beams overhead that gave her handholds as she made her way to a point where she could climb onto Fred's back, and just as she was drawing in deep breaths for courage, a voice came out of the darkness, startling her into a near fall.

"What are you doing, Melissa?"

For long seconds Melissa wavered back and forth on her precarious perch, struggling for balance like a tight-rope walker, before she managed to grab an overhead beam with both hands and steady herself. Once she had, she glared down at the interloper who was standing outside Fred's stall, her thoughts unprintable!

There was something familiar about the figure who stood gazing up at her with his hands hanging limply at his sides while the faint light glinted from his pale eyes.

"For God's sake, who is it?" Melissa demanded heatedly. "Is that Micah?"

"Yes, it's Micah," he answered calmly. "What are you doing, Melissa?"

The sound of her name on his lips gave Melissa cold chills. Micah had a way of pronouncing *s*'s in a sibilant manner that reminded Melissa of a hissing snake.

"I'm visiting Fred!" she snapped ungraciously. "What does it look like I'm doing?" But Melissa was by now contemplating what the consequences might be if Micah told Rob about this midnight visit to the stables, and remembering that the best defense was supposedly a good offense, she put one into effect. "What are *you* doing out here?" she demanded accusingly.

"I couldn't sleep," he responded vaguely before getting right back to the point as tenaciously as a bulldog. "Aren't you afraid of Fred?"

Melissa gritted her teeth in frustration at Micah's per-severence. "No, why should I be?" she said shortly, and began to make her way back to where she could jump down into the aisle of the stable. There was no point in making Rob any madder than he was already going to be by pursuing Fred any further tonight, she decided.

"You have a lot of courage, Melissa," Micah said in a speculative tone. "But sometimes courage can be stupid."

Melissa had the distinct feeling Micah's pronouncement was more condemnation than compliment, and in view of how angry Rob was going to be when—if—he found out what she'd just done, she was in a mood to agree with Micah's evaluation. Rob scared her a lot worse than Fred ever could.

"Yes, it can," she admitted grudgingly, "but I'm usually also careful. The two don't always make a bad combination." And so saying, she jumped down beside Micah to put the careful part of the combination into effect.

She looked into Micah's pale eyes and challenged him directly, hoping that Micah was one of those who was willing to close ranks with his own sort against authority—in this case, Rob. "Are you going to tell Rob I was out here?"

Micah looked at her, his expression calmly impassive. "No, why should I?" he responded. But somehow Melissa didn't feel as encouraged by his answer as she should have. She had the impression Micah had his own reasons for keeping quiet that had nothing to do with a comradely closing of ranks.

"Well…thank you," she said lamely. "I don't think he'd like it."

"Are you afraid of Rob, Melissa?" Micah asked, and again Melissa heard that hissing sibilance that made her want to cringe away from him.

"No," she said as matter-of-factly as she could manage as she began to edge backward in a casual manner toward the open doors of the stable. "It's just that I don't want to have any more run-ins with him than are necessary. It's a drag."

She gave a shrug of nonchalant dismissal as she turned to walk away, looking back over her shoulder at Micah in an indication that he should follow her. He did, but it seemed to Melissa he went about it reluctantly.

"Why doesn't Rob want you around Fred anymore, Melissa?" he asked, and there was a tone of unhealthy curiosity in his question that Melissa didn't like. "He always made the rest of us get back on a horse if we were thrown, and you mastered Fred. So why should you be different?"

Melissa moved her shoulders in a gesture of impatient irritation. "How should I know?" she said shortly. "And call me Mel, will you? I don't like Melissa." *At least not the way you say it,* she added nonverbally as she quelled an involuntary shiver when the sleeve of Micah's shirt brushed her arm.

When they came outside, Melissa heaved a sigh of relief not to be imprisoned in that dark stable with Micah any longer, though she wasn't sure why she was having such a reaction to him. She didn't know what he'd done to get sent to the ranch, and she was puzzled by the fact that her imagination was conjuring up some very ugly explanations that probably had no real basis in fact.

"Well, good night, Micah," she said as she started toward the house, hurrying in her anxiety to get away from him. "You'd better get back to bed too," she added, unconsciously using the tone of an adult toward a child.

She was unprepared for what happened then. She felt a cold hand on her shoulder and then Micah was spinning her around to face him!

"Don't tell me what to do, Melissa!" he hissed in a menacing tone. "I don't like women telling me what to do!"

There was a disturbing glitter in Micah's eyes, and for a moment Melissa had the utter conviction that Micah was not only dangerous, he was perhaps out of control.

She tried to break away from his grip on her shoulder, but he only tightened it until he was actually hurting her with the strength of his hold. Melissa forced herself to calm down and think when all she really wanted to do was scream and struggle.

"All right, Micah," she said in a calm, uninflected tone. "I won't tell you what to do."

He was breathing hard as though he'd been running, and for an instant Melissa thought he wasn't going to respond or let her go. But then he gave a little shake of his head, as though to clear it, and he dropped his hand and backed away from her a few steps. And then he smiled at Melissa, and it was an astonishingly charming smile that denied what had just happened.

"Thanks, Melissa...I mean, Mel," he said, and even his voice was different. He sounded like a normal young man instead of something out of a horror movie. "Good night," he added simply, and with a little wave of his hand, he turned and walked away, leaving Melissa gaping at his back, wondering if she'd imagined the incident that had just taken place.

As she turned and began moving slowly away, she asked herself if she was crazy, or was she right in thinking that Micah might need professional help. She didn't know him well enough to make any snap judgments, and surely if he had serious problems, Rob or Micah's parents or *somebody* would have noticed something and sent him to a psychiatrist for treatment...wouldn't they?

Determining that she would ask Rob about Micah when she got the chance, she continued walking and was almost to the steps of the house when she saw a dark figure move out of the shadows at the side of the house and come straight toward her. Since her nerves had already had their quota of shocks for the night, she reacted by giving a half-strangled scream when the figure marched up to her and grasped her arm.

"What the hell are you doing out this time of night, Melissa?" Rob's voice demanded, and Melissa almost collapsed into a heap with relief, even though Rob's tone was angry. She leaned against him, buying time with which to come up with an answer. She wasn't about to tell him the truth, of course.

"I—I woke up and couldn't get back to sleep again," she said softly, hoping to deter his wrath by not responding to it in kind. "I came out for a walk." Which was only the truth, she thought guiltily. It just wasn't the whole truth.

Rob looked down at her for a moment before tightening his arms around her. "You shouldn't be out here," he said equally softly, and now his irritation was subdued. "It's late and you've had a shock." He paused and shifted his hands to her shoulders so that he could look at her face. "How do you feel, anyway?" he asked in a more gentle tone. "Are you all right?"

"I'm fine," Melissa murmured, beginning to become hypnotized by the warm strength of Rob's hands and by the caring quality in his voice.

"Are you sure?" He moved one of his magnetically charged hands to the back of her neck and began to rub the tender nape with soothing, skillful fingers. "You didn't hurt yourself today?"

His voice was growing huskier, deeper, sexier than Melissa had ever heard it before, and her response to that tone of his was in her own when she answered.

"No, I'm fine. . .really," she sighed.

Rob's fingers tightened on her neck for an instant, then slid around to cup her chin and lift it. Melissa had no idea what her eyes were showing him, but whatever it was provoked a stifled groan from him before he bent his head to kiss her, this time with gentle, stroking magic that was more disturbing than any of his other kisses had been.

In the grip of the soft night, her shaken emotional

state, and Rob's expertise, Melissa responded wholeheartedly. She wrapped both arms around his neck and
leaned into his body, curving herself to him while she
made little purring, begging noises in her throat.

She felt an enormous sense of womanly satisfaction
when he responded to her just as wholeheartedly as she
had to him. He pulled her up harder against his hips and
strained her body to him as though he never wanted to
let her go, unless it was to lie her down somewhere and
take everything she was openly offering.

Melissa was convinced that if someone inside the
house hadn't coughed right then, that was exactly what
Rob would have done. But the noise seemed to bring
him back to reality and made him push her away slightly. When he spoke, it was in a tightly controlled voice.

"You managed to escape me the other night when I
was more than ready for this," he chided gently.

"Aren't you ready now?" Melissa responded, her
tone softly complaining. On one level she was relieved
that Rob apparently wasn't going to take advantage of
what she was offering, since she knew it would be a
mistake when she hadn't yet finished what she'd come
here for. Indeed, she hadn't even made a good start as
yet. But on another level she wanted him with an all-
consuming passion that made her willing to court disas-
ter without a care for the consequences.

"You know the answer to that," he responded in a
dry tone, moving his hips lightly against hers as he did
so to show her his readiness. "But it's late, and I don't
want to start something that will have to be broken off
before we've barely begun." He shook his head, his
smile and his eyes displaying a mocking purposefulness.
"No, Melissa," he said in a soft, meaningful tone.
"When I do make love to you, it isn't going to be a hurried affair. It will be an experience we'll both want to
savor at our leisure, to the fullest extent possible."

Melissa shivered in an involuntary movement of anticipation, the seductive quality in Rob's voice wrapping her in a haze of eroticism.

He let go of her and gave her a little push toward the house. "Go back to bed, Melissa." He chuckled when Melissa's look told him bed was going to be a very lonely place without him. "We'll have our day—or rather our night," he corrected himself with mocking humor, but Melissa was pleased to note that there was a strained quality in his voice that meant he would have preferred sharing her bed to sending her there alone.

"Good night, Rob," she whispered, her tone caressing.

"Good night, honey," he answered, taking a sharp, indrawn breath as he did so. "Now get out of here before I change my mind."

Melissa gave him a wavering smile, but she wasn't ready yet to have him change his mind, and so she scurried into the house and up to her lonely bed before she could give in to the desires Rob Redding provoked in her as easily as he breathed.

Later, she lay cuddled in her bed trying to fight the pictures of what it would be like when Rob finally did make love to her by concentrating on what had happened with Micah that night.

Why does he bother me so? she wondered thoughtfully. She tried to pinpoint some valid reason why she had felt uneasy about him since the first moment she'd laid eyes on him, but other than that unblinking, pale-eyed stare of his, and the way he pronounced her name, she couldn't come up with anything other than his startling reaction to having a "woman" give him orders. And why had he referred to her as a woman? Melissa wondered fretfully. She was supposed to be a teenager.

She thought about his grabbing her and the tone of his voice when he'd said that, but now that she was out from under the influence of the eeriness of the night and her own fear, she couldn't justify her strong feeling that something was definitely out of kilter with Micah Gilroy. So he didn't like to take orders from a woman? Not many males did. And some of them could get pretty violent about the matter.

Sighing her weariness, Melissa turned over on her back, deciding to talk to someone about Micah later. But first she had to get on with her job here. So far she'd accomplished exactly nothing except getting romantically involved with the man who might be the person she would have to expose for his treatment of the kids under his care.

And despite her reluctance to expose Rob Redding to anything other than her own loving gaze, she resolved she would get on with her task first thing in the morning. After all, the sooner she discovered exactly who had beaten Delilah and for what reason—and always supposing Rob was innocent—the sooner she could assuage the heat of the passion she still felt encompassing her after the kisses and caresses he'd given her earlier, which she was glumly certain was going to keep her awake for the rest of the night.

Chapter Seven

Saturday was more or less a "free" day, used for catching up on personal chores. Mrs. Price showed Melissa where to do her laundry, and after stuffing her dirt-encrusted jeans into one of the two washing machines, she wandered back up to the second floor, intent upon doing something about the job she'd been neglecting since she'd arrived at the Rocking R.

Mary Alice Fleming's bedroom door was open, and since Mary Alice had always seemed reasonably friendly, Melissa paused in the opening, hoping for an invitation to come inside. Mary Alice, a blond, bouncy type who rode the range in a pair of designer jeans, was sitting on her bed painting her toenails a bright red. When she looked up and acknowledged Melissa, Melissa smiled her most ingenuous smile.

"Hi, Mary," she said in a mildly friendly tone as she leaned up against the doorjamb. "Getting ready for the dance tonight?"

Melissa had been informed that the usual Saturday night barn dance was scheduled that evening, and she was looking forward to it, not from the standpoint of entertainment, but for the opportunity it might provide to do a little judicious prying.

Mary Alice leaned back to cast a critical eye over the toes she had already painted. "Yeah," she answered abstractedly, her attention focused more on her handi-work than on Melissa. "I'm going with Johnnie."

Apparently having decided that her toes were in good shape, Mary Alice glanced up at Melissa. "Has anyone asked you yet?" she asked in a slyly mischievous tone. "Like Lester maybe?"

Melissa decided not to wait for an invitation and wandered casually into the room as she replied. "Yes, Lester asked me," she said, projecting annoyed boredom into her tone. "But I'm not going with him. I have the feeling I'd spend the evening fighting him off."

Mary Alice giggled her confirmation. "But he's kind of cute," she objected half-heartedly. "Besides, there's no one else to go with—except Micah."

A subtle difference in her tone when she mentioned Micah made Melissa's ears prick up.

"Micah doesn't look like the type who dates," Melissa ventured as she leaned against the shabby bureau in one corner of the room.

Mary Alice frowned, and a somewhat troubled look appeared in her big blue eyes. "No, he doesn't," she agreed with almost evasive hesitancy. "I don't think he likes girls very much...except..."

Melissa waited a second, watching Mary Alice closely. Then she prompted the girl softly, turning as she did so to finger a small stuffed mouse on the top of the bureau. "Except...?"

Mary Alice shrugged. "Well, there was one girl he hung around with some, but she's not here anymore."

Mary Alice gave every indication she was going to return to her toenail polishing without saying anything more, but Melissa wasn't about to drop the subject now.

"Oh, did she graduate?" she asked mischievously, using the term the kids did when referring to being released from the Rocking R.

Mary Alice smiled faintly, but she seemed to be getting nervous, and Melissa's sixth sense started going off like a fire engine siren.

"No, she didn't," Mary Alice said casually. "She...
oh, I don't know. I think her parents got her out or
something," she added vaguely, waving the small polish
dauber in her hand. Then she bent to her toes again with
suspicious industriousness.

Melissa hated to appear overly curious and perhaps
spoil things, but she couldn't let this rest. "What was
her name?" she asked, trying to sound as though she
didn't really care, but was just making casual conversation.

Mary Alice giggled and rolled her eyes. "You won't
believe it if I tell you," she snickered, but when Melissa
prompted her with a smiling look, Mary Alice supplied
the name readily. "It was *Delilah!*"

Mary Alice adopted a sultry pose and batted her incredibly long black lashes at Melissa before dissolving
into giggles again. "Isn't that a scream?" she chortled.
"And the funny thing is, she really did live up to her
name."

Hastily, Melissa played up the situation, rolling her
eyes in turn. "God, what names some parents stick their
kids with!" she said with all the disgust a teenager might
display. "If they were stupid enough to call a daughter
that, I don't blame Delilah for living up to it. It was
probably revenge on her folks for being so idiotic."

Her reaction seemed to spark a common bond of empathy in Mary Alice. "Yeah," the girl said resentfully.
"Parents can be the pits." But there was a wistful quality in her tone that told Melissa the girl had perhaps had
a homelife exactly as Mrs. Price described, with every
material advantage but without the love and attention
she needed.

Melissa hesitated a moment, caught between her need
to find out more about Delilah and Micah, and her desire to help Mary Alice. "Why did you have to come
here, Mary Alice?" she finally questioned gently.

A sullen pout turned Mary Alice's Cupid's-bow

mouth down into a frown. "Oh, not much," she shrugged. "They caught me smoking pot and drinking with one of my boyfriends. They didn't like Mario anyway," she added. "He wasn't on our social level." Her mincing tone apparently was an imitation of her parents' snobbish ones. And then Mary Alice scowled as though she were remembering something. "But at least he listened to me when I talked and he was a warm body to hug."

Her frown turned into a sly smile then. "In fact, I think that was what Mom and Dad really resented. They drink and smoke pot themselves, after all. But they couldn't take me sleeping with Mario." She shrugged off-handedly. "Maybe they thought I'd get a social disease or something."

Melissa managed what she hoped was a convincing laugh of sympathy. She was feeling sympathetic, all right, but she was also feeling a sad sense of anger toward Mary Alice's parents. "Tough," she muttered quietly.

"Yeah," Mary Alice agreed. "But they still might have gotten over it if I hadn't threatened to run away with Mario instead of going to college." She gave a little grimace as she went on. "I wasn't really going to do it. I just wanted them to stop giving me orders when they never really cared what I did anyway. At least they never acted like they did."

Melissa's heart twisted inside her, and she couldn't resist making a suggestion that was much too adult to come from someone who was supposedly here at the ranch for worse crimes than Mary Alice had committed.

"Well, so what if they don't?" she drawled casually. "If I were you, and your parents are willing to pay for it, I'd go to college anyway."

Mary Alice looked at her with surprise, and Melissa cleared her throat and continued, trying to place herself into someone like Mary Alice's shoes and take an approach that would appeal to the girl.

"There are lots of boys at college, after all," she said, giving the girl a sly wink. "And one of them might be somebody you'd want to marry. Once you're married and have kids of your own, who cares if your parents are too wrapped up in themselves to pay any attention. You'll have your own family, and you won't have to depend on them for affection."

Mary Alice brightened visibly. "Yes, I know," she said in an eager tone. "I already figured all of that out, but I don't think I'm going to have to wait for college to find the right guy. I think I'm going to marry Johnnie!"

Dismayed that she might have short-circuited Mary Alice's plans to go to college in favor of marrying a boy who might have as many problems as the girl did herself, Melissa answered cautiously.

"Oh, but you and Johnnie will have to go to school in order to make a living, won't you?"

Mary Alice frowned at her as though she'd just made a stupid remark. "Well, of course, we will," she said disgustedly. And then her eyes grew round and earnest. "Johnnie wants to go to college anyway. He's really smart, Mel. Do you know he's got scholarship offers from *three* colleges?"

Hiding her sigh of relief, Melissa shook her head. "Well, that's great, Mary," she said levelly. "But what about you? What do you want to study at college?"

"Fashion design," Mary Alice said promptly, and then she frowned. "I'm not good at anything else, but if there's one thing I do know, it's clothes." Her blue eyes took on a dreamy expression then. "Johnnie's the smart one. He's really good with chemicals and things like that. In fact, that's how he got into trouble. He was making drugs for his friends so they wouldn't have to go to pushers."

Melissa must have shown by her expression that she disapproved because Mary Alice closed up a little. "Well, *everybody* does it sometime, don't they?" she asked rather petulantly, but at seeing something in Melissa's eyes, she then asked in an incredulous tone, "You mean you've never used anything?"

Melissa shrugged. "I don't like to have my mind messed up," she said casually. "I saw too many friends go down the tubes like that, and I didn't like it."

Mary Alice looked impatient. "Well, of course, it's stupid to get hooked," she said disgustedly. "Johnnie didn't deal for money or anything like that. He just liked messing around with chemicals, and he and his friends didn't do drugs much. Just once in a while when they wanted to get down." She frowned again. "But his father caught him at it and sent him here before he could get into trouble with the police and screw up his chances for college."

Mary Alice shrugged as though there was nothing to get uptight about in what Johnnie had done, and Melissa took another deep breath, hoping that Johnnie would find another outlet for his scientific proclivities, and hoping that Mary Alice would come to realize that even an occasional brush with drugs was a dangerous way to "get down."

She decided to change the subject before she found herself launching into a full-fledged lecture that would blow her cover for sure.

"Tell me about the boys here, Mary Alice," she encouraged. "I haven't really met any of them to talk to besides Lester and Micah."

Mary Alice desisted from painting one small toe and gazed into space, biting her lip thoughtfully. "Well, there's Jason," she offered. "He belongs to Valerie." Melissa knew that Valerie was the tall blonde she'd met first after arriving at the ranch. "He's here for sort of borrowing other people's cars," Mary Alice went on. "He wants to be a race car driver, but his parents took his car away from him because he got too many speeding tickets, so he started wiring up other people's cars to take for drives, and he got caught at it.''

Mary Alice took another swipe at a toe. "I guess it was lucky he was in the car of one of his father's friends when he got caught, so he didn't get sent to jail. He got sent here instead, and he likes riding horses so much, he's talking about riding in rodeos now.'' Mary Alice eyed her handiwork with satisfaction as she continued to talk. "He and Valerie are good together because Valerie's father owns a lot of automobile dealerships and she knows a lot about cars.''

Melissa was contemplating where to go from there when Heather Adamson came to the door. Heather was perhaps the most beautiful of all the girls with her black hair and violet eyes and her charmingly helpless manner. Right now, however, her hair was gathered underneath a towel except for a few dripping strands that had escaped onto her neck.

"Mary Alice, did you take my shampoo again?'' Heather demanded. "I got in the tub and wet my hair, but when I reached for my bottle of shampoo under the tub, it wasn't there!''

Mary Alice looked up with a guilty start. "Oh, yeah,'' she said, making a little grimace with her mouth. "I used it up yesterday. I meant to tell you, but I forgot.''

Heather glared at Mary Alice. "So help me, Mary, if you don't leave my things alone, I'll—I'll—''

Her protest sputtered into ineffectuality as Heather apparently failed to come up with anything suitably intimidating to threaten Mary Alice with.

Mary Alice seemed unimpressed by Heather's irritation. "I'll get you some more the next time we go into town, Heather,'' she said lazily. "What's the big deal?''

Melissa interceded then, thinking it might be more profitable to talk to Heather for a while instead of Mary

Alice. "I have some shampoo upstairs you can borrow, Heather," she offered soothingly.

Heather looked at Melissa with her lovely violet eyes, which now softened with gratitude. "Oh, gee, thanks, Mel," she said in her breathless little girl voice. "I want to look nice for Vincent tonight. He loves my hair," she added shyly.

Not for the first time Melissa wondered what on earth Heather had done to get sent to the ranch. She didn't seem to have the sort of nature one would associate with a troublemaker.

"Come on upstairs," Melissa suggested, resisting the urge to pat Heather on the shoulder like a mother. The girl seemed to inspire a protective feeling, and yet Melissa could picture Heather with a brood of children, enduring as solidly as an earth mother.

"Okay," Heather agreed happily, and as she and Melissa left Mary Alice's room, she began chattering about the dress she planned to wear that night for Vincent and asking Melissa if she didn't think Vincent wasn't the most gorgeous male Melissa had ever seen.

"I'm not sure I know which one Vincent is, Heather," Melissa said as they climbed the stairs to her room. "I don't know all of the boys yet."

Heather's eyes turned dreamy. "Oh, Mel, how could you miss him?" she protested. "He's so *large,* after all."

Melissa had him then. Vincent was well over six feet tall with the build of a professional football player and all the suppressed energy of an express train. He was also dark and had a brooding look about him that Melissa thought must make people give him a wide berth. She wondered how the gentle Heather had taken up with him.

"Oh, yes," Melissa said vaguely. "I think I've seen him. He looked a little...ah...violent to me."

Heather pooh-poohed that. "He's a perfect lamb,"

she defended Vincent. "Oh, sure, he's had a little trouble with his temper in the past," she then admitted offhandedly. "That's why he was sent here. He accidentally beat up some rotten kid who was making nasty remarks about how his father was doing on the football field last season."

Melissa stopped at the head of the stairs and glanced at Heather alertly. "His father?" she inquired, but it was Vincent's propensity for violence she was really curious about.

Heather nodded. "Yes, his father's a professional football player." And then she looked troubled. "And his father taught Vincent to settle differences with his fists. He used to beat up on Vincent himself."

Melissa felt sick for a moment, but at seeing her expression, Heather hastily explained further. "Oh, he never hurt Vincent badly," she qualified. "Vincent says he learned real fast to stay out of his dad's way when his dad was in a bad mood, so things never got to the point where Vincent had to go to a hospital or anything."

"And you're not afraid of Vincent?" Melissa asked casually, watching Heather closely as she answered.

"Good heavens, no!" Heather sounded shocked at the very idea. "We've been dating ever since we both got here, and Vincent would never hurt a female! He treats me like I'm made of glass."

"Well...that's nice," Melissa said, vowing silently to make her own assessment of Vincent, since Heather was obviously prejudiced. And then she looked at Heather curiously, already having a good idea of what the girl's answer would be to Melissa's next question. "How did you end up here, Heather?" she inquired idly.

Heather looked at Melissa with her candid, violet eyes and shrugged. "It was because of my boyfriend at the time," she answered predictably. "That was before I knew Vincent, of course."

Of course, Melissa thought wearily, but she said nothing.

"Alfredo was a little wild," Heather went on, leaning back against the stairwell, seemingly in a mood to chat. "I thought I loved him, because I hadn't met Vincent yet, you see, so there wasn't anything I wouldn't do for him." Her eyes took on a dreamy expression again as she digressed for a moment. "That's what love is all about, you know. You have to give everything to the one you love, and not hold back."

Melissa caught the wistful quality in Heather's tone that said that someone in Heather's life had definitely held back on their love where Heather was concerned, and again Melissa felt angry, yet helpless, at the inability of some people to understand what parenting was all about.

"I guess that's true, within reason," Melissa offered gently. "But only to a point. You can't compromise your own values for someone else."

Heather looked at Melissa as though she didn't know what Melissa was talking about, and Melissa realized the girl had a long way to go before she discovered the truth of what Melissa was trying to tell her. And then she would probably only accept such an idea from whatever male was the current light of her life.

"Anyway," Heather went on, as though Melissa hadn't spoken, "Alfredo needed some money, and he got high one night and decided to rob a store." At Melissa's shocked look, Heather frowned. "Well, I didn't know that was what he was going to do," she protested. "He just took me along for the ride." Her look turned stubborn then as she went on. "But after he'd done it, I wouldn't testify against him, and my dad sent me here out of spite."

Melissa hesitated, not sure what to say. "Well, maybe it wasn't out of spite, Heather," she suggested tentatively. "Maybe he just wanted you to learn that no matter how much we think we love someone, we have to keep our own self-respect. You know what Alfredo did was wrong, don't you?"

Heather looked doubtful, but then she nodded her head. "Yes, I know," she admitted. "And Rob says I shouldn't be so gullible where men are concerned. He says I ought to learn whether a man is worthy of my love before I give it so wholeheartedly."

Melissa felt a little stunned at hearing Heather voice exactly the problem she was dealing with herself right then—and about Rob. But Heather's mood was brightening now, and her next words made Melissa wonder if anything Rob—or she—said to Heather got through.

"But I'm certain about Vincent," she pronounced blithely as she straightened to indicate she was ready to stop talking and get that shampoo now. "He's wonderful, Mel, and I know I'm not wrong about him!"

Melissa sighed and accompanied Heather into her bedroom, hoping Heather was right about Vincent or about the husband she would eventually have if she didn't end up with Vincent. She had a sinking feeling that in Heather's case her whole future would be decided by what type of man she eventually married. If the man was a monster, Heather would probably stand by him every bit as faithfully as she would by a decent, upright man, which left Heather's fate somewhat up to chance.

As Melissa and Heather entered Melissa's bedroom, Heather looked around curiously. "You and Angela are the only ones that have rooms to yourselves," she remarked, sounding somewhat envious. "I share with Valerie, and Mary Alice and Margo room together." She sighed wistfully. "It must be nice to be alone once in a while," she ventured. "Valerie's okay, but she makes fun of the way I feel about Vincent. She doesn't believe in true love."

Score one for Valerie, Melissa thought somewhat cynically. "What did Valerie do to get sent here?" she asked instead of voicing her thoughts.

"Oh, she's like Delilah," Heather said in an absent

tone as she moved to the closet to look at Melissa's things. "She sleeps around a lot."

Melissa's heart missed a beat and then steadied down into its usual rhythm. "Oh, yes," she said casually. "Mary Alice was telling me about Delilah, but she didn't seem to know why Delilah left here. Did you know her very well, Heather?"

"Not really," Heather replied as she took down a hanger containing a gingham skirt and held it up to her body for size. "She roomed with Angela, and they didn't get along very well. When she left, Angela made a fuss about rooming by herself, and that's why they put you in here instead of in with her." She smiled mischievously then. "Angela can get her way about almost anything when she puts her mind to it. She's very smart."

Melissa nodded absentmindedly, wondering how she was going to get to talk to Angela and get anything out of her. Angela was smart—maybe too smart to fall for any story Melissa could come up with to get her to talk.

"Here's the shampoo," she said, offering the bottle she'd fished out of a drawer for Heather.

Heather clutched the bottle eagerly and then started to leave the room, apparently eager to begin her beautifying session.

"Thanks, Mel," she said over her shoulder, her voice light and prettily girlish. "I'll bring it back when I'm through."

"Fine," Melissa answered, smiling though at the moment she felt burdened at hearing the stories about how the kids at the Rocking R had ended up there. She also felt frustrated because it was obvious that neither Mary Alice or Heather felt there had been anything strange in Delilah's leaving the ranch the way she had, and the only explanation Melissa could come up with for that attitude was that they hadn't *known* why Delilah had left.

She waited a few moments, then returned downstairs

to go in search of Angela. Melissa found her in the library poring over an intimidatingly thick book on philosophy. She looked up irritably when Melissa entered the room, then her face cleared when she saw who it was.

"Hi," Angela drawled in a cynical tone. "Looking for somebody?"

Melissa decided that Angela pictured herself as an intellectual who had little patience for the average run of humanity, and Melissa had had enough experience with that type during her college and working days to know how to deal with such an attitude.

"Actually, I was looking for a good book," she replied, managing to sound as cynical and bored as Angela had. "Is there anything worth reading in here?"

"Some." Angela shrugged, placing a finger in her book and closing it partly to hold her place. "Redding may *look* like a macho man, but he seems to have a mind as well." There was a grudging sort of admiration in her tone that Melissa was pleased to hear, though she immediately chided herself for experiencing that pleasure an instant after she felt it. "What do you like?" Angela asked suspiciously.

"Oh, anything, as long as it's written for someone over the age of twelve," Melissa replied with a note of disparaging superiority.

Angela seemed to relax then, and Melissa congratulated herself on having judged the girl correctly. Angela was obviously an idealistic fanatic determined to move and shake the world through the strength of her intellect. Melissa knew that usually Angela's type eventually adapted to a realistic decision to do what she could without expecting miracles.

"I'm glad to see you're not like those other featherbrains," Angela now said with scathing contempt. "I've never come across such a bunch of self-centered, emptyheaded centerfolds in my life!"

Melissa hid her smile when she looked at Angela and realized that while berating her companions for their attention to their looks, she herself obviously took pains to enhance her own attractions. She was neat and clean and her makeup was applied as skillfully as if it had been done at a salon.

"Have you got a cigarette?" Angela then asked companionably as she tossed her book aside and moved over to make room for Melissa on the couch.

Melissa shook her head as she sat down. "Sorry, I don't smoke," she said.

Angela adopted a bored look. "That's too bad," she shrugged. "I'd really rather have a joint anyway," she added nonchalantly. "I find pot relaxing. It clears my head and lets me concentrate on important things."

Melissa gave an inward sigh, readying herself for a long siege of hearing all the solutions to the world's problems Angela probably thought she had. Melissa had heard it all before in college bull sessions and from Washington politicians, but if it took listening to it all again to win Angela's confidence, Melissa was prepared to endure.

"What matters to you, Angela?" she asked, struggling for a bright tone to mask the resignation she felt.

"Oh, injustice...politics...philosophy," Angela tossed off blithely, as though she were naming the latest rock stars. "I'm an anarchist," she added in a tone of confidentiality. "What are you?"

Melissa considered that a good question, and she gave an honest answer. "A realist," she said dryly. Then she deviated from the truth in order to cement the burgeoning trust she could see in Angela's brown eyes, though it hurt her conscience to do so. "I tried anarchy, and it got me sent here."

Well, it's not exactly a lie, Melissa thought, annoyed by her guilt feelings. *I did try to exercise a little anarchy to get out of coming here. It just didn't work.*

Angela looked at her as though startled for an instant, then dissolved into giggles like any ordinary schoolgirl. "Me, too," she chortled with eager comradeship. "What did you do?"

Melissa told her what she figured Angela would most like to hear. "I went to the town library and tore up all the fascist books on the shelves," she answered, feeling a grim revulsion at voicing the lie.

Angela's eyes widened with respect and excitement. "That's just what Larry did!" she said eagerly. "And I got in trouble for painting socialist slogans on the cars belonging to the members of our local school board!"

"Great," Melissa forced enthusiasm into her reply. "Who's Larry?" she then asked.

"Larry Wingate," Angela said impatiently. "Brown hair, brown eyes—kind of small, but wiry."

Melissa nodded, placing Larry in her mind. She decided she should have known just from looking at him. He was as intense as Angela and went about looking as though he carried the weight of the world on his thin shoulders and ached to remove it and remold it with his bare hands.

"He's the only boy here who's got a mind." Angela sniffed. And then she fixed Melissa with an intent look. "But you said at the dinner table that you shoplifted, too. Why did you do that?"

Melissa groaned inwardly, feeling trapped in her web of lies, but she managed to come up with an appropriate answer. "Why should I have to pay for what should belong to everybody just so some capitalist can make a dishonest dollar?" she lied, inwardly wincing.

She wasn't feeling very proud of herself by now, but for the life of her she couldn't figure out how else to handle things. Teenagers were not known for being broadminded where their own ideas were concerned, and she knew she wouldn't have a chance in hell of getting any information out of Angela if the girl knew what Melissa really believed.

Melissa stifled her conscience by telling herself that what she was doing was for the good of all these kids, whether they would believe it when the truth came out or not. The justification rang hollow, but it was too late to back out now.

"Good for you!" Angela said fiercely, making Melissa wonder if she was going to turn out to be an unwilling role model for Angela. God forbid! Deciding that before she left the ranch she would make it very clear who she was and what she stood for, Melissa decided to quit beating about the bush.

"Say, Angela," she said, trying to keep the grimness she felt out of her voice, "fill me in on the characters around here. I'm going to be seeing everyone at the dance tonight and I'd like to know something about them first."

Angela leaned forward giving the impression that she now considered herself and Melissa bosom buddies. "Oh, most of them are just a bunch of punk kids!" she condemned her fellow inmates summarily. "Larry's the only one who thinks about anything besides himself. All the others are mental and emotional lightweights."

"What about Micah?" Melissa asked casually, watching Angela closely to see if the girl had the same reaction at the mention of Micah's name that Mary Alice had.

Angela didn't seem to be as wary, but it was plain Micah made her uneasy. "Micah's...different," she said with a thoughtful frown. "I can't figure him out, but I think he's a latent homosexual."

Angela tossed off the phrase with such practiced ease that Melissa automatically discounted the observation, considering the source. She imagined that Angela had come up with that evaluation simply because Micah didn't seem interested in girls, but Melissa thought Micah might just be a late developer.

Angela backtracked a little then. "I think there was

something going on between him and Delilah, though,'' she mused thoughtfully, ''and Delilah wasn't the type to waste her time on a guy who wasn't interested in her body. Of course, it could have been that. . . ''

But then Angela broke off and looked at the door. ''Did you hear something?'' she asked so innocently that Melissa wasn't positive she was putting on an act, though she wondered if Angela had broken off on purpose before she said too much about something she wanted to keep hidden.

''No, I didn't hear anything,'' Melissa answered, trying to keep the impatience she felt out of her voice. ''What's Micah's background, Angela?'' she asked returning immediately to the subject that interested her.

Angela giggled. ''He's a preacher's kid,'' she sneered. ''His daddy has some big church in Missoula. Opium for the masses and all that.'' She waved her hand contemptuously, and her tone grew intense and disapproving.

Melissa didn't want to get into Angela's opinion about religion, so she launched another question quickly. ''What was he sent here for?''

Angela shrugged. ''I don't know,'' she said in a tone of disinterest. ''I don't think anybody does. He was here before anybody else got here, and he doesn't talk about himself.''

Angela discarded the topic of Micah quickly then, in favor of discussing Larry. She disclosed that neither she nor Larry believed in romantic love, but they did believe in sex, and she then proceeded to outline in detail the sort of sex the two of them favored, while Melissa listened until her eyes glazed over, shocked in spite of herself at being the recipient of such intimate confidences.

She was acutely grateful when Mrs. Price appeared at the door to the library to remind Melissa that her jeans had finished washing and needed to be put into the dryer so that someone else could use the washers, and she got up with alacrity to escape hearing more than she'd ever wanted to hear about Angela's and Larry's private lives.

Angela spoke a cheerful farewell and returned to her book, while Melissa left the room, wondering if she was hopelessly old-fashioned or if the new morality made it all right to discuss one's sex life with such casual ease. And she was also wondering why she suddenly felt less enthusiastic about conducting an affair with Rob Redding unless there was some hope that more would come out of it than mutual physical pleasure.

But that was a question for later, and right now Melissa had enough food for thought to last her the rest of the afternoon before the barn dance would give her an opportunity to overload her brain further.

Chapter Eight

Within seconds of entering the wide doors of the barn where the dance was to be held, Lester swooped down on Melissa with all the salivating eagerness of a cat pouncing on a particularly delectable mouse, and stifling a resigned sigh, she gave him as bright a smile as she could manage and submitted to his demand that she dance with him.

There was a popular song playing on the record player set up near the refreshment table, and as Lester clutched her to his skinny chest, fondled her back with roaming hands, and whispered erotic suggestions into her unwilling ear, Melissa determinedly tuned him out while she surveyed the rest of the partygoers to see how things were developing.

Mary Alice and Johnnie were swaying together in blissful rhythm to the music, each wearing contented, somewhat fatuous smiles that made Melissa smile with amusement. Valerie and Jason were giving a good imitation of a bored married couple who had no commitment to one another other than sex. Angela and Larry could barely follow the steps of the dance due to the ferocity of their no doubt earthshaking argument about things that *mattered*, and Heather, her head barely reaching the midsection of Vincent's chest and tilted at an impossible angle so that she could stare soulfully into his eyes, was clearly in seventh heaven. Vincent's rugged, normally somewhat pugnacious expression now bore such gentle regard for the lovely girl in his arms that Melissa began to believe that Heather had tamed the beast that had hitherto lived in his savage breast.

The one fly in the ointment, other than Lester's increasingly evident hormonal disturbance at having Melissa in his clutches, was seeing Rob dancing with the girl named Margo, a dark-haired, dark-eyed exotic-looking beauty who had a somewhat superior attitude that put Melissa's back up. Melissa frowned as she saw Rob smiling down into Margo's sultry dark eyes. He looked entirely too content to be where he was for Melissa's taste, and she felt a surge of jealousy that surprised her with its strength.

Melissa had never actually spoken a word to Margo and knew nothing about her other than the fact that right now the girl was looking up at Rob as though she'd been on a strenuous diet for about a year and he was a hunk of perfectly cooked steak. Which wouldn't have mattered, of course, Melissa thought sulkily, if Rob hadn't been looking back at Margo as though he would enjoy being eaten down to the last morsel.

Melissa was so wrapped up in watching Rob and Margo that she almost missed seeing something else. If Lester hadn't moved one of his hands dangerously low on her back, distracting her for an instant while she pointedly moved the hand to a safer location, she would have missed the expression on Micah's face as he also watched Margo and Rob.

Micah was the only one not dancing, but he seemed far from bored. Apparently he was more upset by the Margo-Rob combination than Melissa was herself. A gasp of surprise left Melissa's lips, and she stumbled a little when she recognized the sheer rage animating Micah's normally impassive features and pale eyes.

Melissa thought shakenly that if a look had as much physical as emotional power, Margo and Rob would be writhing their death throes at that very moment—or at least one of them would have. The funny thing was that afterward, Melissa couldn't be certain whether Micah's animosity was directed at Rob or Margo or both.

As she continued to stare at Micah, he suddenly switched his deadly gaze to her, and Melissa didn't have time to cover the fact that she'd been watching him. And as had happened on the night he'd caught her in the stables, his features underwent a bewilderingly fast transformation. Suddenly he no longer resembled a psychopath in the grip of a killing rage, but was all charmingly shy boy, and then he started toward her, and Melissa felt a sort of helpless panic that made her jerk backward in Lester's arms.

To her surprise, Lester looked down at her with a sheepish little grin on his immature face. "Ah, come on, Mel," he said coaxingly. "Don't play hard to get. I didn't say anything I haven't been saying since we started dancing, so why the sudden panic?"

After an instant of disorientation, Melissa realized Lester thought she was reacting to his pornographic mutterings in her ear rather than to Micah's approach, and since she couldn't explain her reaction satisfactorily to herself, much less to anyone else, there was nothing to do except pretend Lester was right.

"Cool it, Lester!" she grated out shakenly. "I'm *not* going out into the bushes with you later!"

Lester pouted, looking like a three-year-old who'd just had a cookie snatched from his grubby little hand. "Then why have you been leading me on?" he complained sulkily. "That's not fair!"

But Micah was beside them by then, and it was too late to explain to Lester that far from leading him on, Melissa had just been disastrously inattentive to his erotic blandishments. Micah tapped Lester on the shoulder as Lester was opening his mouth to complain further, and Lester swung around in a display of irritated aggressiveness that disappeared quickly when he saw who had interrupted him.

"Oh...hi, Micah. Did you want something?" Lester asked politely.

Melissa had the sudden eerie impression that Micah had the same kind of effect on other people that he had on her. An effect that made one want to walk cautiously around him, as though he were an emotional volcano subject to eruption at any time, given sufficient provocation.

"I would like to dance with Mel," Micah said, shyly polite. His demeanor and tone were now so different from what Melissa had glimpsed as she had watched him staring at Rob and Margo a few moments earlier that she felt disoriented by the change and found herself wondering how he had this Jekyll and Hyde ability to switch personalities so suddenly. Too, his present mood was so mild as to make her doubt she'd ever seen the other side of him.

"Sure," Lester said with a shrug, giving Melissa a sullen look of rejection as he did so. "You can *have* her," he added, giving a slight emphasis to his statement that Melissa would have found highly insulting if she had given two pins for Lester's opinion of her.

Lester stomped away, and Micah moved closer to put his arm around Melissa's waist in a gingerly fashion while he took her slightly shaking fingers in his other hand. He kept a respectable distance between them as they started to dance, for which Melissa was grateful, and he didn't speak. Melissa was grateful for that as well. She needed time to regain her composure.

The first song came to an end before the two of them had taken more than a dozen steps, but since another one began almost immediately, Micah didn't let her go, but continued to dance.

"Are you having a good time, Mel?"

His question was delivered in such a shyly sweet tone that Melissa almost couldn't believe her ears.

"Oh...ah...yes, I suppose so," she managed to reply weakly. "Are you?"

Micah gave a charming little duck of his head that Melissa thought meant yes, but which was belied by his answer. "I don't care much for social occasions," he said, giving her an apologetic smile. "I don't dance very well, as you can see."

Melissa mustered a trace of cheerfulness. "You dance all right, Micah," she assured him. "You haven't stepped on me once so far."

"Thank you," was his grave reply. "It's kind of you to say so, but that's because I'm holding you so far away. If I held you closer, you'd soon have stumps where your feet used to be."

Micah's sweet gravity and his unexpected display of a pleasantly dry wit made Melissa smile more genuinely at him, even though she still felt bewildered by his personality. She had a sudden image of him as a reversible quilt with a crazy pattern on one side and a delicate, pleasing design on the other, and she wondered with a trace of helpless confusion which was the real Micah.

"How are you settling in, Mel?" he then asked in a gentle way. "Are you beginning to feel comfortable here?"

He sounded as though he really cared whether or not she was adjusting well to the Rocking R environment, and in spite of her doubts about Micah, Melissa responded to his tone.

"Pretty well," she replied with a rueful smile. "Some of my muscles still hurt, but they're getting better."

"You'll get used to it," Micah assured her. "It just takes time."

The conversation between the two of them was trivial for the rest of the dance, but Melissa felt strangely soothed by it and by Micah's attitude. Aside from his bewildering shifts in mood, he seemed more like an adult than any of the other inmates Melissa had talked to—except perhaps Margo, whom Melissa hadn't as yet spoken with and who certainly *looked* adult, but who was an unknown quantity so far. Melissa found herself hoping Margo would stay an unknown quantity, then chided herself for her irrational jealousy.

When the song ended, Micah escorted Melissa to the refreshment table and stayed by her side until Vincent lumbered up to ask her to dance. Melissa looked around for Heather, surprised to see that she was dancing with Rob. Despite her irritation at her own foolishness, Melissa's heart gave a curious little jump at the thought that perhaps Rob's dancing with Margo was nothing more than the first of his duty dances. And if that was true, she would have her own turn before the night was over, a prospect that both pleased and alarmed her, since she knew she wouldn't be able to keep her mind on anything except what it felt like to be in his arms.

Vincent grasped her rather clumsily and led her into the dance, but it quickly became evident that the song's rhythm was much too complicated for his sense of timing. Melissa distracted both of them from their awkward progress by talking to him while she tried to judge if the violence in him might extend to beating up a girl like Delilah.

"Heather is very nice, isn't she, Vincent?" she ventured pleasantly.

Vincent stumbled slightly, quickly recovered himself, and smiled in an apologetic way that revealed the gentle side of his nature. "She's. . ." He groped for words, and Melissa supplied them, instinctively sensing Vincent's difficulty at expressing his feelings verbally.

"Beautiful? Sweet? Charming? Loyal?" she teased, grinning when Vincent's face flushed bright red.

"Yeah," he mumbled embarrassedly. "She's all of those things."

"Do you plan to see each other when the two of you

leave here?" Melissa asked gently, taking pity on Vincent's embarrassment.

Vincent looked mildly astonished. "Well, sure," he said. "We only live a few miles from each other back in California."

Melissa surprised herself by feeling happy that Vincent and Heather wouldn't be separated. Now that she had actually spoken to Vincent, she thought that he and Heather seemed to complement one another, each supplying what was lacking in the other. Heather calmed Vincent's violent tendencies, and Vincent projected an ability to protect in the manner of a strong male, something Heather could respond to wholeheartedly. Melissa also discarded the idea that Vincent might have beaten Delilah. He just wasn't the type, she decided, almost sorry that she was back to square one.

One by one Melissa danced with each of the other boys as their girls were appropriated by Rob. Margo and Micah had disappeared from the scene, a fact that made Melissa frown in puzzlement as she wondered where they could have gone and why Rob was making no attempt to round them up.

She found Jason to be hyperactive and self-centered. He talked about himself, driving fast cars, and roping steers, never waiting for an answer except when he delivered a proposition to "get it on," which was slipped in at the end of the dance. Melissa declined, Jason shrugged, and they parted, neither feeling the least regret at the separation.

Larry was exhausting as he expounded on the state of the world, and Melissa was grateful that he didn't seem to require replies.

Around midnight Mrs. Price brought in sandwiches, and as Melissa munched on chicken salad, she reflected somewhat sourly that, as yet, she was the only one Rob hadn't asked to dance. She was nursing her wounded vanity over that fact as she watched him sort through records, then was distracted from her thoughts when she saw Margo slip in through the open barn door and head for Rob like an arrow heading for a bull's-eye.

Melissa watched, her mood deteriorating, as Margo clung to Rob's arm and brushed her lovely bosom against it, then reached up to pull his head down to whisper something in his ear. Melissa considered Rob Redding a rotten swine when he had the nerve to laugh at whatever Margo had said, then favor the girl with a warm hug.

Deciding that now was definitely a good time to slip outside for some air, Melissa tossed her sandwich away and started toward the door. She was almost to it when she felt a warm hand descend upon her shoulder, making her jump like a startled rabbit.

She knew who it was, and she was about to give in to the urge to express her irritation when Rob spoke first, his voice both soothing and gratingly amused.

"You can't leave yet, Melissa," he drawled silkily. "How would it look to the others if you were to leave before we'd had our 'duty' dance?"

Melissa curled her lip and was about to tell him what she thought about some of the "duties" he'd been performing that night, but he was already gathering her into his arms, and she was suddenly having to concentrate on concealing her reaction to his touch from anyone watching.

She had unthinkingly gone stiff and unyielding to keep herself from melting into him like butter on a warm piece of toast, and Rob glinted a sardonic look down at her.

"Relax, Melissa," he murmured in a half threat, "or I'll kiss you right here in front of everyone and destroy your reputation as the frigid witch of the East."

Melissa's eyes widened, startled at his description, and he chuckled mockingly. "That's right," he drawled, tongue-in-cheek. "Lester's been spreading the word that you're as cold as a Montana winter." He stifled a laugh at Melissa's indignant expression and shrugged. "Well, he apparently hasn't had the benefit of direct encouragement the way I have," he teased, "but I suppose you could always change his mind."

Melissa stiffened again before a reluctant smile curved her lips, making Rob's eyes shift to her mouth and take on a hungry expression that pleased her enormously. "Maybe I could make Lester change his mind," she said, trying to sound serious. "I'm sure he'd be willing to. . ."

But Rob's possessive look stifled her teasing, and as he pulled her harder against him, she lost the desire to tease altogether. She rested her head in the hollow of his neck, exulted in the warm strength of his fingers on her back, and commenced to drown in the sea of emotion he evoked from her every time he touched her.

They danced silently and with perfect rhythm for a while before Melissa was able to surface from her erotic daze sufficiently to pay attention to the song that was playing. The record on the turntable was Mac Davis's "Baby, Don't Get Hooked on Me," and Melissa thought sadly that there couldn't be a more appropriate title to describe her dilemma.

Here she was, intent on exposing whoever had beaten Delilah and knowing full well that that person could be Rob. On top of that, she hadn't the faintest idea if he cared for her in any way other than as a potentially exciting bedmate, and she was rapidly falling under his spell to the extent that she was beginning to dread the idea of a merely casual affair with him. She had the distinct feeling that where he was concerned, *casual* was not the expression to use. *Commitment* was beginning to sound much more appropriate, and that was a foolish idea at this point.

A mild sense of depression descended on Melissa as she tried to fight the delicious sensations that leaning against Rob's strong, hard body evoked. She felt his sexual magnetism in every cell of her body, but it was foolish to be seduced into thinking anything more might ever come of their attraction than an easing of physical needs. And that just wasn't enough, Melissa thought, made uneasy by the inner revelation.

Rob chose that moment to move the hand that had been stroking her back up to the nape of her neck, where he began a gentle massage that wrung a shudder of sensual response from Melissa.

On feeling that shudder, Rob tightened his muscles and gathered her closer against him. Melissa felt a vague sense of danger about how they must look to anyone watching them, but she was helpless at maintaining a facade of indifference in the face of what he was making her feel.

She did half-open her languid eyes and murmur, ''Rob... we shouldn't...''

But he whispered, ''Shhh,'' on a husky note from deep within his chest, and Melissa subsided meekly, melting against him again.

She didn't even realize the music had stopped until Rob gently withdrew from their embrace and turned her toward the open barn doors. Melissa didn't know if he intended to let her go alone outside, where she'd been headed when he'd caught her, or if he meant to come with her and do something about what they'd aroused in one another, and she didn't get the chance to find out. Margo was suddenly beside him, and flashing Melissa a resentful, jealous look from her glittering dark eyes, she pulled Rob away with her toward the refreshment table.

Melissa watched them go, her dancing dream shattered, even though there was a look of annoyance in Rob's blue eyes she supposed meant he didn't appreciate Margo's interference. Then Melissa turned and hurried outside to hide her own disturbed feelings in the shadows of the night.

She wandered to the corral railing to stand leaning against the wooden slats while she waited for her mind to exert its dominance over her body again. Eventually, under the soothing balm of the night, the earthy smells all around her, and the peace of the open sky, her emotions calmed.

She stayed there a long time trying to come to terms with the conflict between her intellect and her emotions, her duty and her desires. She vaguely heard the sounds that meant the dance was over, but they made no real impression on her, locked as she was in the battle between her head and her heart. Her head was telling her to be careful...to find out a lot more about Rob Redding before she lost her heart to him. But her heart was telling her that she knew all she needed to know about the man who was affecting her more profoundly than any man ever had before.

She heard a step behind her, and then two arms encircled her body from behind to come to rest on the railing in front of her. Unconsciously Melissa leaned back against Rob's body, feeling a sense of homecoming as she did so that was strangely peaceful despite the excitement that coursed through her veins when he dipped his head to caress the line of her neck with his lips.

"It's late. You should be in bed," he murmured huskily, but his voice contained no imperative, and his lips coaxed her to stay.

Rob shifted his weight, put an arm around Melissa's waist and half turned her to face him. He stroked her cheek with one hand while he looked down at her, his eyes sleepily half closed as they roamed her face with leisurely approval.

"You're lovely, Melissa," he murmured quietly. "There's something childlike about your face, except that it's a seductive childishness. You make me want to protect you from others and from things, but at the same time, I want to make love to you in every way a man can make love to a woman...gently...fiercely. I want to cuddle you, and yet I want to crush you to me and ravage that beautiful mouth of yours...handle every part of you both tenderly and with savage passion.''

Melissa sighed her permission as Rob lifted her into his arms and carried her a short distance away to the dark shadows beneath a weeping willow. When they were enclosed within the sheltering branches of the tree, Rob lowered her to her feet, then pulled her against him with a slow, unhurried purposefulness that built the excitement within her. And then his mouth closed over hers, shaping her lips to his, lingering, molding, stroking until Melissa forgot everything except the thrill of his subdued mastery of her mouth.

He trailed kisses down her neck as one of his hands moved up to shape her breast to his palm and the other pressed her hips more firmly against his own with slow, arousing circular movements that ignited a fire in Melissa's loins, making her shudder against him. She clung to his shoulders, then moved her hands to his neck to thread his thick mane of hair through her fingers before she made an incoherent sound and moved his mouth back to hers.

His tongue entered her mouth and she accepted it with an eager thirst for the taste of him. Her response brought a growling sound of arousal from him, and then his strong arms were crushing her to him as though he wanted to impress her body into his permanently. Melissa moaned as her knees buckled, and then Rob was lowering her to the ground and stretching out beside her without breaking the kiss.

She felt his fingers at the knot of her halter top, and then he was tugging it down to expose the pale smoothness of her breasts to him. He did break the kiss then, so that he could look at what he'd uncovered, and Melissa gasped as he stroked the burning skin of her breasts with warm fingers...and then with the warm moistness of his tongue.

His seduction was incredibly restrained, when Melissa could sense the power of the passion that engulfed him. And it was incredibly skilled. She was helping him unbutton her skirt without giving the least reflection to what she was doing or why. She was simply caught up in a primeval force as old as time and as compelling as magic.

"Sweet darling," he murmured as he raised his head to kiss her mouth again. "My sweet Melissa..." There was a catch in his voice as he said her name, which enchanted her. His breath was labored, his eyes warmly glazed with passion, and his body was taut with the desire that raged through him. Yet still his every movement was unhurried and so warmly caressing that Melissa felt a burst of love spring into life inside her to accompany the physical arousal he had built to fever pitch.

"Rob..." Melissa said his name with aching wonder, and even in her dazed state, she could hear the revelation she was making in saying his name like that and wondering if he could hear it too.

Apparently he did, because his passion broke the bounds he had put upon it then, erupting into an almost convulsive movement as he slid over her and crushed her mouth and her body beneath his. Melissa clutched him to her, and for the first time in her life she wanted to give her soul as well as her love and her body to a man. She wanted to give Rob everything...everything... everything....

"Rob?" Micah's voice intruded into Melissa's dreamworld vaguely at first, but when he continued to call Rob's name and Rob abruptly lifted his head to listen, reality crashed in on her with devastating force!

"Rob, are you out here?" Micah persisted, and there was a note of desperation in his tone now that brought a frown to Rob's face.

He looked down at Melissa and whispered, "Stay here...out of sight. I'll go see what he wants."

Melissa nodded shakenly and suppressed a groan of denial when Rob lifted himself from her. He stood for a moment adjusting his clothing and taking deep breaths to calm his arousal while Melissa huddled where she lay, unable to think for the moment...unable to dispel the desire that Rob had awoken in her.

"I'll be back in a few minutes," Rob murmured, and then he stepped through the sheltering tree branches and disappeared.

Melissa lay still for a little longer until she felt able to sit up. And it was only then that she realized she had done it again. She had been about to make love with a man she might have to expose to the world as an abuser of the young people placed in his care.

As she fumbled with her halter top to retie it, then refastened the button of her skirt, she fought the idea that Rob could be guilty of such a thing with a ferocity that, had she been capable of clear thinking, would have told her all she needed to know about how deeply Rob Redding had encroached upon her heart. And as she got to her feet to move unsteadily to the outer limits of the branches to peer out, she determined that she now had two reasons to find out exactly what had happened to Delilah. Her original assignment was sufficient reason in itself...but clearing Rob of any suspicion that he might have hurt Delilah was equally important...vitally important. For until she did clear him, she couldn't afford to give him the love and commitment she wouldn't be able to take back if she found too late that he was actually capable of an act she shrank from with every principle she had.

Rob and Micah were nowhere to be seen, and Melissa slipped out from among the willow branches to speed across the open ground toward the house. She refused to wonder what Rob would think when he came back to find her gone. She refused to wonder what had brought that note of desperation into Micah's voice. She simply wanted to finish her investigation, and if the results were favorable, get on with discovering whether she had really, at last, found the one man she could love forever.

Chapter Nine

Since Melissa had forgotten to set her alarm the night before, and since her sleep had been fitful until almost dawn, she woke very late the next morning, but when she did wake at last, she had a plan in mind.

She hashed over the details while she bathed and dressed and then wandered down to the dining room to eat a cinnamon roll and drink some coffee. There was no one else in the house, but Melissa was so caught up in her planning that she scarcely noticed. After she'd eaten, she wandered outside to sit with her back to one of the porch braces. Stretching her legs out and lifting her face to the September sun, she continued her thinking.

Her first priority was getting to know Micah better. According to gossip, there had been something going on between Delilah and Micah, and while Micah might not know exactly what had happened to Delilah, he was the most likely candidate—besides Rob—to know something that might prove helpful to solving the mystery of who had hurt the girl.

Melissa also wanted to explore why she, and apparently others, reacted so strangely to Micah. That split personality of his was enough to make anyone wary of crossing him, of course, but why was it there?

In a strange way Micah both appealed to and repelled Melissa. When he was behaving "normally," whatever that term meant, she found him delightfully intelligent, witty, warm, and shy. But at other times he frightened her. Micah was an enigma Melissa intended to unravel. If he was dangerous to himself or others, something needed to be done about him. If he was in need of professional help, he needed to get it.

Normally, of course, Melissa would have discussed Micah in detail with Rob. But she was not in a mood to discuss much of anything with Rob for the present. She was in a mood to stay completely out of Rob Redding's way until she could come to him unfettered by doubts.

Melissa stirred, trying to find a more comfortable position, as she reflected that Micah had seemed to like her last night. If she could build on that and get to know him—find out what went on behind those eyes of his that could freeze into near madness, burn with rage, or soften into sweetness so swiftly—she was certain she would be a great deal closer to knowing the truth of what had happened to Delilah than she was now. And it was becoming imperative that she solve the mystery soon.

Having decided upon a course of action, Melissa got up and wandered toward the stables, wondering where everyone was. Even Mrs. Price had been absent when Melissa had breakfasted.

The horses were all in their stalls, but the stables were quiet and deserted, as though everyone had disappeared from the face of the earth. The tack room was off to one side, and Melissa poked her head in the door, feeling relieved when she spotted Parker sitting quietly and contentedly mending bridles. A cigarette hung loosely from his lips, and his eyes were screwed up as he concentrated on his work, making the wrinkles around them even more pronounced.

Melissa coughed delicately to disclose her presence, and when Parker looked up, his weathered lips split into a grin. "Well, missy, so you finally hauled yourself out of bed, did you?" he said good-naturedly.

"Yes," Melissa responded with a faint smile. "I guess the dance last night tired me out." She glanced around the tack room with interest. "Where is everybody, Parker?" she then asked in an idle tone. "Is there something I should be doing?"

Parker took a deep drag of his cigarette, then squashed it under his booted heel. "Naw," he said laconically. "The boss said to let you sleep in this morning since you've been working so hard all week. Said you could go to church with the rest of 'em next Sunday."

"Church?" Melissa's mouth fell slightly open. Somehow she couldn't picture a least likely bunch of churchgoers than the group residing at the Rocking R.

Parker noted her reaction and gave a sly grin. "Yeah," he explained. "It's part of the program. Rob takes the kids and Mrs. Price regular as clockwork every Sunday mornin'."

Parker tossed the bridle he'd been working on aside then and patted the bench beside him, inviting Melissa to sit down. Surprised by his friendly manner, Melissa did so, while she wondered if his sudden friendliness sprang from the afternoon's entertainment she'd provided him during her battle with Fred. Remembering that episode made her feel a twinge of guilt, and she asked a tentative question as she joined Parker on the bench.

"Did you get in trouble with Rob over my battle with Fred, Parker?"

Parker gave one of his snorting laughs and slapped his knee in remembered enjoyment. "Hell, yes, missy!" he chortled. "Rob like to tore a strip out of me for puttin' you on that nag!"

Since Parker didn't seem unduly concerned about his chastisement over the matter, Melissa relaxed somewhat. "I'm sorry, Parker," she said with a smile of her own, even as she wondered why she was apologizing to

Parker for his part in almost getting her maimed for life.

"Ah, shucks, missy," Parker chuckled, shaking his head. "Don't make no never mind. The boss's bark is a lot worse than his bite, and I'm used to it."

He pulled another cigarette out of the pack in his shirt pocket and offered it to Melissa, but when she declined, he lit it for himself.

"I knew he'd be mad about it before I ever put you on Fred," Parker went on expansively. "But I wanted to see what you were made of."

Melissa looked at him uncertainly, and he shrugged. "Ain't no better way to see if a body's got grit than to put 'em up against old Fred," he said matter-of-factly. "You did right good, missy. Better 'n most I've tried that on, though I don't pull that too often nowadays. Just on the ones I take a shine to."

Melissa gaped at that. Not only did it seem a strange way to express approbation for someone, but she hadn't been aware that Parker had "taken a shine" to her, as he put it. At seeing her expression Parker winked at her and patted her knee.

"I don't waste no time on them that don't warrant it, missy. You looked like there was more to you than showed, and I wanted to see if I could still spot a winner like I used to."

Melissa smiled wryly and raised an eyebrow. "A winner?" she queried doubtfully.

"Yep," Parker said, complacency in his tone. "You come through just fine, missy. Thought you would, and I was right." Then he gave her a grudging look of admiration. "I'd like to know where you learned all that language you was usin' on Fred, though. You sure picked up some good un's somewheres."

Melissa grinned at Parker's admiring tone. "Oh, here and there," she said with mischievous casualness. "But

I've been trying to tone that sort of thing down. It doesn't fit my image, does it?" she teased.

Parker snorted his agreement. "Nope, it sure don't, and if I know Rob, he'll get around to puttin' a stop to it one of these days." His look turned innocently sly then as he added, "Especially since he seems to have taken a liking to you himself."

Melissa shifted uneasily at that observation and hastily changed the subject. "Is *everybody* gone, Parker?" Her thoughts were turning to Fred and her unfinished business with him. If there was no one around but Parker, this might be the perfect time to see if she could actually ride Fred in a civilized manner or whether it would turn into a battle royal again.

"All but Micah," Parker replied as he got to his feet to fetch another bridle to work on. "He's over by the dormitories practicin' his ropin'."

Melissa greeted that information with surprise. Since Micah's father was a minister, she would have thought the boy would be a prime conscript for church services. Parker saw her look of surprise, and his look turned thoughtful and a little grave.

"The boy don't go to church, missy," he said quietly. "He's got a few problems to be worked out on that score."

Melissa would have liked to question Parker about the "problems" Micah had, but since the older man's face had an expression that precluded asking questions about the matter, she got to her feet to leave instead, having decided that now was a good time to encourage a friendship with Micah. Before she left, however, she did sound out the possibility of being allowed to ride Fred again.

"Parker, can anyone actually ride Fred?" she asked innocently.

Parker shot her a look of mingled amusement and suspicion. "Sure, missy," he answered. "Once he learns you ain't gonna' take nothin' off him, he settles down pretty good, though he's always a mite unpredictable.'' He gave Melissa an inquiring look from beneath his shaggy brows. "Why?" he drawled. "You thinkin' 'bout givin' him another try? The boss said no to that, you know.''

"I know, I know,'' Melissa muttered, rolling her eyes to the ceiling as she remembered the look on Rob's face and the tone in his voice when he'd issued his prohibition about her going near Fred again. "But...well...'' She bit her lip and shot Parker a pleading look. "It's hard to get as far as I did with Fred and then just walk away. You understand, don't you?''

Parker chuckled, shaking his head in a way that could have meant sympathy for her feelings or the fact that he thought she was crazy. "Missy, I understand,'' he drawled, "but if you decide to get up on that cuss again, you better make sure Rob's not around. Where you're concerned, his protective instincts twitch all over the place.''

Melissa grinned with satisfaction, pleased that Parker hadn't actually forbidden her to try riding Fred again. She nodded and winked. "Don't worry, Parker,'' she assured him. "I'll be careful...that is, if I do decide to give Fred another run for his money.''

She flicked Parker a wave and left him shaking his head again, but he had a rather pleased expression on his weathered face that Melissa hoped meant he was proud of her for persevering.

She found Micah twirling a rope around and around, his face a study in concentration on what he was doing. She stood back and watched him awhile before he realized she was there, giving him a thorough inspection.

Melissa decided that Micah wasn't ugly or handsome—he was just an average-looking young man. His brown shock of hair was in an untidy mess at the moment, and his gray eyes were clear and untroubled. His small, rather prim mouth was pursed into a thin line and, at the moment, his rounded chin looked endearingly childish. Dressed in jeans and a plaid shirt, his stocky frame held taut with the effort he was making, he looked like any normal, healthy teenager, if slightly younger than his age.

Melissa watched as Micah drew the rope up, pulled the large circle into a smaller one, and then began to practice roping the end post of a nearby fence. When he succeeded on the second try, his mouth relaxed into a happy grin and his eyes sparkled with pleasure in his achievement. It seemed like a good time to make her presence known, and Melissa strolled toward him.

"Hi, Micah," she called in a casual tone. "That was a good throw."

Ignoring the startled jerk and then the narrow-eyed consideration Micah gave at her appearance on the scene, Melissa pointed toward the rope in his hand. "Will you teach me to do that?" she asked hopefully.

Micah coiled the rope carefully, watching Melissa with a speculative, closed expression. "Why aren't you at church?" he asked impassively, ignoring her compliment and her question.

Melissa shrugged both shoulders casually. "You've got me," she said in an offhanded tone. "Nobody invited me."

Micah hesitated, then relaxed and gestured Melissa forward. "You're lucky, then," he commented somewhat grimly. "They will next time."

Melissa came closer and looked at Micah with what she hoped was normal curiosity. "Is it compulsory?" she asked. "Does Mr. Redding make us go?"

Micah seemed pleased at her question. "Yeah, he makes everybody go except me," he answered, pride in his statement.

"How come you get off?" Melissa asked, projecting

a little jealous envy into her tone. "Are you Rob Redding's pet or something?"

Melissa watched as Micah's chest swelled and he straightened his shoulders further, and it was at that moment that a nasty little idea began growing in her head—an idea she didn't like one bit.

"We have a. . .a *special* relationship, yes," Micah answered, obviously trying to subdue his pride in that relationship but not succeeding very well. And then he frowned, and his tone turned bitter. "He knows I hate church!" There was a savage bite to his declaration that made Melissa decide to go carefully in her effort to get to know Micah better.

"Do you?" she asked quietly. "Why is that?"

Micah looked at her uncertainly for a moment, then evidently decided she could be trusted somewhat. "I had it rammed down my throat for too many years," he said, his tone grim. "My father is a minister."

Melissa gave him a sympathetic look, encouraging him to go on, and after an instant's hesitation Micah did so. "He made me sit out there and listen to him every Sunday and he'd preach about all the *virtues* when all the time he. . .''

But there Micah caught himself up, biting off what he'd been about to say, and Melissa decided to let the matter drop for the time being. If Micah ever trusted her enough to tell her about his family life, she had the feeling it was going to be a pretty gruesome tale, judging by the tortured anger in Micah's eyes.

He changed the subject abruptly. "You want to learn to rope?" His tone indicated he was struggling for normality, and Melissa played along.

"Yes, will you teach me?" She smiled, looking at the rope he held with eagerness in her expression.

For the next half hour or so Micah worked with Melissa on the art of roping, which she found fun and fairly challenging. She also found Micah to be a good instructor. He was patient, articulate, and understanding during her first fumbling attempts, and by the end of the session, she had made a good deal of progress, which seemed to please Micah as much as it did Melissa.

"It's almost lunchtime," he said, finally calling their session to a halt. "The others will be back in another half hour or so, and I'd better go clean up. Rob likes us to be neat."

"Okay," Melissa agreed, happy that Micah seemed to be behaving a good deal warmer toward her than he had previously. She gave him a friendly smile that made him color a little. "Thanks for your help, Micah," she said sincerely. "I really appreciate it. You're a good teacher."

The compliment appeared to please Micah enormously. His skin flushed a deeper pink, and his eyes sparkled at the boost to his ego.

"Ah, you're just a good learner," he declaimed with shy modesty, and Melissa's heart went out to him suddenly. At that moment she saw him as a sweet, shy, potentially affectionate young man who needed the encouragement and friendship she could offer.

She laughed and made a face at him. "Sure," she drawled teasingly. "It had nothing to do with you, huh?"

Before he could reply, she started walking away from him. "Thanks again anyway, Micah," she called as she waved good-bye to him. "See you later, okay?"

He returned the wave, and a charming little grin tugged at his mouth as he took his rope and headed toward the dormitory. Melissa headed for the stables, intending to renew acquaintance with Fred and—depending on Fred's mood—perhaps even ride the horse during the half hour she had before Rob returned to the ranch.

Fred was placidly munching hay when Melissa approached his stall, and he seemed totally uninterested in

Melissa's presence. That fact gave her the courage to inch past his side to his head and begin her efforts to win him over.

"Hi, Fred, you cussed old reprobate," she cooed at him in silky tones that were designed to fool him into thinking she was praising him. "You remember me, don't you?"

She patted his head and noted that his brown eyes didn't seem to have that wild look in them that indicated his temper was aroused.

"I'm sorry I don't have any sugar or a carrot," she crooned, "but I'll bring you some next time I see you, all right?"

Fred didn't indicate whether he cared a flip whether Melissa brought him culinary goodies, but she ignored his lack of enthusiasm and continued her blandishments and petting until it seemed that Fred was actually willing to take an interest in her. He watched her from eyes that were beginning to take on a sleepy look of contentment, and finally he gave her a little butt with his head that Melissa supposed was a sign of affection. At least she hoped it was.

Mentally patting herself on the back for the effectiveness of her seductive technique, Melissa decided to go one step further.

"You don't mind if I sit on your back, do you, Fred, honey?" she purred as she began to slip a bit into his mouth. "I don't weigh much, and I promise I won't wear spurs."

Melissa didn't want to take the time to saddle Fred, and after she had the bit fastened and the reins in her hand, she took a deep breath and used a nearby bale of hay to mount the horse, expecting at any moment to be bucked clear out the door of the stables. Apparently, however, she had caught Fred on one of his good days. He just stood where he was, giving no indication that he was even thinking of bucking Melissa off.

So far, so good, Melissa thought as she gave a gentle kick with her heels. "How would you like some nice fresh grass, Fred?" she encouraged as he began to amble toward the door of the stables.

Fred must have thought he'd enjoy some grass because he allowed Melissa to guide him toward a nearby fenced pasture. She leaned down from his back to open the gate, not wanting to tempt her luck by getting down from Fred's back again.

Once in the pasture, however, Fred forgot that it was grass he'd come for. He elected to have a good run instead, which suited Melissa just fine as his sedate walk turned into a trot, and then into a pleasant gallop. She laughed out loud as she clutched Fred's belly with her legs and leaned over his neck, and after they'd had a good run, she sat in perfect contentment while Fred cropped the grass she'd promised him, enjoying the beautiful surroundings and the fresh smell of the day.

Unfortunately Melissa became so caught up in her enjoyment that she lost track of the time, until she was brought out of her somnambulant communing with nature by the sight of a cloud of dust on the road to the ranch, signalling that Rob and the others were returning from church.

One of those words that Parker had assured her Rob wouldn't approve of slipped from her mouth as she urged Fred to return to the stables pronto. Fred apparently got the message and did his part by fairly flying over the pasture back to the open gate leading into the grounds surrounding the ranch buildings. It was unfortunate that Melissa's warning had come too late. If she had noticed the time even five minutes earlier, she would have made it. As it was, however, she and Fred came galloping up to the gate right about the time Rob approached it in the car from the other side.

As Rob climbed out of the car the expression on his face was thunderous, and Melissa sat frozen on Fred's back, unsure whether it would be better to keep quiet and take her medicine like an adult or launch an offensive in her best teenaged style.

"Get down!" Rob ordered, making Melissa abandon any idea of taking the offensive. Stung by his tone, she climbed down rapidly, then turned and looked up at Rob with cautious wariness.

"What are you doing on that horse?" he demanded, no trace of humor in his tone. Melissa tried to inject some into the situation.

"Riding?" she responded, grinning rather weakly and encouraging Rob to join her in that grin. Her grin faltered when he didn't.

"You know what I mean," he said, quietly dangerous.

Melissa quickly decided that honesty was the best policy, since it didn't look as though a lie would do her any good in this situation.

"Rob, I couldn't let Fred get away with it," she explained in what she hoped was a reasonable tone, though it came out more pleading than reasonable. "I won our battle fair and square and yet *he* was going to get the reward of never having me ride him again. Now is that fair?"

Melissa thought for a moment that Rob was going to explode, and she was relieved when she saw him fight down his rage. But his mouth was drawn into a grim line, his eyes shot sparks at her, and his hands were clenched into fists, so she knew she wasn't going to be let off scot-free.

"Did Parker help you with this?" he asked grimly.

Melissa shook her head in violent negation. "No," she said firmly. "I did it all on my own."

She pleaded for his understanding with her eyes, and for a moment she thought she saw a flicker of something favorable move behind those beautiful, clear blue eyes of his, which made her catch her breath against the yearning to be taken into his arms. But if that was what he wanted, he did a good job of hiding the fact.

"Melissa, you disobeyed me," he said with cold authority, making Melissa realize for the first time that they had an audience around them. The kids who had ridden to church and back with Rob were standing around, eyeing the proceedings with avid curiosity, making it impossible for Melissa to answer in the way she would have liked to. "Do you expect to get away with it?" Rob demanded then.

Melissa dropped her eyes from the stony look in Rob's. "No," she answered quietly. "You must do what you have to, Rob."

Her simple acquiescence seemed to make Rob even angrier for some reason. "Very well," he clipped out. "Since you seem to have such an attachment to this horse, you can take care of him from now on."

Melissa's startled look of pleasure died quickly as Rob disabused her of her mistaken notion that he was being kind.

"I didn't say you could ride him," he continued. "I said you could take care of him. That means you feed him, curry him, and sweep out his stall."

Melissa fought hard to control her resentment as Rob went on, but apparently she didn't succeed, because at something he saw in her face, he tacked on another punishment.

"You can also clean out the rest of the stalls for the remainder of the week," he said, finishing his sentencing with cold implacability and ignoring Melissa's dismayed wince as well as the gasps of incredulity from the kids gathered around.

Melissa recovered quickly and presented Rob a face stony with acceptance of his punishment. "Very well, Mr. Redding," she said without expression. "Shall I start now?"

Melissa saw Rob's jaw tighten at her tone and her

cold look, and she thought she also saw a look of regret over his unexpected harshness in his eyes. But having set the punishment, even if he hadn't meant to be quite so harsh, he wouldn't back down.

"No, it's lunchtime," he grated. "You can start this afternoon after we let the horses out to pasture."

Melissa nodded, letting her eyes show the sense of outrage she felt. "All right," she agreed coolly. "May I go now?"

Rob gave a sharp jerk of his head, indicating his permission for Melissa to leave, and she grabbed up Fred's reins and walked away, her back ramrod straight and her head held high.

As she put Fred back in his stall, she had to brush away a few tears of anger and disbelief at how harsh Rob was being after what had happened between them the night before. But maybe that was behind it all, Melissa thought an instant later, her bitterness increasing. Maybe Rob was angry because she hadn't waited for him and was taking this way to punish her.

Disgust was added to her bitterness as she stomped from the stables toward the house. At lunch she was surprised to find that there were others who thought Rob was being unbelievably harsh with her, though it didn't do much to alleviate her sense of outrage at his perfidy.

"Gee, Mel, that's rough," Mary Alice sympathized, her tone muffled from the bite of sandwich she'd just taken. "I can't understand why Rob is being so mean to you. He's usually very fair."

"Yeah!" Angela chimed in indignantly. "The punishment should fit the crime, but in your case, Rob's making a mountain out of a molehill!"

Melissa shrugged as though she didn't care, noting that aside from Valerie, who was indifferent, Margo was the only one of the girls who wasn't sympathetic.

"It doesn't matter," Melissa said casually. "By the time I get through, I ought to have muscles to spare."

She flashed a big grin. "Anybody want to challenge me to some arm wrestling next week?"

The girls laughed at that, and everyone seemed to accept that Melissa was a good sport. But if they could have read her mind, Melissa knew they would revise that opinion fast. As she went upstairs to change into her grubbiest clothes, she was in a mood to kill Rob Redding.

Her anger lent strength to the thrusts of her pitchfork into straw, and she made progress a lot faster than she had on her first venture into muckraking. In fact, she finished the whole row of stalls in time to get back to the house for supper.

It was Rob's night to eat with the girls, and after Melissa had bathed and changed clothes, she joined the rest of the household in the dining room, ignoring Rob, as though his chair was empty.

The other girls looked warily back and forth from Melissa to Rob for a while, but when it became apparent that nothing was going to happen, they relaxed into their usual chatting and eating.

Melissa felt Rob's brooding gaze on her throughout the meal, but she refused to look at him. When dinner was over, she went back upstairs, changed clothes, and left the house to return to the stables.

The boys had brought the horses back in for the night, and Melissa grabbed a brush and began to curry Fred with a violence that might have wounded an animal with a thinner skin. Fred seemed to enjoy the vigorous brushing, however, and Melissa had the impression he would have liked to roll over on his back and let her have a go at his stomach.

"Dumb horse!" she muttered under her breath as she put the brush away and prepared to return to the house. But her words had an undertone of affection that reflected her changed feelings toward Fred, and when Fred reached his great head around to butt her rear end in a farewell gesture, she laughed and decided Fred had changed his feelings toward her as well.

Micah came into the stables as Melissa was leaving and noted the remnants of the grin Fred had inspired. He stopped and looked at Melissa in surprise.

"What's funny?" he asked. "I thought you were in the doghouse, but you sure don't act like it."

Melissa reached up a hand and patted Micah on the cheek. "I just found out Fred likes me," she explained happily. "And I like him. So let Mr. Rob Redding make what he wants to out of that, the big bully!"

Micah raised his eyebrows, but he seemed pleased that Melissa's attitude toward Rob was hostile. "Doesn't Rob like you?" he asked in a curiously stilted voice.

"Hah!" Melissa snorted disgustedly. "Does it look like he likes me?"

Melissa had the impression her answer pleased Micah enormously, and that fact sobered the good mood she had begun to develop. The idea she'd had earlier in the afternoon returned with renewed force, and as it was a singularly unpleasant idea, she had to force herself to maintain her cheerful exterior.

"I'm tired," she said, managing a big yawn. "I'm going to bed. Good night, Micah."

"Good night, Mel," Micah said, his tone almost affectionate.

Micah went on into the stables then as Melissa trudged her way toward the house deep in thought. She didn't notice Rob coming toward her until she almost ran into him.

"What are you doing out here?" he asked roughly as he stopped her by gripping her upper arms.

Melissa shook off his grip. "What you told me to do, Mr. Redding," she answered levelly. "I've been currying Fred."

Rob's jaw tightened with annoyance. "You could

have waited until tomorrow,'' he said with irritation. ''You were through for the day.''

Melissa gave him a cool look that made his jaw tighten further. ''I wanted to do it, Mr. Redding,'' she informed him coldly. ''I like Fred.''

With that she brushed by Rob and continued toward the house, glad in a way that she and Rob were at odds, since it would make it easier to delay what was eventually going to happen between them. At the same time she hated the discord between them, and she felt depressed because of it and because of the idea concerning Micah that wouldn't let go of her.

But as she climbed the stairs to her room on tired legs, she knew she wouldn't be able to rest until she proved or disproved that idea. Too much depended on finding the truth and upon acting as soon as possible to repair any damage that might already have been done.

Chapter Ten

Melissa spent the second week of her stay at the Rocking R cleaning stables in the mornings, learning to be a cowgirl in the afternoons, getting to know Micah at every opportunity, and avoiding Rob Redding whenever possible. Rob was showing definite signs of regret over the coolness between them, and Melissa was fairly certain that if she gave him a chance, he would apologize for overreacting and lift some of the punishment he'd meted out. But since she felt it was far better at this stage to keep her distance from Rob so that she could concentrate on her real reason for being at the ranch, she avoided him assiduously and stifled the pangs of longing and regret she felt as she watched him grow more frustrated and angry about her attitude day by day.

Meanwhile, though Micah was slow to trust and parceled out his confidences in cautious doses, Melissa was beginning to learn something about his family life before he'd come to the ranch, and what she was learning depressed and discouraged her.

Apparently Micah viewed his father as a very weak and ineffectual man who was directed, humiliated, and thoroughly henpecked by Micah's mother. The mother, according to Micah, was cold, unloving, and devoted to maintaining control over the men in her life, to the point where she dominated her husband completely and alienated Micah to a degree that he could barely mention her name, and then he stuttered over it.

It was not surprising to Melissa, therefore, when it became more and more obvious that Micah worshipped the ground Rob walked on. Apparently Micah had substituted Rob into the strong father role he craved from his real parent, but who had disappointed Micah so badly. But while that fact didn't surprise Melissa, Micah's obsession with Rob did bother her considerably.

Micah was jealous, possessive, and myopic where Rob was concerned. He didn't see Rob simply as a strong human being, but elevated him to a status of godlike infallibility that Melissa considered unrealistic and unhealthy, since Rob was bound to disappoint Micah someday, and she wasn't certain the boy could handle such a disappointment. Too, though Micah hid his feelings fairly well generally, Melissa was certain there might be something else in Micah's feelings for Rob that was even more unhealthy—something that would require a great deal of professional help to resolve.

But she considered she had too little hard information from which to draw absolute conclusions, and she was as yet reluctant to talk to Rob about Micah until she knew more. It wouldn't be fair to Micah to paint a picture of him to Rob that might be false. Besides, she wasn't sure what Micah's personal problems had to do with Delilah, and she had to be content to wait and watch until her relationship with the boy was firm enough to allow her to question him specifically about anything. Her role for the present was to listen when he cared to share, because she had already learned that if she pressed, he shut up like a clam.

Meanwhile she took what enjoyment she could from the afternoon sessions with Parker—and often Micah— while they taught her to be a cowgirl. She had managed to persuade the two of them to let her ride Fred in those afternoon sessions, and though she felt somewhat guilty at first at putting them in jeopardy with Rob, Parker didn't seem to object and Micah seemed certain that nothing he did would make Rob withdraw the "special" relationship he and Rob shared.

By the end of the week, however, Melissa's guilt feelings had reached the point where she decided it was time to challenge Rob over his dictum about Fred. She had proof now that Fred had settled down and accepted her as his rider, and she had developed such a fondness for the horse that she had no intention of letting Rob Redding's protectiveness separate her from the animal.

Therefore, on Friday afternoon, after Melissa had unsaddled Fred and she, Parker, and Micah were standing together talking for a few moments, she broached the matter with the two of them.

"Parker, do you know if Rob is going to let me go out on the range next week?" she asked.

"He hasn't said, missy," Parker replied, his gaze sharpening as he eyed the stubborn tilt to Melissa's chin. "I'm gonna be talking to him about assignments tonight, though." He hesitated, then drawled, "You ain't thinkin' about askin' him to let you ride Fred out there, are you?"

"Yes, I am," Melissa stated firmly. "You've seen for yourself that Fred is behaving himself with me, and I like Fred. I don't want to ride any other horse but him."

Parker sighed and shook his head in resignation. "Well, I wish you luck, missy," he said doubtfully, "but I wouldn't count on much, if I was you. Rob's usually a fair man, but he has his stubborn spots, and seems like you and Fred is one of 'em." He looked at her from under his bushy brows, and there was a twinkle in his faded brown eyes. "I think maybe he's afraid Fred will damage that purty little hide of yours, and I've told you before Rob has taken a liking to—"

Melissa, seeing an alert tenseness coming over Micah, hastened to interrupt Parker. "Well, it won't hurt to try, will it?'' she asked spiritedly. ''All he can do is say no.''

Micah spoke up then, his voice very quiet and level. ''If you want me to, I'll speak to Rob, Melissa,'' he offered. ''I'll tell him you and Fred work well together and that I think you'll be safe with Fred.''

Melissa flashed Micah a look of gratitude and smiled at him, though something about his offer bothered her. ''Thanks, Micah,'' she said, ''but I don't want to get you in any trouble.''

Micah seemed to swell up with pride then, and his look was cool as he gazed at Melissa, his gray eyes going remote. ''It won't get me in trouble, Melissa,'' he objected. ''Rob doesn't get mad at me.''

Melissa glanced at Parker and saw that the old man was frowning and that there was a troubled light in his faded brown eyes. He didn't say anything about what was troubling him as he turned to go, however. He merely offered some advice to Melissa.

''Like I said,'' he tossed over his shoulder as he strode away. ''I wish you luck, but don't count your chickens before they're hatched.''

As Melissa turned back to Micah she spotted Rob and the rest of the riders who had been out that day returning, and she frowned as she straightened her shoulders determinedly.

Micah's question came very softly, and when she looked at him, the gray impassivity in his eyes was disconcerting.

''Do you really not like Rob, Mel?'' he asked in a deceptively casual tone.

For a moment Melissa debated over how to answer him. If she told Micah that far from disliking Rob, she was close to being in love with him, she had the instinctive feeling that Micah would freeze up on her totally and forever. Yet if she protested the opposite too heartily, he might decide that anyone who disliked Rob was unworthy of Micah's trust and affection. A middle ground seemed the safest way to take.

"Oh, I don't dislike Rob," she ventured as casually as Micah had spoken. "He's been hard on me, but it hasn't really hurt me, and I suppose he's just doing his job."

She could see that her answer pleased Micah, and she felt depressed that it had. Micah apparently was unwilling to share a scrap of Rob's "special" regard with anyone else, which could turn out to be a serious problem when the matter of Delilah was cleared up—if Rob and Melissa did get together—and especially when Micah learned that she and Rob had lied about who Melissa really was. Would the boy do anything drastic when he found out his hero, Rob, and his friend, Melissa, had broken trust with him? The prospect worried Melissa.

"Yes, that must be it," Micah said with a great deal of satisfaction. "Rob's just doing his job." And then he looked at Melissa in almost a superior manner and added, "But it doesn't matter anyway, does it, Mel? You won't be here forever."

Micah's words affected Melissa in a strange way. Suddenly the thought of leaving the Rocking R—and Rob Redding—was unbearable, and she greeted that reaction with silent alarm. She had been trying not to fall in love with Rob—at least not yet. But had she already gone over the edge? Was it too late to be cautious where her heart was concerned? And if it was, what was she going to do about it if Rob turned out to be the one who had attacked Delilah?

"Here they are," Micah said, breaking into Melissa's thoughts.

Rob and the kids and two regular ranch hands who worked for Rob were almost upon them, and Melissa felt a sense of despair as she looked at Micah and saw the gleam of adoration for Rob in his gray eyes.

Taking a deep breath, she spoke quietly. "I'll wait for

Rob and speak to him about Fred now, Micah. It will get harder the longer I wait.''

Micah's jealousy had apparently abated, because he grinned at Melissa and gave her a thumbs-up sign. Then he wandered away to a vantage point where Melissa knew he would watch Rob with complete concentration while giving the impression he was doing something else. Melissa had discovered this habit of Micah's the previous Monday and had seen it every day since.

After her conversation with Micah, and her alarm over her true feelings for Rob, Melissa was not in the best of moods at the prospect of tackling Rob on the subject of Fred, but she was not going to back away from the confrontation...nor from the chance to have a few minutes alone with the man she had missed terribly throughout the preceding week.

As she watched Rob and the rest of the riders unsaddle their horses, she wondered if she should say something to Rob about the way Micah felt toward him. She was still reluctant to make an out-and-out statement, but perhaps she could skirt the issue a little.

When Rob came striding out of the stables, Melissa intercepted him. ''May I talk to you, Mr. Redding?'' She kept her tone level and unhostile, and yet Rob's eyes narrowed and his jaw tightened as he paused beside her.

''Go ahead,'' he invited flatly as he stopped beside her.

She hadn't counted on the fact that his frustration and anger with her might have grown to the point where he no longer wanted to be alone with her. Melissa licked lips suddenly gone dry.

''Ah...I think it would be better if we talked in your office,'' she suggested, and felt her heart sink when Rob's expression hardened further. But he nodded and turned toward the house.

''Come on, then,'' he said shortly. ''I haven't got all day.''

Rob walked so fast that Melissa had to practically run to keep up with him, and his rudeness began to ignite her own temper. She reflected bitterly that if Rob Redding was the sort who lost interest simply because he ran into a little opposition to what he wanted, then he wasn't worth all the upset she was feeling at his attitude.

But after they entered his study and she watched him pull off his gloves, seat himself in the large chair behind his desk, and light up a cheroot, her heart continued to ache at the sight of his long, lean body and beloved face, so untouchable right now.

"May I sit down?" she asked dryly, trying to hide her feelings.

Rob inclined his head, watching her through unrevealing blue eyes that showed no trace of desire or warmth.

Now that it was time to speak, Melissa didn't know how to begin. She wanted to talk to Rob about more personal matters, but his attitude made it impossible to do so. He merely sat silent, giving her no encouragement at all, until Melissa's nerves began to scream and she had to say something.

"Have you decided yet what work you're going to assign me next week?" she finally asked in an abrupt, ragged tone.

Rob's gaze was impassive. "Yes," he answered without elaborating.

Melissa fought down a wave of irritation, gritted her teeth, and somehow managed to keep her voice level. "Does it involve riding a horse?" she added.

"Yes," he drawled, again without expanding on his answer.

Melissa took a deep breath to calm her temper and plunged. "Then I want to ride Fred!" she challenged, giving Rob a defiant look.

His answer took her by surprise. He merely shrugged and gazed at her coolly. And then a harsh smile curved his mouth and Melissa got ready for the explosion she suspected was coming.

"Why should next week be any different than this one?" he drawled sarcastically.

Melissa misunderstood him, thinking he was referring to his prohibition against riding Fred.

"I've done everything you ordered without a murmur all week," she challenged him again. "Don't you think I deserve at least a chance to prove I can ride Fred safely now?"

"I'd say riding him for five afternoons straight gave you plenty of chances to demonstrate that," he said, dropping his bombshell in a quiet, dry tone that had an undertone of anger.

Melissa gaped at him for an instant, then became aware of her open mouth and shut it with a snap. She looked at Rob cautiously then, and he looked back at her like a sleepy, tawny mountain lion ready to attack at any moment.

"How did you know?" she said, her defiance weakening.

"I know everything that goes on at this ranch," Rob answered with hard assurance. "I can tell you what time you get up, what you eat for breakfast, when you go to the bathroom, and even. . ." He looked Melissa up and down then, a blue flame beginning to flicker in those devastating eyes of his, bringing an answering warmth in Melissa's body. "Even what color nightgown you wear—that is, when you wear one," Rob finished in a silky, seductive tone that made Melissa's breath catch in her throat.

Unbidden, however, a silent question intruded on her fascination with Rob's masculine sensuality. *And who beat Delilah Muller-Smyth to the point where she's afraid to name the person even now?*

After swallowing nervously, she responded in a shaky tone. "You can?"

"I can." Rob's affirmation was positive.

Melissa tried to shake off the disquiet her silent question had provoked and concentrate on the issue at hand. "Why did you let me get away with it?" she asked, looking straight into his eyes.

Rob shrugged his shoulders and gave her a wry smile. "I didn't want Micah and Parker to be punished because of you," he said.

In the face of the guilt she felt at his answer, Melissa dropped her eyes. "Am I going to be punished again?" she asked, sounding discouraged. She forgot for the moment that Rob Redding had no right to punish her for anything.

"Don't you think you deserve it?" he answered in a mild tone.

Abruptly Melissa recovered her sense of who she was and why she was here, and she faced Rob defiantly.

"No, I don't!" she replied levelly. "You seem to forget that I'm not one of your kids, Rob. I'm a grown woman, and I can make decisions for myself. I've ridden Fred all week, and we get along famously. Ask Parker and Micah, if you don't believe me!"

Rob's expression had grown thoughtful at Melissa's reminder of who she was. "Oh, I believe Fred has behaved himself temporarily," he said almost absently. "But he's been known to take spells of agreeableness before. They don't usually last."

Melissa shrugged, wondering why she suddenly felt uneasy about the disparity in Rob's expression and in his words. His mind didn't really seem to be on what he was talking about.

"What can he do except throw me?" she asked practically. "He's done that before and I survived. And there will be people around to help if he acts up— though I don't think he will."

"I don't want to see you hurt, Melissa!" Rob grated, his voice taking on a harshness that startled Melissa. "I have a responsibility to you while you're here," he then added, but Melissa thought his last statement was a coverup for the strong feelings he had displayed in his first reaction. The knowledge made her relax somewhat while a warm glow threatened to cut off her ability to think at all.

"Rob, I promise I'll be careful," she said softly. "I don't want to be hurt either."

Rob stared at her at hearing that softness in her voice, and Melissa thought he seemed to be fighting something inside himself. She was positive of it when he changed the subject abruptly.

"You seem to really be getting into the life out here," he drawled almost sarcastically. "Aren't you forgetting that you came here to observe—not to participate?"

Melissa felt a sudden sadness at his question and realized she was guilty of wanting to participate in a more permanent fashion than might be permitted her. "I haven't forgotten," she said quietly, though that was not strictly the truth. "That's why . . ."

She stopped abruptly, fearing she'd been about to say too much, but Rob caught her up on her unwitting revelation.

"That's why you've been avoiding me like the plague," he stated harshly. "That's why you call me Mr. Redding in that snotty little voice and act as though you never melted in my arms the way we both know you have!"

Melissa looked up, startled by the bitterness in his tone. He looked back at her without relenting for a moment, before his expression softened. "Or have you just been waiting for me to apologize for going overboard with the punishment when I caught you riding Fred because I was worried sick he might really hurt you?" he asked softly.

The admission stunned her, though she had suspected the truth on some level for quite a while. She just hadn't allowed herse   deal with the knowledge that Rob cared to that   nt when she was unable as yet to put her private li   rst.

He got u   m his chair abruptly and came around the desk to   her up into his arms. "What the hell are we fightin   out?" he asked in a low, harsh tone. "You kno   amned well *this* is what we both really want!"

His kis   s savagely hungry at first, and Melissa's response   equally so. She couldn't imagine how she had sur   d for an entire week without touching him...   ing him...feeling his strong arms around her and   body against her. She held on to him as though   were drowning and he was her lifeline, and her lip   d tongue devoured his every bit as greedily as his di   s.

He   w back at last, his eyes two sleepy blue expressions   unabated desire. "God, Melissa, don't look at me   that," he muttered raggedly, telling her her exp   on echoed his. "I'm not made of stone, you kno

       ther am I," she gasped weakly as he closed her ey   y kissing the lids. "You're looking at me the same w

       chuckle was deep and satisfied. "Tell me what a   is supposed to look like when he's been starving for   ek and finally gets what he wants," he growled.

       elissa countered, her voice shaky. "If you'll tell me   at a woman is supposed to look like under the same   cumstances," she said.

"Exactly the way you do," Rob murmured, dipping s head to slide his mouth over her neck. "And she's upposed to taste the way you do...and feel the way ou do...."

He seized her mouth again before she could reply to that, and for several long moments the two of them strained against each other and took their fill of each other's mouth. Then a knock at the door made them break the kiss simultaneously, while each jerked their head toward the door, their expressions identical with irritated frustration.

"Who is it?" Rob roared, making Melissa jerk in his arms.

Margo's voice answered, sounding muffled. "Mrs. Price wants Melissa in the kitchen," she said sulkily. "It's her turn to help fix dinner."

Rob's mouth tightened for an instant, but his answer was quieter. "She'll be there shortly, Margo," he called. "We're busy right now."

Melissa could almost feel Margo's jealousy coming in waves through the door, but the girl finally gave a short "Okay!" before they heard her moving away.

Rob turned back to Melissa and a smile smoothed away his irritation when he saw her anxious gaze. "This is no place to conduct an affair," he whispered with amusement. "There's no privacy."

He was about to kiss her again, Melissa knew, but his words had brought a breath of sanity back to her. "Rob..." She stopped him by placing her hand gently over his mouth. "I still haven't finished the job I came here to do. Until then, I don't think—"

Impatience returned to his face. "Damn it, Melissa!" he interrupted in low, fierce tones. "I'm not a saint! I want you!"

"I want you, too," Melissa answered with quiet sincerity. "But as you said...this is no place to have an...an affair." She almost choked on the word that described a relationship she was fast losing her taste for. She hated to admit it, but even if she proved that Rob was innocent in the *Delilah* matter, she didn't want simply to have an *affair* with him anymore. She wanted a lot more than that. She wanted...

But she shut off that thought for the present. "Besides," she added with a fatalistic shrug, "I really do have to finish the job I came here to do before. . ." She stopped, her look finishing the thought.

"Well, how long is it going to take?" Rob asked frustratedly. "You've been here almost two weeks now, Melissa! I thought reporters could throw an article together in an afternoon."

Melissa ducked her head, knowing her guilt was showing in her eyes. "This. . . this is not one I can throw together," she prevaricated. "I. . . it's more complicated than that. I need more time."

"And I need you," Rob stated harshly, tightening his arms around her. "I need this." He kissed her again, and Melissa melted into him, unable to control the sensations coursing through her at his touch. At her reaction, Rob pulled back slightly, and his gaze was triumphant. "You need it too, Melissa," he grated huskily. "Don't you? *Don't* you?" he demanded when she tried to avoid answering.

"Yes." She gave him the answer he wanted, and it was nothing but the truth. Her desire for Rob was rapidly growing into a need. . . a need that was threatening to grow into a compulsion and that she was not at all sure she was going to be able to resist if he kept up the pressure he was now exerting.

"Then get it done, Melissa," he ordered, his tone half demand, half entreaty. "Get it done and come to me before I'm forced to stop paying attention to your ethics and take what we both want!"

Melissa looked at him, drowning in the desire blazing forth from his clear blue eyes. "All right, Rob," she whispered achingly. "I'll. . . I'll get it done. Are you going to let me ride Fred, Rob?"

He snorted his opinion of her perseverence. "Hell, yes, ride the damned beast if you want to!" he gave in, though his permission was given grudgingly. "But you stay close to someone at all times, do you hear?" he demanded. "I don't want to have to seduce you in a hospital bed!"

Melissa smiled at the thought. "I think you've already seduced me, Rob," she admitted weakly.

"Not the way I want to," he grated, unappeased by her attempt at humor. "And not the way you want it either," he added as he inspected the soft passion still evident in her eyes.

"No," Melissa sighed. "This is definitely not the way I want it," she said, wishing she could explain to Rob exactly why it was so imperative she delay what was going to happen between them. And then she remembered that she had been going to ask Rob about Micah, and she opened her mouth to do so when both of them heard a noise outside the study window.

"What was that?" Rob muttered as he left Melissa to stride to the window and look out. It was almost dark outside, however, and though Rob looked both ways, he saw nothing. Giving a shrug, he turned back to Melissa. "I guess it wasn't anything," he dismissed the matter as he crossed to his desk.

"You'd better go help Mrs. Price if you're going to maintain your image as just another inmate, Melissa," he then said as he reached for another cheroot.

"All right, Rob," she agreed, sounding as tired as she felt.

Rob looked up sharply at hearing that tone. "Are we being too rough on you, honey?" he then asked more calmly and with genuine concern, Melissa felt.

"No." She shook her head and smiled. "Now that my stable duty is over—it is over, isn't it?" she interrupted herself to ask mischievously, and at Rob's shamefaced nod, she went on. "I'm not doing anything the rest of the girls don't do. And I enjoy a lot of it, Rob. Really I do."

An alert expression came into his eyes then, and his smile was genuinely pleased. "You do, huh?" he asked thoughtfully. And at Melissa's nod, he added casually, "You don't miss the bright lights and advantages of city life?"

Melissa shrugged. "Rockport doesn't have many advantages of city life," she reminded him. "And no, I don't miss it. I like it here, Rob."

Her sincerity was obvious, and Rob's gaze turned even more thoughtful in reaction to it. "Well, well," he murmured. "Who would have thought it? Maybe I'd better work on . . ."

But another knock on the door interrupted whatever he'd been about to say, and Margo's voice was imperious this time. "Mrs. Price wants Melissa, Rob!" she stated petulantly. "Is she going to stay in there all night?"

Rob raised one eyebrow in a humorous expression, and looking at Melissa, he replied in a way that made her blush. "Not tonight, Margo," he called. "She'll be out in a minute."

He grinned as Melissa gave him a chastising look, and he crossed to her to give her a lingering kiss on the mouth before he pushed her toward the door. "Sometimes a man gets pushed too far," he whispered teasingly. "It makes him want to do something dangerous."

"So I see," Melissa drawled.

"No, sweetheart," Rob disputed that. "You haven't seen anything yet. But you will . . . you will . . ."

And his last kiss gave her a taste of his meaning before he pushed her out the door to begin the mundane task of putting together a meal when she would rather have been dining on love.

Chapter Eleven

Since there was a trip to Missoula planned for the kids the next day, the weekly dance was scheduled for that night. Melissa had bathed and was dressing for it when Mrs. Price appeared at her door to tell her her father was on the phone and to hurry downstairs to take the call.

Alarmed that something might be wrong at home, since her father had never been an overly anxious parent even when she'd been younger, Melissa raced downstairs to Rob's study and picked up the receiver from the desk.

"Dad?" she said anxiously. "Is something wrong?"

"This is not your father, Melissa," came the rasping growl of her friendly editor. "It's Malcolm Keller."

"Mr. Keller!" Melissa squeaked, darting a nervous look toward the door of the study to make sure she'd closed it behind her. "What's the matter?" she then asked almost in a whisper.

She heard an exasperated sound at the other end of the line. "That's what *I'd* like to know, Melissa," he answered impatiently. "I haven't heard a word from you since you sent me that note saying you were going to pretend to be one of the inmates there, and that was over a week ago!"

Melissa winced at his tone. "But there hasn't been anything to report," she defended herself. "I still don't know who beat up Delilah."

"Hmph!" Mr. Keller snorted. "That doesn't sound like the vaunted investigative reporter you used to be. What have you been doing, punching cows?"

"Not yet, but I will be next week," she replied saucily.

She heard another sound of annoyance and stifled a sigh at her employer's impatience. "Then it's a good thing I've been doing your job for you, isn't it?" he growled.

Melissa frowned, then looked hopeful. "What do you mean?" she asked.

"Delilah let down the barriers a little today, that's what I mean," Mr. Keller informed her in a long-suffering tone. "She found out where you were from her mother, and it shook her up a little."

"It did?" Melissa's response was eager. "What did she say?"

Mr. Keller's voice sobered at that, taking on a graver note. "She said you'd better be careful out there, Melissa," he said. "She wouldn't name any names, and she skirted the subject like a hummingbird on a flower, but from what I could gather, somebody out there is dealing in drugs, and he won't take kindly to any interference. I gather that may have been what happened to Delilah, but she wouldn't admit to it."

The idea left Melissa flabbergasted. She hadn't seen any signs that would indicate the kids were using anything. Angela had indicated she liked to smoke pot occasionally, but Melissa had never smelled it, nor had she been able to spot the telltale signs that Angela had a source for it out here.

"Is that all she said, Mr. Keller?" Melissa queried. "Did she say what kind of drugs are being used?"

"No," he drawled. "She didn't go into any details at all. The only way I knew there were drugs being dealt out there is that she said. . ." Mr. Keller hesitated then, and Melissa grew impatient for his reply.

"Yes, yes. . .?" she urged him. "What did she say?"

"Well," Mr. Keller went on, "don't get your feelings hurt, but she said if Miss Goody Two Shoes—meaning you—didn't have any drug habit now, you might after you'd been there awhile."

As Melissa was digesting that unexpected—and unwelcome—information, Mr. Keller went on. "She said something else, too, Melissa," he drawled. "She said you'd better keep your hands off of Redding. She said it like she was warning you off her territory, but that doesn't make any sense, because I don't think wild horses could drag her back out there."

Since Mr. Keller had never seen Rob and was unlikely to have the same reaction to him as a woman would, even if he had, Melissa didn't think it would serve any purpose to explain to her editor that Rob was very good at inspiring jealousy in females. She dismissed Delilah's warning as sour grapes, while she felt a lightening of her heart in regard to Rob's innocence in beating Delilah. Surely the girl wouldn't be jealous of a man who had beaten her and who still inspired the sort of terror Delilah was laboring under? Unless, of course, Melissa thought with a returning sense of gloom an instant later, Delilah was the sort of female who became enthralled with a man regardless of the treatment she received at his hands. Delilah had run away from the ranch, presumably because of her beating, but might she be having second thoughts about Rob now?

Then Melissa remembered that Delilah had supposedly been involved with Micah when she'd been at the ranch, and she asked Mr. Keller about it.

"Did Delilah mention anything about a boy named Micah, Mr. Keller?"

"No, why?" he asked in his turn.

"Oh, there's been some talk about her being involved with him while she was here," Melissa answered abstractedly, her mind still on what Mr. Keller had told her earlier about drugs on the ranch.

"Well, she didn't mention him," Mr. Keller said, dismissing the subject. "Now, Melissa," he went on determinedly. "I've been thinking it might be better to pull you off this story and get the police involved. Drug dealers are dangerous, and I didn't send you out there to—"

"No!" Melissa protested strenuously. "I haven't seen so much as a joint while I've been here, Mr. Keller. No one has approached me to sell me anything either. I don't want to get the authorities in here on a witch hunt just on the strength of Delilah's hints. It could damage the reputation of the place for no good reason if it isn't true!"

Mr. Keller went silent as he thought about what Melissa had pointed out. "Well," he said gruffly, "you may be right. But those fellows play rough, if it is true, Melissa. We've seen what was done to Delilah. Do you really want to take the risk that the same thing could happen to you?"

Melissa shrugged, then remembered that Mr. Keller couldn't see her response. "I've faced worse things, Mr. Keller," she said dryly, thinking of an enraged pimp who had resented having his picture splashed on the pages of the Washington newspaper where she'd worked and had come after her for revenge.

"Have you?" Mr. Keller sounded doubtful. "Like what?"

"Never mind," Melissa cut him off. It was getting late, and she didn't want anyone wondering why she hadn't shown up at the dance—especially Rob. "Listen, Mr. Keller," she went on hastily. "Do me a favor and throw the name Micah Gilroy at Delilah. If she won't talk about him, at least see how she reacts to the name."

"Micah who?" Mr. Keller grunted, and Melissa could hear his chair squeaking as he leaned forward to his desk to write down the name.

"Gilroy," Melissa repeated, and spelled it for him.

"We're going into town tomorrow," she added, "and I'll call you from there in the afternoon. I ought to be able to slip away long enough to phone you without anyone knowing about it. Meanwhile, I think I'm going to let it be known that I'm in the market for a little something to ease my sentence here."

"You be careful, Melissa," Mr. Keller instructed sternly. "This could turn out to be dangerous for you, you know."

"I know," Melissa said impatiently, wondering what Keller had thought she'd been doing all these years on the Washington paper. She was also wondering how she was going to appear to be convincing about wanting to buy drugs when she'd already made it clear, at least to Mary Alice and Angela, that she hadn't ever used drugs before. But she could worry about that later, she decided as she glanced at her watch.

"Tell my parents and Grandma hello for me, Mr. Keller," she said. "Let them know I'm all right."

"Sure," he agreed with a snort. "I'm the only one who has to know that may not be true much longer if you get too nosy, right?"

"Don't worry," Melissa assured him gently. "I've been in tight situations before. I can take care of myself."

"I hope so," he growled. "Your folks will have my hide if you can't, not to mention Kate."

Melissa could hear the concern in his voice, which meant that his own conscience would suffer a severe blow if anything happened to her, and she smiled affectionately.

"I'll be in the office all afternoon waiting for your call, Melissa," he went on sternly. "And from now on you keep in touch more frequently than you've been doing. I don't want to be left in the dark again."

"I will," Melissa assured him. "But I've got to go now, Mr. Keller. Thanks for calling, and I'll talk to you again tomorrow."

"You'd better!" was his succinct reply before he hung up.

Instead of hurrying to the dance as she'd meant to, Melissa wandered to the window as she mulled over what Mr. Keller had told her. She was staring out abstractedly when she saw a movement out of the corner of her eye and turned her head to see what looked like a shadowy figure just disappearing around the corner of the house.

Melissa frowned, wondering if it had been her imagination or if she really had seen something. But even if she had, it didn't necessarily mean that someone had been listening to her conversation, did it?

She glanced down at the window casement and saw that the window was raised a few inches. So if anyone had been out there, they could have heard her part of the conversation, she reflected thoughtfully as a cold chill went down her back. And then she shook her head, deciding that she was becoming paranoid after her conversation with Mr. Keller. She didn't trust Delilah enough to tell the truth about anything, much less what had happened to her here at the ranch, so until she came up with some hard evidence, Melissa decided, she was not going to go off half-cocked!

As she made her way to the barn, however, she ran over in her mind the most likely suspects. The only admitted user was Angela, but Melissa had never seen Angela using anything. The only person who had a history of distributing was Johnnie, but Mary Alice had said he only did it because he liked working with chemicals, and that he hadn't done it for money. And Johnnie was not the type to have someone beaten up. He was too gentle.

So who did that leave? Melissa fretted as she stopped just inside the barn doors to look around. And why hadn't she seen any indication that there were drugs being used by the kids on the ranch?

And then she remembered the peculiar glitter in Margo's eyes at the dance the preceding Saturday night. Melissa had thought it was an indication of jealous anger, but was it really? There had been a certain look in Margo's pupils. . . .

At that point Melissa's eyes were caught and held by Rob's blue-eyed gaze from across the room, and he raised one eyebrow in a silent inquiry about where she had been. Melissa managed a smile, which she hoped was brighter and more cheerful than she actually felt, and gave a slight shrug of her shoulders to indicate the delay in her arrival at the dance had been caused by nothing important. Rob shrugged his shoulders in return before his attention was reclaimed by Margo, and Melissa's smile abruptly departed as she saw the smile Rob gave the girl. Objectively, of course, Rob had to be on her list of suspects. But in her heart, Melissa rejected the idea vehemently. It *had* to be someone else!

Determining that she would watch Margo closely that night, Melissa turned away from the sight that was diverting her attention from the job at hand and headed toward where she saw Mary Alice and Johnnie cuddled together in a dark corner.

"Hi!" Melissa greeted the two brightly. They returned the greeting, and for a few moments Melissa made small talk with them, until she felt enough time had passed for her to risk a casual question.

"Say, you two," she drawled in a bored tone, "if I wanted to get my hands on a joint or something stronger here, who would I talk to?"

Mary Alice and Johnnie both looked startled at the question, and then they immediately exchanged a glance that looked so conspiratorial, Melissa's heart plunged. It looked very much as though she had hit bull's-eye with her first bullet.

"I thought you didn't go in for that sort of thing,"

Mary Alice said with a brightness that didn't quite cover a nervous quaver in her voice.

"I don't, normally," Melissa responded, using the disgust she was feeling in her tone for effect. "But this place is getting to me. After a week like I've had, I need some relaxation."

Johnnie looked troubled. "I wouldn't start on that stuff if you're not already into it, Mel," he advised hesitantly. "It just means trouble...I should know." He gave a rueful twist of his gentle mouth and there was a sad look in his warm brown eyes.

"Oh, I don't expect to make a habit of it," Melissa assured him breezily. "I've been around it enough to know it can get heavy if you let it take you over. I just wanted something tonight."

Mary Alice looked even more nervous as she exchanged another look with Johnnie. "I'm sorry, Mel," she then said firmly. "We don't know how you can get anything out here."

Melissa had heard enough lies to know when she was being told one, and she knew immediately that Mary Alice was lying. The question was, *why* was Mary Alice lying? Melissa decided to apply a little subtle pressure.

"Okay," she said casually. "I'll ask some of the other kids. Maybe they'll know."

Mary Alice grabbed Melissa's arm to stop her as Melissa started to walk away. When Melissa turned back in surprise, she saw that Mary Alice's big blue eyes contained an anxious look.

"It won't do you any good, Mel," Mary Alice stated. "He told us..."

And then Mary Alice stopped speaking as Johnnie made an admonitory sound, and she shot him a look of apology. Her cheeks were flushed when she returned her gaze to Melissa, but her speech was firm.

"You won't get anything from the others either, Mel, so you might as well forget it." Her gaze sharpened for an instant as she saw Melissa looking speculatively at Johnnie. "And you can forget any ideas you might have that Johnnie messes with that stuff anymore, Mel," Mary Alice went on, "because he doesn't!"

Melissa believed her. She also believed someone had given instructions that Melissa was not to be trusted enough to be told who the local pusher was. But why? she wondered as she watched Mary Alice and Johnnie walk away from her abruptly. What had happened to make the pusher decide she was an outsider? Unless someone *had* been listening at the window when she'd been talking to Malcolm Keller.

She quickly caught up with Mary Alice and Johnnie and stopped them before they got near anyone else. "Who's *he*?" she demanded heatedly. "And how come he's down on me?"

Johnnie looked sympathetic but resigned. "You don't want to mess with him, Mel," he said quietly. "Leave it alone. He's not going to sell you anything, and he—he says we shouldn't trust you."

Melissa's eyes opened wider as she looked at Johnnie and Mary Alice in astonishment. And then her jaw relaxed, and her gaze was steady and angry. "Do you two think I'm the sort of person who can't be trusted?" she demanded.

The two looked at each other for a moment, then both looked back at Melissa. "I like you, Mel," Mary Alice said. "And I think you can be trusted." But then she shook her head. "But I'm not going to argue with him about anything. He scares me too much."

Johnnie nodded his agreement, and from the expression on his and Mary Alice's faces, Melissa realized she wasn't going to get anything else out of either of them. She shrugged and tried to rescue the situation as best she could.

"Well, thanks anyway," she tossed off with a faint grin. "I guess I'll just have to get high on lemonade."

The relief Mary Alice and Johnnie displayed at her remark told Melissa she'd done the right thing, but inwardly she was seething. If she'd known the identity of the pusher at that moment she thought she would have horsewhipped him for jeopardizing the future of these kids!

Hoping she wasn't displaying what she was feeling, Melissa gave a friendly wave and moved away toward the refreshment table to cool her temper with a glass of the lemonade she'd mentioned.

As she stood sipping the cool liquid, however, Melissa searched the barn's occupants with her eyes, picking out and rejecting possible suspects. The problem was, she was suddenly unsure of her own judgment, since it had taken Mr. Keller's efforts to make her aware there was a drug problem on the ranch at all.

When she spotted Angela and Larry, she felt a surge of hope. Since Angela had openly admitted that she used marijuana, and Larry's philosophy seemed to be that anything that felt good was all right, perhaps they could be persuaded to override the pusher's edict? But then another thought hit her an instant later. What if Larry was the pusher?

She decided to risk it anyway, in the hope that she might spot something from their reaction to her questions, and was heading determinedly toward them when Rob's voice echoed through the barn.

"How about some square dancing?" he called out, and there was an answering cheer from the kids that startled Melissa. She wouldn't have thought these modern sophisticates would go in for square dancing so enthusiastically. But she had begun to lose faith in any conclusions she might draw about these kids now, and in any case, Lester appeared and grabbed her arm to pull her into a square.

"Come on, Mel!" he said eagerly. "Let's dance!"

There was nothing for it but to agree. Fortunately

Melissa had a nodding acquaintance with square dancing because of an elective college course she'd once taken. She only hoped she could remember the steps when her mind was so preoccupied with other things.

Melissa did a double take when she looked over to the next square and saw that Margo and Micah were paired together. They gave the impression of being old friends, and Melissa suddenly remembered that they had disappeared together at the last dance for a while. So what had been the significance of the blazing look Micah had directed at Margo and Rob that Melissa had intercepted at that same dance? Who exactly was he jealous of?

At the thought, Melissa felt a lightening of her worries for a few moments. She hoped fervently that Micah did have a crush on Margo...a nice, normal adolescent crush that was as healthy as apple pie and the Fourth of July.

And then Melissa had no time for further thought as her head began spinning for an entirely different reason. Lester, it seemed, was addicted to violent twirling when the caller on the record directed the square dancers to "swing your partner!" and when it came to allemande lefts, he was positively wicked! Melissa thought he was going to jerk her arm right out of its socket and she would be left crippled in body as well as in heart before she left Montana for a saner—and duller—life.

The first dance turned out to be only an appetizer for things to come. Rob was not dancing himself. He was busy relentlessly playing square dance after square dance on the record player, and since it developed that the procedure was to change partners at each new set, Melissa was subjected to toe stompings from Vincent, Larry's exhausting energy, Jason's bored leers, and Johnnie's nervous, perspiring palms. Micah turned out to be the only partner with no noticeable defects, but by the time *he* got around to dancing with Melissa, she was too far gone to care.

Of course, there was no opportunity to question anyone about anything for the rest of the evening, and when Rob called a halt earlier than usual because of the planned trip to Missoula the next day, Melissa was in no shape to tackle anything but her bed. As she started in the direction of the house with the rest of the girls, and then looked back to see Mary Alice and Johnnie exchanging a hasty good night kiss, it reminded her of something else she hadn't seen on the ranch so far besides drug use.

She had had the impression from listening to Mary Alice and Angela and Lester that absolute orgies went on between the sexes here. But *when*? Melissa wondered crossly. Did everyone pile out of their beds at 3:00 A.M. in the morning, have a quick assignation in "the bushes," as Lester had said, and then come in slightly before 4:30 A.M. to start a grueling day?

Somehow Melissa doubted it, and since she was experiencing a bewildering sense of self-doubt about almost everything right then, she crawled into her bed for some recuperative sleep to restore her brain's capacity to function.

But as she lay there staring up at the dark ceiling, wondering if the square dancing had maimed her for life and whether she'd lost every facility to carry out a successful investigation she'd ever had, she couldn't help the insidious thought that she wished this evening's dance had ended the way the last one had—in Rob's arms under the willow tree and without Micah Gilroy's interruption. That conclusion to an evening beat tonight's by a wide margin.

And as she drifted into slumber at last, she wondered faintly just what Micah's problem had been that night, when he had sounded as though he'd lost his last friend.

Chapter Twelve

The trip to Missoula was made in two vehicles, and by the time the drive was over, Melissa felt like a sardine who'd been shut up in a can with a bunch of other chattering, excited sardines. It didn't help matters either that Rob drove the station wagon containing the girls and Melissa had to sit in the backseat watching while Margo snuggled up next to him as cozily as though the two of them were alone together. Parker drove the boys in the van, and as Melissa glared at the back of Rob's head, she wished she'd ridden with Parker instead of him.

When Rob and Parker had drawn the two vehicles into parking spaces at a shopping mall, Melissa was the first one out of the car. She would have walked right off, but Rob's stern voice stopped her.

"Remember to stick together, girls," he instructed. "It's bad enough I have to trail you through all the women's-wear departments. I'm not about to waste my time trying to round you up when it's time to go."

Melissa was torn between laughing out loud at the thought of Rob escorting six giggling females on a shopping trip encompassing ladies' underwear and cosmetics, and chagrin at hearing that he expected to keep her under his eyes. She didn't have a thing to buy, and if she hadn't wanted to avert suspicion, she would have stayed at the ranch to call Mr. Keller while everyone else was away.

She thought she saw a gleam of amusement in Rob's eyes as he caught her disgruntled expression, and her mood slipped another notch. So he thought it was *funny* that her little masquerade was going to cramp her style, did he? she thought crossly as she watched the jostling between the males and the females of the group, who were instinctively trying to pair off. Well, he would get a lesson in how a determined reporter went about things then, she decided grumpily.

Rob deftly squelched the attempt at pairing off and directed Parker to take the boys inside to various men's stores to do their shopping while he himself herded the girls in another direction. The moaning and groaning that resulted from this arrangement didn't last long, however, as everyone knew they would all meet for lunch and an afternoon movie later. Melissa thought that movie would probably be the least-watched film in history on this particular afternoon, but she also thought there was no harm in the necking that would go on in the darkened theater. The kids worked hard all week, and she figured they deserved a chance to blow off steam.

In the large department store Rob led them to, the girls immediately headed for the dress department to look over the latest styles. Melissa imagined that most of them were accustomed to shopping in exclusive little boutiques where the prices would have given her a heart attack on the spot, but you couldn't have told it from the way they attacked the racks of ready-mades. They were as happy as clams.

Melissa trailed them, noting that Rob seated himself in a chair near the dresses and pulled out a ranch magazine to read while he waited. Melissa made a show of flipping through the dress racks for a few moments, but her attention was really focused on locating a convenient restroom nearby. It was still morning, but she thought she'd better try and reach Mr. Keller at the first opportunity if Rob was going to watch everyone like a hawk all day.

After spotting a familiar sign down an aisle in a cubbyhole area, she began to inch in that direction. She had to pass Rob on the way, but she planned to detour around behind him and pray he didn't look to his right as she approached or to his left as she passed him.

Melissa blessed her luck as a man dressed in typical Western attire approached Rob just as Melissa was in a dangerous spot on her journey. Rob and the man greeted each other familiarly, and Rob stood up to shake hands. As he did so Melissa slipped behind the post backing the chair Rob had been seated in. Then her luck ran out as he turned to face the direction she wanted to go as he stood and talked to the stranger. Melissa had no choice except to stay where she was and listen and hope that Rob would shift in the other direction soon.

"I see you've got the dirty dozen with you, Rob," the stranger said on a good-natured chuckle. And at Rob's nod and wry grin, the man continued. "But I heard you're getting out of the rehabilitation business soon. Is that true?"

Melissa's heart gave a funny lurch at Rob's reply. "Yes, I don't need the money anymore, and I need a break from the responsibility. I haven't had a vacation in the five years I've been doing this." Rob shrugged and shifted his weight from one booted heel to the other. "I'll miss the kids in a way, but I have other things on my mind right now."

The man nodded his agreement. "Yeah, I imagine they have been a big responsibility. You've done good work for them from what I hear, but it's about time you had a chance to think about yourself. Isn't it time you got married and had some kids of your own?"

Melissa's heart gave another lurch as she saw that Rob was looking thoughtful in response to the man's question. And then it stopped beating entirely for a second at Rob's answer.

"Yes, it is. As a matter of fact, I've been thinking about it a lot lately."

Melissa wasn't entirely certain *she* was responsible for Rob's thinking about marriage and children, but she hoped so. She saw the stranger slap Rob on the back. "Well, good for you!" he said to Rob. "Have you got someone in mind or are you still looking?"

At that moment Rob turned in the direction Melissa had been hoping he would, and Melissa was torn between her desire to hear his reply and the chance to make her escape and get to a telephone.

In the end she chose escape in case Rob named someone other than herself that he was thinking about marrying. If he did have someone else in mind, Melissa didn't want to hear anything about her rival, not even her name. She would have enough trouble getting over Rob Redding without being burdened by the added torture of knowing who had won him. And if he did have Melissa in mind, she would find out soon enough, she reassured herself stoically.

She reached the restroom undetected and slipped inside, scanning the room eagerly with her eyes for the expected telephone. She wanted to curse a blue streak when she discovered this particular restroom had no phone, but a second later she was grateful when the door was thrust open behind her, and Mary Alice and Angela trooped in, giggling like two magpies.

Their chorused "Hi's" were cheerfully unconcerned, though Melissa thought she saw a waver in Mary Alice's blue-eyed gaze. Deciding that she'd better justify her presence in the room, Melissa slipped into one stall while Mary and Angela went into two others.

So much for the glamour of investigative reporting, Melissa thought sourly, and then remembered the conversation between Rob and the stranger she'd overheard and decided to see if the girls had heard anything about Rob getting out of the rehabilitation business.

"Hey, you two," she said, lifting her voice. "Have you heard anything about Rob not working with people like us anymore?"

Angela piped up from behind the wall of her stall. "Yeah, I heard that," she said irreverently. "Too bad we couldn't have gotten in trouble a little later than we did, huh?"

Mary Alice disagreed. "There are a lot worse places than the ranch, Angela," she protested. "Personally, I'd rather chase cows than be sent to one of those really rough places."

Melissa broke in with another question. "How come he's not going to do it anymore, do you know?"

Angela sounded bored with the subject, but she answered. "He only started it because he needed the money to keep his ranch," she said cynically. "But I think he's come into funds now, and he doesn't need to do it anymore. So much for the kind-hearted capitalist!"

Mary Alice had a frown in her voice as she protested. "Oh, come off it, Angela! Rob's a good guy. He may have started all this because he needed the money, but he's really good at it."

Angela snorted her disgust. "Oh, you'd take up for anyone wearing pants, Mary Alice, and Rob fills his jeans better than most men."

Mary Alice and Angela started a mutual wrangling session then, but Melissa's mind was on other things. This was the second reference she'd heard today about Rob "not needing the money" anymore. *Why* didn't Rob need the money anymore? Melissa wondered, a cold foreboding piercing her heart like a knife. Had he inherited some? Or gotten over whatever temporary financial difficulties he'd been experiencing by wisely using the money he'd made taking in the kids? Or did he have another source of income that had put him ahead sufficiently to erase his money troubles—a source such as selling drugs to the kids in his care?

Melissa felt sick at the thought. But as she thought about it, Rob was the only person she could imagine who had sufficient authority to order the kids not to say anything to her about drugs. Surely Mary Alice and Johnnie wouldn't have been so nervous and so inclined to obey the edict if one of the other inmates had ordered them to keep quiet, would they? And if Rob was guilty, the mere fact that he knew Melissa was a reporter would explain the edict. And if he was romantically interested in her as well, which seemed evident, wouldn't he be even more inclined to keep the truth from her?

Melissa didn't want to believe it. The very possibility made her shudder with revulsion. But Delilah had been so scared...and she had told Mr. Keller to tell Melissa to stay away from Rob. Had Delilah been trying to issue a warning without spelling out the details? And hadn't Melissa felt the strength in Rob's arms and the power of his charismatic authority? Surely Delilah wouldn't be afraid that one of the kids would come to wreak revenge upon her if she talked about what had happened...but she might very well be afraid that a fully-adult man with the type of dominant personality Rob had would do so.

The other girls were leaving their stalls, and Melissa joined them, deciding that now was not the time to do or say anything out of the ordinary. If she stayed gone too long, Rob would become concerned, and she didn't want him watching her any closer than he already was. She still had that call to make.

Her reasoning proved correct when she found Rob outside the restroom door waiting for them. He looked at Melissa rather piercingly, Melissa thought, and she managed to smile at him, hoping her inner misery didn't show. But as she stared into Rob's beautiful clear blue eyes, she wondered despondently if eyes really were the window of the soul. Right now Rob's were indicating he was one of the finest men she'd ever known. But what if they really hid the soul of a pusher?

God, she hoped not! She prayed not. Even if she hadn't already been more than halfway in love with him, she would have hated to see him involved in such a dirty business. It was too despicable to be contemplated. Yet it had to be contemplated if she had any integrity as a reporter left at all.

The next couple of hours dragged by for Melissa as her thoughts churned and twisted. The girls were obviously well-trained in Rob's maxim that they stay together, making it impossible for Melissa to slip away, and by the time Rob's patience had worn thin with the shopping trip, Melissa's was practically nonexistent.

The meals at the ranch were undeniably delicious, but the kids were dying for a taste of junk food, so lunch was eaten at a fast-food place specializing in hamburgers, hot dogs, and gooey confections that guaranteed the addition of five pounds just to look at.

Parker and Rob were unwilling to join their charges at such a feast, however, and they ate together at a restaurant across from the fast-food place that had a more varied menu, yet still allowed them to keep an eye on the kids.

Melissa had a hamburger, which she couldn't finish, then ordered a hot-fudge sundae to soothe her troubled soul. Micah was seated beside her, and as she ate the rich confection, Melissa stared out the window at Rob across the way and wished with all her heart that all of this were over and he had been proved innocent. Then perhaps he would take her by the hand and lead her somewhere...anywhere...where she could really find that peace she had been looking for when she'd come home to Rockport.

Melissa gave an unconscious sigh, then noticed that Micah was watching her with an unfathomable look in his gray eyes that was new and disconcerting, though not hostile. She reminded herself to keep a tighter rein on her expressions, however, and launched into a funny story about an incident that had happened at a fast-food place in her college days, though she left out the fact that it had happened then.

Micah laughed in all the right places, but Melissa had the disorienting feeling that he was acting a part, just as she was. But there was nothing she could grab hold of to support her feeling, so she shrugged it away as nonsense.

The movie was about a rock band, and all the kids were looking forward to seeing it, but Melissa was definitely not looking forward to pretending to drool over the lead singer while enraptured by the music he played. However, when she found out that Rob wasn't accompanying the kids to the movie, and when she spotted a telephone in the lobby, her mood lightened somewhat. Here was her chance to make that call.

Parker did accompany everyone into the theater, his elderly face creased into the lines of a long-suffering martyr, but Melissa was relieved when he seated himself, tipped his hat over his eyes, and leaned back to nap through the entertainment.

She was careful to sit behind Parker and in an end seat. Lester was on her left, and she had no doubt that he was planning to pay more attention to her than to the movie, but she wasn't about to worry about him when she had more important matters on her mind.

Fifteen minutes into the movie, after Melissa had fended off a number of Lester's inexpert passes, she whispered to him that she was going to the ladies' room and eased herself quietly from her seat. Then she hurried up the aisle, slipped out the double doors, and headed straight for the row of telephones she'd spotted on the way into the theater.

She was standing in front of one of them, scrambling

in her purse for a coin, when a hand descended onto her shoulder. She thought later she must have jumped three feet into the air. The coin fell from her fingers onto the floor, and she gave a shriek that was loud enough to wake the dead.

"For God's sake, Melissa," Rob growled impatiently. "It's only me. What the hell is the matter with you?"

He bent to retrieve the coin, and Melissa unconsciously backed away a few steps. When he straightened and looked at her white face, his expression changed to one of concern.

"What is it, honey?" he asked quietly. "Has something happened? Who were you about to call?"

"I . . . ah . . . my dad!" Melissa improvised, remembering that since Rob had said he knew everything that went on at the ranch, he must know that her father had supposedly called her the preceding evening. "My grandmother isn't feeling well, and I was just going to check on her."

It sounded like every lie she'd ever told all bundled up in one package, but apparently Rob believed her, and Melissa felt a twinge of guilt when he looked at her sympathetically.

"I'm sorry, honey," he murmured. "Go ahead and call. I'll wait, and then I'll take you to get a cup of coffee."

Melissa decided she wasn't up to dissembling over the telephone with Rob listening, however, and she shook her head. "Oh, no . . . that's all right," she said hastily. "It wasn't anything serious. I can call from the ranch later."

Rob hesitated, then shrugged. "You know best," he said simply. "Now come and have some coffee with me. I've been going crazy to get you to myself since yesterday. In fact, I didn't dare dance with you last night because I was afraid I couldn't keep from kissing you in front of everyone."

In spite of her suspicions about Rob, his smile and his tone warmed her from head to foot, and she felt a weakening softness toward him that made her despair of her ability to keep her objectivity firmly in place.

"Is that why you had us doing all that square dancing?" she asked weakly as Rob turned her toward the doors of the theater.

"Why else?" he chuckled warmly. "You noticed I didn't dance, didn't you? I didn't even trust myself to behave in that sort of innocent exercise."

"Oh," Melissa faltered, then caught her breath as Rob wrapped his arm around her waist and pulled her close to his body.

"Oh, indeed," he murmured intimately, and his warm breath wafting over her face made Melissa close her eyes against a wave of desire.

He didn't speak again until they were seated at a small, nearby restaurant and had ordered coffee. He just watched her, and Melissa couldn't help looking back at him, feeling a combination of helpless love and desire...and heartbreak...as she let her eyes travel over his rugged, handsome, deliciously male face.

Please, God, she reiterated over and over again while they were engaged in their mutual, intimate inspection. *Please don't let him be guilty. Please let him be just what he seems to be...a caring, warm, strong, and moral man of principle.*

Then he spoke to her and broke her concentration on her prayer. "How is the story coming, Melissa?" he asked quietly. "I'm trying to be patient, but I don't know how much longer I can keep up this farce. Every time I see you, I want to take you into my arms. I'm even beginning to resent the kids because they're the reason I can't behave with you the way I want to."

Melissa swallowed. "I...it's coming together, Rob," she replied faintly. "It shouldn't be too much longer."

"But when do you work on it?" Rob asked in puzzlement. "You never use the typewriter in the den. Do you write it all out in longhand?"

"Oh...ah..." Melissa faltered. "I can't use the typewriter where someone might come along and see what I'm doing, Rob," she improvised, sticking as closely to the truth as possible. "I mostly keep things in my head; it will all come spilling out when I get the chance to write it."

He shrugged, then shook his head impatiently as he reached across the table to take her hand in his. "Melissa, how important is your career to you?" he asked, looking directly into her eyes. Melissa groaned inwardly, wishing with all her heart that this conversation, with all its implications, could have come later on in their relationship. When she hesitated about replying, Rob grimaced slightly and went on.

"I guess what I'm trying to ask is if you're a hardcore career reporter," he said. And then he took a deep breath and held her gaze intently. "What do you want out of life, Melissa? Is your career all-important to you, or is there room for...other things."

Melissa took his meaning clearly, and decided instantly that she could answer him honestly on this point whether anything ever came of it or not.

"No, my career isn't all-important to me, Rob," she replied sincerely. "I can write articles without being a full-time reporter. Or I can try to write a book." She didn't say that the subject of the book, which she had contemplated before, would be her experiences as an investigative reporter on a big Washington newspaper. "I...want to love one man...marry him...have babies...live happily ever after...." She faltered slightly before she finished in a soft, choked voice, her heart in her eyes. "Just like in the fairy tales."

"I love fairy tales, Melissa," he said in a low, deep voice. "And I love..."

But the waiter appeared at that moment to refill their

coffee cups, and the words died on Rob's lips. Melissa closed her eyes against the disappointment she felt at not even getting the opportunity to hear him say those words to her once. But an instant later she regathered her willpower and was glad Rob hadn't spoken them under these circumstances. She would far rather hear them when there were no dark shadows to cloud the occasion.

When the waiter departed, she immediately changed the subject, determinedly hardening her heart against the disappointment Rob displayed at her action.

"Rob, I heard you talking to a man in that department store this morning." She rushed into speech before he could. "You were saying you're going to stop taking kids in soon. Is that true?"

"Yes, it's true," Rob said impatiently, then opened his mouth to get back to more intimate matters, but Melissa cut him off.

"Why?" she asked as she searched his face, praying he would have a good explanation she could believe in.

Rob shifted his shoulders impatiently. "I don't need the money anymore, and I need a break." He looked at her meaningfully, and his voice dropped lower as he added, "I have some things I want to do with my own life for a change."

But Melissa wouldn't be diverted. "What...ah... happened?" she persisted. "Did you inherit a fortune from a long-lost relative or something?" She tried to inject a teasing note into her question, but it wasn't a particularly successful attempt.

"Something like that," was Rob's brief reply, given in a way that indicated he definitely wanted to cut off that line of conversation. Melissa didn't know what she was going to do or say if Rob got to the point of making a proposal of marriage to her, and she was desperately searching her brain for some way to head him off temporarily when the man Rob had spoken to in the department store that morning paused by their table.

"Hello, again, Rob," the man said in a hearty tone. He shifted his curious gaze to Melissa after Rob had acknowledged the greeting—somewhat reluctantly, Melissa noted. "Who's your friend?"

Rob performed the introductions without going into any details about who Melissa actually was or why she was with him, and after the man chatted a few moments, he moved on. As Rob turned back to Melissa, she hastily introduced a new line of conversation.

"Rob, what did Margo do to get sent to you?" It was all Melissa could think of to divert Rob from more intimate matters, and since she was unable to keep a note of jealousy from her voice as she spoke, it proved to be a good diversion.

A twinkle appeared in his blue eyes and a slow smile curved his masculine mouth under the mustache. "Nothing," he answered innocently, though it was clear he was having a hard time keeping from laughing.

Melissa looked at him first in astonishment and then with suspicion. "What's she doing at the ranch then?" she said crossly, chagrined to realize her jealousy was showing but unable to help herself.

Rob gave her a bland look tinged with an understanding that made Melissa slightly uncomfortable. It was clear he knew exactly why she was asking about Margo, and furthermore, that he was enjoying her display of jealousy. Finally, however, in the face of Melissa's growing discomfort, he relented.

"Her parents are good friends of mine, Melissa," he explained. "Her father works for an oil company and was recently sent to one of the Middle Eastern countries for an assignment lasting six months. He wanted his wife with him, and she wanted to go, but Margo didn't. So they asked me if I'd take care of Margo until they get back."

Melissa relaxed a little in the face of Rob's patient explanation, but not completely. "Weren't they afraid she'd be contaminated by associating with the rest of the population at the Rocking R?'' she asked dryly.

Rob shook his head, and his lips were twitching with amusement now. "No," he said. "They know the background of the kids I take in, and they trust me. And they also know Margo's...ah...fond of me and likes to please me. They figured I could handle things.''

"I'll bet!" Melissa clipped out spontaneously, and at that reaction Rob laughed outright.

"Oh, Melissa," he chuckled when he got his laughter under control. "I could have sworn your eyes were blue, but they have a distinctly green cast at the moment.''

Melissa glared at him and opened her mouth to tell him what she thought of his smug humor, but instead she saw something over his shoulder that made her eyes widen in surprise. Micah was seated at the table next to theirs with his back to them, and the tenseness of his posture made it clear he was listening to every word they were saying. Melissa had been so involved with Rob, she hadn't noticed when Micah had come in, so she wasn't sure how long he'd been there or how much he'd heard of the conversation. She wasn't sure why he was interested enough to have left the theater to eavesdrop either, but the possibilities made her uneasy.

Rob was looking at her curiously and was about to turn his head to see what she was staring at when Melissa hastily caught his attention. She didn't think this was the time or the place to provoke a confrontation. Rob might not object to Micah being where he shouldn't have been, but on the other hand, he might, and Melissa knew instinctively that Micah would be deeply hurt if Rob got on to him in front of her.

"Rob, I'm sorry about that last remark," she said quickly. "It's none of my business why Margo is at the ranch, and it's none of my business if she's...ah... fond of you.''

That last statement almost stuck in her throat, but

Rob's reaction was tender. "Isn't it, honey?" he asked, quietly mocking. "I thought I'd given you the right to be a little jealous."

He had caught her hand in his again, and was now engaged in stroking her palm with the fingers of his other hand while he held her eyes in a gaze so explicitly meaningful that Melissa couldn't look away for the life of her. She began drowning in that blue gaze that told her she was important to Rob Redding in a way she longed to be important—the way she'd always wanted the man she finally loved to look at her. And the distant protest in her mind—the "if only" questions—began to retreat further as she was wrapped tighter and tighter in the web of love he was casting just with his eyes.

Their total concentration on each other was at last broken as Rob shifted his gaze slightly when people started pouring out of the movie theater across the way. He took a frustrated breath and squeezed Melissa's hand.

"We'll have to finish this later, sweetheart," he said, his voice softly caressing. "It's time to get the kids and start for home."

He released her hand to fish in his pocket for money to pay for the coffee they'd had, and as he did so Melissa saw Micah get to his feet and hurry out of the restaurant to join the rest of the kids. As she got up to accompany Rob out of the restaurant, she felt a sad sense of unease that Micah had been witness to the conversation between she and Rob. She wasn't sure why the idea upset her so much, though she'd had her suspicions that Micah's feelings for Rob bordered on being unhealthily obsessive, but she would have much preferred that Micah hadn't seen and heard what he did.

On the ride back to the ranch Margo again appropriated the place next to Rob, but this time Rob occasionally caught Melissa's eyes in the rearview mirror, and it was hard for Melissa to remain jealous in the face of his nonverbal messages. Once he even grinned when Margo rested her head on his shoulder, provoking a glare from Melissa that dissipated when Rob winked at her in the mirror.

But aside from that, Melissa's thoughts were taken up worrying how the man who had captured her heart could possibly be a corrupter of youth. She reflected that while it was said love was blind, she couldn't imagine it being that blind.

She tried to imagine Rob beating Delilah or any other female, and was unable to come up with an image of the event. He had a temper, true, but she had also seen him control that temper. She couldn't even imagine him having someone else do the actual beating at his orders. The idea was ludicrous.

But then she sighed as she realized it was almost impossible for her to be objective about Rob. And better judges of character than she was had been fooled by charming con men for centuries. So how could she be certain that Rob was as innocent as he appeared...as she *wanted* him to be?

And how was she going to find out the truth? she thought an instant later, her frustration mounting. She hadn't been able to phone Mr. Keller that day, and she hated to think what his reaction to that would be when she did get hold of him. But perhaps Delilah had let go of another piece of the puzzle and he would have some news that would mute his irritation.

Deciding that she would try to call Mr. Keller that night, or if that proved impossible, the next morning, she leaned her head back against the seat, shifted slightly to relieve the pressure of Mary Alice's elbow in her ribs, and dropped off into a doze to relieve the pressure of her worries and the anticipation of a possible heartbreak that would put any she'd suffered in the past to shame.

Chapter Thirteen

Melissa's hopes of being able to use the ranch phone to call Mr. Keller were dashed that evening when Rob announced that he was going to do some paperwork in the study and didn't want to be disturbed. She was too preoccupied with her dismay over that development to notice that Rob seemed unusually preoccupied as well.

Resigning herself to wait until the next morning to make the call, Melissa did her evening chores, then tumbled into bed, certain she wouldn't sleep. Apparently she did sleep, however, because the next thing she knew, Mrs. Price was shaking her awake to tell her to get ready to go to church.

Melissa thought about pleading a sudden illness, thinking that would give her the whole morning alone in the house, but Mrs. Price cut off her first tentative complaint in a way that convinced Melissa she would get nowhere with that particular ploy.

"Come on, Melissa," Mrs. Price instructed firmly. "I've heard every excuse ever thought up by one of you youngsters to get out of going to church, and my ears are closed. Now get up out of that bed and get ready. You missed last week, which means you probably need to go all the more this week."

Melissa glared at Mrs. Price's retreating back, then grudgingly did as she was told, thinking it was going to be great to assume her rightful role as an adult once more when all this was over.

When she came downstairs and saw Rob dressed in his blue suit, white shirt, and patterned tie, however, she went weak at the knees at the sight, forgetting for the moment that all that perfection might be hiding the soul of a man she couldn't respect. She was puzzled when Rob again seemed preoccupied, so much so in fact, that he barely glanced at her before disappearing into his study again to put in another half hour's work before it was time to leave for church.

The church was of such picturesque quaintness that, despite her worries, Melissa was glad she'd been forced to come after all. Built of logs, it had hand-hewn wooden pews, a carved wooden altar, and a huge picture window behind the choir pews that gave a panoramic view of rolling Montana hills and the big sky for which the state was famous.

The pastor was a rancher who preached part-time, and his message was eloquently simple—and particularly apt in Melissa's case. It emphasized the fact that humans had only a short time on earth, and it behooved them to find out quickly how they wanted to live that time in accordance with their consciences and get on with it.

On the drive back to the ranch Melissa reflected wistfully that she knew exactly how she wanted to spend her time. She wanted all the mystery at the ranch cleared up as quickly as possible, with Rob found innocent of any wrongdoing. Then she wanted him to ask her to marry him and spend the rest of her days surrounded by Montana's beauty and Rob's love, with a couple of little Robs thrown in. In her spare time she would write that book about her experiences in Washington. She decided she wouldn't even mind Rob's continuing to take in kids for rehabilitation, though she thought she would prefer he take in ones who were less affluent so that they would have the benefit of time spent in this beautiful country in the bosom of a loving family.

After lunch she was jolted back into reality as she found out for the first time where the kids conducted their orgies—or rather what passed for orgies in their estimation. There was a river about a mile away that served as a swimming pool for the kids on Sunday afternoons, and though it was September, this particular day was warm enough to permit use of it.

Rob had ensconced himself in the study again, making it impossible for Melissa to get to the telephone, so she grudgingly accompanied the rest of the Rocking R contingent to the river for a swim. She consoled herself with the thought that she would at least get to talk to some of the kids again and perhaps find out something useful.

She shortly found out that was not going to be the case. No sooner had everyone gotten out of sight of the ranch buildings than the various steady couples paired off with a vengeance. And by the time they arrived at the river, Melissa decided Romeo and Juliet would have been shocked to the core at the way modern couples played the game of teenage love. She was a little shocked herself.

The kids did pay lip service to their ostensible reason for the outing by dipping themselves briefly in the river, but then they disappeared into the surrounding foliage with a speed that made Melissa's head spin. Soon the only people still swimming were Micah, Lester, Margo, and herself.

Lester had apparently given up on seducing Melissa and was concentrating his attention on Margo. She seemed amused by his pantings, but Melissa was surprised when Margo consented to wander off with him into the local Garden of Eden, and Melissa reflected in bewilderment that anyone who could settle for Lester when they were supposedly enamored of Rob was too much for her to fathom.

Micah seemed determined to make the outing a success, however. He seemed more relaxed and cheerful than Melissa had ever seen him, and she couldn't help but join in when he laughingly splashed her, then ducked out of the way of her expected retaliation.

After a while they tired of their game and crawled out onto the grassy bank to lie in the warm sun and rest. Melissa was drowsily daydreaming, picturing herself lying there with Rob instead of Micah, when Micah inched over closer to her. She opened sleepy, unsuspecting eyes to see him leaning over her and looking at her with a good imitation of Lester's leer. That woke her up fast.

"You like me, don't you, Melissa?" he asked in a soft, coaxing voice.

Melissa nodded warily, wondering how she could move away without hurting his feelings. "Sure, Micah," she answered in a casually friendly tone.

Her thoughts were churning, however, and she felt anything but casual. She had thought Micah didn't particularly like girls. In fact, she had wondered if he didn't like Rob a little too much, and not just as a father figure. But he *had* been involved with Delilah somehow, she remembered, and he and Margo seemed to have some kind of a relationship.

Micah smiled at her then—a charming, little-boy-on-the-verge-of-manhood smile—and Melissa felt drawn to him as an older sister might be drawn to a sibling. She wondered desperately what she was going to do if he made a pass at her. If he were a late developer and was on the verge of discovering girls, might a rejection from her tip him in the wrong direction again? That is, if he *were* inclined toward the other direction. Melissa wasn't certain of anything at that point.

She decided the best course of action was to try to

avoid any kind of involvement at all of the sort Micah obviously had on his mind. If she could head him off tactfully, perhaps he would find his way with a girl his own age eventually.

"Let's go swimming again, Micah," she suggested quickly and started to get up from where she lay. But Micah's arm came across her body and kept her where she was.

"Not now, Mel," he said in a tone that brooked no opposition. "I want to talk to you."

Melissa looked at him in alarm, and then she frowned slightly. In spite of all the signals Micah was throwing out that he was on the verge of a pass, his eyes were strangely blank of expression. She had the feeling she was looking into an empty well covered by a swirling gray mist.

"What about, Micah?" she asked cautiously.

And then she heard the sound of a horse approaching and felt an upswelling of relief. If there was one thing she needed at the moment, it was time to think up a way to divert Micah's sudden sexual interest in her without hurting him in the process.

She started to sit up, but Micah held her where she was as he raised his head almost casually to watch the approaching rider. And then as the hooves came closer, he turned back to Melissa, smiled an enigmatic little smile, and quickly bent his head to kiss her with all the fire and inexpert passion of a young man caught up in the grip of his first infatuation.

Melissa was so caught off guard that for a few fatal seconds she just lay there, her eyes wide open and her body frozen in Micah's strong grip. By the time she had recovered enough to try to push Micah away, the horse was beside them, and Melissa looked up into Rob's face to see such thunderous contempt that she wanted to sink right down into the ground.

She started to struggle then, not caring whether

Micah's fragile ego was damaged in the process, and Micah let her go easily. He then looked up at Rob, his expression denoting surprised chagrin, as though Rob's arrival had taken him completely by surprise.

Micah got to his feet quickly, but Melissa was on hers a lot faster. She stood facing Rob while he towered over her like one of the Four Horsemen of the Apocalypse, and Melissa was at a loss as to what to say or do. If she tried to explain what had happened in Micah's presence, she might damage his self-image irreparably, yet Rob didn't look as though he was going to give her a chance to explain in private. She wanted to shake Micah silly for getting her into this ridiculous position, but since that was impossible, she simply stood and stared at Rob while he stared back at her in a way that made her want to curl up and die.

The rest of the kids must have heard Rob's arrival, because they started spilling out of the bushes like prairie dogs popping out of their holes, and that only increased the impossibility of Melissa's explaining anything.

Rob looked around at them, and if looks could have shriveled anyone on the spot, Melissa thought they would all have been clumps of dust.

"Get back to the ranch—all of you!" he ordered in a tight, grim voice that had everyone looking at one another in amazed anxiety. Rob looked like a blond, tight-lipped volcano that could blow at any second, and in reaction to that look and his tone of voice, everyone started to scatter toward the ranch as rapidly as possible. Even Vincent, as huge as he was, looked cowed.

Micah deserted Melissa as rapidly as everyone else did, and then it was just Rob and she, with Rob looking at her so coldly Melissa began actually to be afraid of what he might do. But when he started to turn his horse and leave her without saying a word, she sprang into action herself. She dashed forward to grab his leg and delay him.

"Rob, wait!" she demanded. "It isn't what you think!"

The blue of his eyes was like ice. "How do you know what I think, Melissa?" he bit out with cold contempt. He dug his heels into his horse's flanks, and Melissa had to jump backward to get out of the way.

"Rob, damn it!" Melissa yelled, her temper aroused by his action. "You're so arrogant!"

"No, I guess I'm just old-fashioned," Rob bit out. "I didn't realize eastern women liked to play such amusing games with men. You had me dancing on your string, but I guess that wasn't enough for you. You obviously wanted to see if you could catch someone Micah's age as well." His mouth curled into a sneer beneath his mustache. "What's the matter, Melissa? Did you get so caught up in your role you wanted to try to relive your own youth? Or are you just accustomed to having more than one male in your bed at a time?"

Melissa stared at him in shock, and Rob didn't wait around for a reply to his insulting remarks. He spurred his horse into a gallop and took off for the ranch as though he were being chased by a pack of hounds, and Melissa watched him go, her mind roiling with conflicting emotions.

Damn him! she cursed as she wiped angry tears from her eyes and started off after him. *Where does he get off condemning me when he's probably guilty of far worse than having to submit to a kiss from a kid who's so mixed up, he doesn't know who he is yet!*

But at that thought Melissa's tears dried and her expression turned grim as she thought over what Micah had done. He had known Rob was coming, she was certain of it. He had heard the hoofbeats as clearly as Melissa had, and Micah had even looked up to see who was coming before he'd kissed her. That much was clear, as well as the fact that he obviously had the purpose in mind of driving a wedge between Rob and herself. What was not clear was why Micah wanted to come between her and Rob. Who was he jealous of exactly? Melissa wondered as she stomped her way back to the ranch. Rob? Or herself?

A week ago she would have said Micah was so obsessive about Rob, he would fight anyone for Rob's affection. But there had been something in Micah's kiss today that made her wonder if she was wrong. She could have sworn Micah had felt something while he'd been kissing her other than malicious satisfaction at causing trouble.

The downstairs was quiet when she entered the house, and she thought the girls were probably cowering in their rooms away from Rob's wrath. She hesitated, then decided she'd try the study to see if she could at last get in touch with Malcolm Keller to ask his advice and see if he'd learned anything further from Delilah.

Unfortunately, when she pushed the door to the study open, she saw Rob standing at the window looking out. She almost backed out again, but Rob's back had a curiously vulnerable look to it that made her close the door behind her instead.

"I need to talk to you, Rob," she said quietly as he turned around at hearing the door shut behind her. "I want to explain what happened today. I think we have a problem with—"

"You're the one with the problem, Melissa," Rob said in a hard, flat tone. "My only problem is getting you out of here as fast as possible."

Melissa stared at him, close to tears at his stubborn resistance to hearing her side of the story. And then she remembered that he might have another reason for wanting to get rid of an inquisitive reporter, and she hardened her heart.

"Do you have a psychiatrist or psychologist you use when you need advice about one of the kids?" she asked abruptly, thinking that it was useless to try to explain anything to Rob in his present mood, but that if there was a professional in Missoula she could talk to about Micah, she might be able to get some insight into just what was going on with that young man.

"Why do you want to know?" Rob demanded coldly.

Melissa looked at him, and suddenly her temper erupted full blown at how ridiculous he was being in thinking she would encourage Micah the way he obviously thought she had.

"I thought you knew everything," she snapped. "Surely you can figure out the answer to that without my having to tell you."

At the look of furious anger her remark provoked, Melissa gave up, jerked open the door, and left the room to climb the stairs to her room and reflect upon how useless all her efforts had proved to be so far. No story she'd ever worked on had ever made her feel so inadequate—or so depressed.

And as she flopped onto her bed and stared unhappily up at the ceiling above her, she knew the reason she had accomplished so little since coming to the Rocking R to conduct an investigation that should have been a piece of cake compared to some of the ones she'd done in the past. Rob Redding was that reason. He twisted her up in knots, confused her thinking, and left her as helpless as one of the kids in his charge to sort out facts from fiction. And now he was apparently going to try to get rid of her before she could ever hope to find out the truth.

Chapter Fourteen

By the next morning Melissa still hadn't been able to get to the telephone, and when she got downstairs at the normal ungodly hour, feeling as though she'd spent the night in a cement mixer, it was to find Parker waiting for her to tell her she was to debut as a working cowgirl that day out on the range.

"Hurry up and eat, girl," he instructed over his shoulder as he left the house. "You don't want to be late your first day."

The hell I don't! Melissa grumbled inwardly, even as she wondered why Rob hadn't instructed Parker to escort her off the ranch pronto instead of allowing her to continue to masquerade as one of his inmates.

The important thing was that she still had a chance to accomplish something before Rob did send her on her way, however, and Melissa hurriedly downed two aspirins and a cup of coffee before she excused herself from the table to try to get to that damned telephone before she had to start learning to herd cows.

As she came out into the hallway on her way to the study, a knock sounded on the front door, and since there was no one else around to answer it, Melissa snatched the door open, a frown on her face at whoever was delaying her. The frown deepened when she saw who was there.

"Hi, Mel," Micah greeted her happily. "I came to

ask you if you'd help me get some fresh hay down from the loft so whoever's on stable duty can clean out the stalls today. Will you?''

Micah had helped Melissa innumerable times during her sojourn as stable mucker, and she couldn't bring herself to turn down his request for help now, although she was still angry at him for what he'd pulled the day before. But if he was as mixed up as she thought he was, she couldn't hold him accountable for what he did, even if his confusion did cause a lot of problems for other people, including herself.

"Ah, okay, Micah," she agreed reluctantly. "Just let me run up and get my jacket and gloves."

"I'll wait," Micah offered, stepping inside the house. And that put an end to Melissa's plan to delay joining Micah until she'd had a chance to make her phone call.

Her mood was therefore bordering on surly by the time she and Micah were climbing into the hayloft above the stables, and she was ready to disabuse him strongly if he tried anything other than exactly what he'd said they were going to do.

To her relief Micah merely started grabbing bales of hay and tossing them over the side of the loft to the floor below. Melissa began to help him, but the bales of hay weighed considerably more than she'd expected them to, so she had to scoot hers to the edge and topple them over rather than lift them, as Micah was doing.

Melissa had just gotten to the edge of the loft with her third bale of hay and was preparing to push it over when something gray and furry that squeaked menacingly and had little red eyes landed smack on her arm from an overhead beam and dug its sharp little claws into her skin.

She went into a state of instant panic. She screamed, flung her arm out to get rid of the creature, tripped over the bale of hay in her flailing about, and sailed over the edge of the loft. For once since coming to the Rocking

R, fortune smiled on her and she landed in the middle of a pile of smelly, manure-laden hay that cushioned her fall enough so that she only had the breath knocked out of her. But for long moments, as she lay gasping to try to get that breath back, she thought herself a goner for sure.

Finally her lungs began to function again, and as she heard shouting and yelling, she opened her eyes to see a pair of jean-covered legs standing by her side. Rob just stood there staring down at her while Micah knelt by her other side, asking her over and over again if she was all right.

Melissa managed a nod to shut Micah up and raised her eyes to look at Rob's face. He may have looked a little white and strained, she decided, but mostly he looked as though he felt she'd gotten no more than she deserved, and when he simply turned and walked away, her temper flew through the roof.

That's it! she snarled inwardly as she began to attempt to sit up. *Any man that cold-hearted deserves to remain a bachelor to the end of his days!*

She brushed away Micah's helping hand and got to her feet, wavering unsteadily for a few seconds until she got her equilibrium back.

"What happened?" Micah asked, and Melissa turned and snarled at him.

"I was attacked by one of Rob Redding's pets, that's what happened! He probably trains them to keep people like me in line!"

She had time to see that her outburst had astonished Micah before she turned on her heel and stomped toward the house to wash off the smell of manure that clung to her like a bad excuse for perfume, but at that point she didn't care what Micah or anyone else thought about her mood.

"You tell the *boss* to start without me!" she called back over her shoulder as she strode away. "And if he doesn't like the idea, tell him for me he can ride off to perdition for all I care!''

Once inside the house, she scrubbed herself with soap and water, changed clothes, and marched back downstairs to head for Rob's study, determined to get her business here finished and done with and get back to civilization as quickly as possible. But when she opened the door to the study, Mrs. Price was dusting in there, and Melissa wanted to scream her frustration.

"What are you doing here?" Mrs. Price demanded disapprovingly. "Aren't you supposed to be working?"

Melissa did a neat about-face, not even bothering to answer. If she'd opened her mouth at that point, she knew she would spew abuse like a rocket, and Mrs. Price didn't deserve to be the recipient of the foul language hovering on Melissa's tongue right then.

Micah had Fred saddled for her when she got back to the barn and was waiting for her, but everyone else had already left. Melissa put her booted foot in the stirrup and swung up onto Fred's back.

"Let's go!" she snarled, and headed out without waiting for a reply.

Micah soon caught up with her and led the way, which Melissa considered fortunate, since she didn't have any idea where she was supposed to be going. Furthermore, in her present mood she didn't much care. She would have kept riding indefinitely if it had been left up to her, preferably to the other side of the world.

Micah remained silent until they'd ridden for about half an hour. Then he reached over and grabbed Fred's reins.

"We have to split up here, Mel," he informed Melissa quietly when she looked at him with an inquiring frown on her face. "You ride on over that hill over there until you see some of the others. I have to go in another direction to mend fence."

Melissa nodded absently. Her thoughts were still fuming, and she didn't feel like being civil. She barely even noticed when Micah rode away. Since she was headed in the right direction, she let Fred have his head, trusting him to take her where they were going while she continued to think about how cruel and hardhearted Rob was. Strangely, however, she was not one whit more inclined to believe him guilty of selling drugs to his kids or of harming Delilah. She was simply furious with him for personal reasons that had nothing to do with her job here.

She wasn't aware of anything around her, and she supposed she would have ridden on for hours if Fred hadn't put his hoof in a hole and stumbled, nearly tossing her off his back in the process. Melissa came alert with a start.

"Hey, Fred!" she said with some concern as he staggered on, favoring his right leg. "What's the matter, boy? Did you hurt yourself?"

Fred made a gallant effort to continue, but Melissa soon decided she shouldn't be riding him when he was limping so badly. She pulled on the reins and stopped him, then got off his back to inspect the leg. She thought it looked swollen, but she didn't know enough about a horse's anatomy to be certain. Then she looked around her for help, and suddenly realized there was no one around and she didn't know where she was.

She didn't panic, though she was distinctly nervous. She was certain the others must be around somewhere but that she just hadn't reached them yet. Micah had said over the next hill, and there was one just ahead of her, but she couldn't remember if she'd already crossed the one Micah had mentioned or whether this was it.

She took Fred's reins in her hand and pulled him after her, setting a slow pace. His stumbling gait looked as though it were painful, however, and Melissa finally dropped the reins.

"You stay here, Fred," she told the horse firmly. "I'll walk on ahead to see if I can find somebody."

She patted his head once, then started off on foot toward the nearby hill. But each time she looked behind her, it was to see that Fred was trying to follow her, and she wished she knew how to make him stop, but there was nothing to tie him to out here. So she kept walking, hoping Fred wasn't going to do any permanent damage to his leg.

An hour later she had not only crested the hill that had been her first goal, but several more besides, and she had to admit that it was beginning to look as though she was on the wrong track entirely. The Montana countryside stretched for miles around her, but the gently undulating land made it impossible for her to get a clear look around to try to spot the others, and she didn't know what else to do but to keep walking.

Two hours later she was footsore, thirsty, hungry, and close to tears as she began to accept the fact that she was well and truly lost. She decided it was time to stop walking and rest awhile, and hoped that someone was missing her by now and would come look for her.

She had only meant to rest for ten minutes, but it was half an hour before she could force her stiffened muscles to move again, and she then decided she would try to retrace her steps, though by now she wasn't certain if she was choosing the right direction. She was beginning to feel totally disoriented—and frightened. This was an awful lot of empty country to be lost in, and Melissa thought it might be like searching for a needle in a haystack even if the others were looking for her by now.

The dry, cottony taste in her mouth caused by fear and thirst increased as she walked, and she was developing a blister on her left heel that added to her misery considerably. Furthermore, she had lost Fred, so she didn't even have the comfort of her horse's company.

All in all, she reflected bitterly, she'd had better days. And then she brightened somewhat as she spotted a clump of trees that looked invitingly shady in the lee of a hill. The September sun wasn't unduly hot, but when one had been out in it for hours without a drop of water, it felt like the height of summer, and Melissa was ready for some relief.

Her hope that the trees concealed a stream proved to be unfounded, and Melissa gazed around forlornly, thinking that she wouldn't have cared if she'd gotten typhoid or cholera if there had only been one little sip of cool, delicious water to ease her thirst.

She slumped down at the base of one of the trees to rest, stifling the tears that threatened, when the thought hit her that she didn't remember seeing this clump of trees on her way out, so she must have taken the wrong direction instead of heading back toward the ranch. And with that realization Melissa faced the fact that she was totally lost, totally disoriented, and there was nothing to do but stay where she was and hope for rescue—which might or might not be forthcoming. She was by now so weak from hunger and thirst and walking for hours that she didn't think she had the strength to move anymore anyway.

The only thing that saved her from dissolving into a fit of weak tears was that her body decided sleep was a better antidote to her problems, and Melissa finally stretched out on the ground beneath the tree and cradled her head in her arms until she fell into a deep sleep, which lasted until the shadowy coolness of evening woke her to the misery of her abused body again.

The dim half-light she woke up to stirred the beginnings of the first really panicky fear she had felt since childhood. She cursed herself for sleeping instead of staying awake to listen for anyone calling her. And then she cursed herself for believing that anyone was looking for her at all. It was possible that no one would know she was missing until everyone gathered at the dinner table and found she wasn't among them. And when they did realize she wasn't there, would they try to find her in the dark, or wait until morning? she wondered.

She fought to keep her spirits up, but the next four hours were the loneliest, coldest, most frightening ones she'd ever endured in her life. She had no difficulty staying awake now. Her thoughts wouldn't have let her sleep if she wanted to, and she definitely didn't want to. If she was going to die soon, she wanted to spend her last few hours awake.

She was grateful that at least there was a moon and thousands of stars, and at last, as Melissa scanned the area around her with widened eyes, she saw a dark, horse-shaped blot appear at the top of a hill outside the trees, and she burst into a sob of relief and stumbled out of the shelter of trees, yelling in a hoarse voice to attract the attention of whoever was riding toward her.

And as she ran, she knew she wanted her rescuer to be Rob. She wanted it as she'd never wanted anything in her life before. She wanted him to hold her in his strong arms, rock and comfort her, warm her body with his own and kiss her senseless. Suddenly she knew he wasn't guilty of any of the things she had suspected, and she wanted to tell him so. She wanted to confess everything—tell him her background, why she was really here, what had happened between her and Micah and most of all... that she loved him. She loved him as she'd never expected to love a man, and she wanted him as badly as she wanted to live right then.

She was babbling all of that and more as she came closer to the horse, and then she stopped dead still, the words dying on her lips as hopeless despair filled her heart. She was close enough to see now, and what she saw was Fred, his reins dangling uselessly and his saddle... empty.

Fred came up to her and butted her with his head. Melissa wrapped her arms around his neck and clung to him, glad at least to have something warm to hang on to—something alive and nonthreatening to share her loneliness. She stood like that for quite a while before she recovered sense enough to begin to think again.

Then she petted Fred and murmured endearments to him through her cracked lips. She praised his faithfulness while an idea began to form in her head—an idea that might not work, but which was worth a try. Fred was still lame, so that she was afraid to ride him, but he wasn't so lame that he couldn't walk, or he would never have found her. And if he could find her, could he possibly find his way back to the ranch?

She began to talk to Fred urgently then, begging him to lead her home. And home held a whole new connotation for her, as she associated home with the ranch and Rob. She prayed that if Fred did lead her back, she would never have to leave "home" again...nor Rob, either.

Her urging seemed to be accomplishing something, as Fred turned in a direction Melissa hadn't even contemplated going. But she trusted him, and she was starting to walk by his side when another shape appeared on the horizon, and this time the horse shape had a man's shape on its back. Melissa gave one fierce, glad cry of joy before, for the first time in her life, she fainted dead away.

When she woke up, she groggily searched for Rob with her eyes, expecting him to be nearby. Instead she found that she was back at the tree, her hands bound behind her around the bole of it...and Micah Gilroy was standing over her with a faint gleam of moonlight glinting in his gray eyes that struck the most deadly terror in Melissa's heart she had ever known.

Chapter Fifteen

"Good," Micah said when he saw that she was awake. His mouth moved in a rictuslike grin. "I don't know how much time I have, and I want to talk to you."

Melissa licked her dry, cracked lips and swallowed down the terror that was trying to close her throat. "How did you find me?" she asked, striving for a casual tone, which was somewhat ridiculous under the circumstances. It was obvious that Micah hadn't tied her up out of any benign reason, but she had to pretend a calmness she didn't feel or else dissolve into a bout of hysteria that would accomplish nothing.

Micah grinned his unholy grin again. "I found Fred and let him find you," he answered smugly. "I knew he'd track you down."

Melissa cleared her throat before she could speak. "What's going on, Micah?" she said in a cracked voice. "Why have you tied me like this?"

"You got too big for your britches, Mel," he sneered. "You got careless." He shrugged his shoulders in a contemptuous movement. "You had me fooled for a while until I heard you on the phone the other day, but I know all about you now."

Melissa had a flash of instinct that told her Micah wanted to brag about what he was doing. There was no one else he would ever be able to tell about it, and the urge to have someone know seemed to be as important to him as the actual doing of...whatever he had in mind. Melissa didn't know exactly what that was yet, but she had a good idea it wasn't going to be anything she was going to enjoy. Far from it. But it would be in her best interests to keep him talking as long as possible in the hope that someone would find them before he began whatever he planned to do.

With the full realization that there might not be any rescue, however, Melissa could only hope Micah didn't plan to do any more to her than he had done to Delilah. For she was certain now that it was Micah who had beaten Delilah. She just wasn't certain why, and she meant to find out.

"What are you talking about, Micah?" she croaked. "I don't know what you mean."

"Don't you?" Micah said on a nasty laugh. "You're no delinquent kid, Melissa...and you're in love with Rob."

Melissa was silent for too long, unable to decide whether it would be best to lie about her feelings for Rob or confess them but pretend Rob didn't feel anything for her. But then she remembered that Micah had overheard Rob that day in the restaurant, so he wouldn't believe that.

"You've got him all hot and bothered for you, too," Micah spat with venomous anger. "You've got him wrapped around your little finger, just the way my mo—mo—" He broke off, shook his head violently and abruptly, and changed direction. "Just the way Delilah and Margo thought they could, but I fixed them. And I'm going to fix you, too, Melissa."

The hissing intonation he gave to her name made Melissa shudder, but she kept her wits about her. "Delilah?" she rasped questioningly.

Micah's eyes narrowed dangerously, and he reached up and gave Melissa a light slap across the face that stung. "Don't lie to me, Melissa!" he hissed. She had jerked her head around in an attempt to avoid the blow, but it hadn't done any good, and now Micah seized her chin in his hand and forced her to look at him.

"That's just a sample of what you'll get if you try to play dumb," he said in a soft, menacing voice. "I heard you talking to someone on the telephone about Delilah. Enough to know she's the reason you came out here in the first place. What happened, did she forget what I told her would happen to her if she talked about me?"

When Melissa didn't answer immediately because she was trying desperately to think of what to say, Micah reached behind him and picked up a long, hefty stick of wood, which he began to tap against his palm threateningly. "Talk to me, Melissa," he encouraged her softly. "Talk to me voluntarily, or I'll have to make you talk."

"All right, Micah!" Melissa spoke hastily, eyeing the stick in Micah's hands with dread. "I do know Delilah. And I did come out here to find out what had happened to her because she wouldn't tell anybody."

Micah relaxed slightly. "That's better," he said in a bullying tone. "Now tell me more...and don't lie to me! I'll know if you do!"

Melissa eyed him fearfully and started talking. "Delilah and I are from the same town, Micah," she said. "Her cousin runs a newspaper there, and I work for him." She stopped when she saw Micah stiffen, afraid that she had just lost any chance of reasoning with him. But maybe not, she thought an instant later. Maybe she could make him afraid of the consequences of what he was doing.

"My editor and Delilah's family sent me out here to find out what happened to Delilah since she wouldn't tell us herself," she went on cautiously. "And if anything happens to me, Micah," she added after taking a deep breath, "they'll send the police to investigate this time. They already know that someone's selling drugs here, and if I get hurt, that will be that much more reason for them to investigate.''

She could see that her words were having an effect on Micah, and she pushed her advantage. "Listen, Micah," she said, urging him to see reason with her tone. "If you'll tell me everything and let me go, I'll do everything I can for you. I like you, Micah," she said softly. "I don't want to see you go to jail."

But that didn't seem to worry Micah, as evidenced by his soft chuckle. "What, for selling a little marijuana and amphetamines?" he asked with nasty amusement. And then he shrugged as though he were unconcerned. "They wouldn't put me in jail, Melissa. All I'd have to do is give them the names of my suppliers and they'd let me go."

Melissa reflected that what Micah said was probably true. She even actually hoped it was true. She considered Micah a very sick young man who needed a psychiatrist more than a jail cell.

"Maybe you're right, Micah," she answered him as calmly as she could manage. "But what about your beating Delilah? And what do you think they'll do to you if you compound that by hurting me?"

Micah looked at her with cold consideration. "You must think I'm a fool!" he sneered. "Delilah didn't tell anybody I hurt her, did she?" he pointed out reasonably. "And you won't be able to tell anybody anything when I'm finished with you."

Melissa swallowed down another wave of nauseous fear. "Delilah will tell if you hurt me that badly, Micah," she persisted, but he merely laughed at her.

"Do you think so?" he chuckled. "You don't think she'll be even more afraid of me when she finds out I'm willing to kill to keep Rob?"

Almost paralyzed by terror at hearing what Micah intended, Melissa closed her eyes briefly as she thought out her response to that. Then she opened them and faced Micah directly. "What makes you think you have Rob, Micah?" she asked shakily. "He doesn't love you that way."

She had known it was a dangerous thing to say, and she wished she hadn't when she saw the effect of her words on Micah. His gray eyes glittered with rage, and his grip on the stick in his hands tightened.

"He will!" he spat venomously. "He would already if you hadn't corrupted him with your evil woman's body! But once you're gone, he'll turn to me! I'll make him turn to me!"

Melissa hastily tried to divert him. "Maybe so, Micah," she said soothingly. Realizing that topic was too dangerous, she switched direction. "How did you meet Rob, Micah?" she asked, hoping to keep him talking. "How did you come to love him?"

Micah looked at her suspiciously, but as she had suspected, he wanted to tell someone about his feelings for Rob. They must have been bottled up inside him for a long time, and here was his chance to get them out.

"Rob came to my father's church about a year ago, while he was in Missoula for the weekend," he started out slowly. "And he talked to me for a while that day. He talked to me like I was on his level and like I mattered."

Melissa shifted her eyes to scan the horizon while Micah delved into his memories. But there was no one around as yet. No one at all.

"He looked just the way I'd always wanted my father to look," Micah went on dreamily. "He was strong and smart, and nobody could tell him what to do." Micah's voice radiated pride, and Melissa pictured how Rob must have looked to him on that day. She was proud of Rob, too, but she found herself wishing he hadn't made quite such a strong impression on Micah.

"I made up my mind then and there Rob and I were going to be the best of friends," Micah went on, sounding like a little boy all of a sudden. "But I had to find some way to be around him, so I went into one of the deacon's houses one night and tore it up."

Micah was looking at her blankly, and Melissa could imagine him methodically going about his vandalism to achieve what he wanted.

"I made sure I got caught, of course." Micah laughed almost happily. "And then I made sure I got sent here. I've been here ever since, and I'm never going to leave here."

He frowned then, and his childish-looking mouth curved into a grim line. "They tried to make me leave once," he said tautly, "but I fixed that. I made them think I'd kill myself if I didn't get to stay here, and my parents were glad to send me back." He shrugged offhandedly. "They never wanted me anyway. Rob's the only one who's ever wanted me."

Melissa felt the most profound pity she'd ever experienced when Micah said that. Poor unwanted, lonely Micah, she thought sadly, but then she remembered that Micah intended to harm her—perhaps fatally—and she got back to the task of keeping him talking.

"Do you hate your mother and dad, Micah?" she asked.

Micah stiffened slightly. "I hate my mo-mo—" But again he couldn't voice the word *mother*. "I don't hate my dad," Micah skipped on. "I just...he's just so *weak*!" he got out in a choked voice. "He let *her* tell him what to do all the time, and I thought he hated her too, but then one night I went into their bedroom and saw them..." He broke off, the memory of what he'd witnessed twisting his face into an ugly caricature of his normal expression.

"Micah, don't!" Melissa tried to comfort him, but it was the wrong thing to do, apparently.

"That's enough out of you!" he snarled, shaking the stick at her. "I'm not going to fall for your tricks and your lies. I'm going to fix you just like I did Delilah, and then I'll finish getting control of Margo!"

"How are you getting control of Margo?" Melissa asked sharply, praying he wasn't going to tell her that what she suspected was true.

"The same way I control everybody else," Micah sneered. "All those rich kids want drugs when they first come out here, and I get them what they want. Then they're afraid to cross me because they're afraid I'll tell Rob, so they leave me alone to do as I please." He chuckled nastily. "Margo wants to be like the others," he said matter-of-factly, "and I've already got her experimenting with drugs. She'll be hooked pretty soon, and she'll do anything I tell her."

Melissa suspected the kids feared Micah for other reasons than his threats to tell on them. Kids were remarkably sensitive to the sort of aura Micah had, and she thought they were more afraid of his underlying violence than of his ability to get them in trouble. But she didn't say that. She simply continued to keep Micah talking.

"Did Delilah take drugs too, Micah?" she asked quietly. "Or did she just want Rob?"

His glare was ugly. "She was all over him," he said with disgust. "And she wouldn't stop even when I warned her." He shook his head, remembering. "So I had to show her I meant what I said," he said simply, and his mouth curved into a smile. "That fixed her. She's so scared of me now, she won't talk, and she won't come back."

A sudden thought hit Melissa and she voiced it. "Do the other kids still take drugs, Micah?" she asked, despising him in spite of her pity for him, if that were true.

He looked at her contemptuously. "Hardly at all," he said shortly. "After they've been here with Rob for a while, they mostly stop, although a few still want a joint now and then. And I don't care," he added without interest. "All I care about is that they buy from me at first, so that I can control them. After they get to know Rob, they don't want him to find out they did that, so they treat me with respect. I've never had to tell on any of them so far."

Melissa launched another question. "What about you, Micah?" she asked softly, thinking if he was an addict, it would explain some of the deterioration of his personality. "Do you take any of that stuff yourself?"

"I'm not hooked!" Micah flared up, his face contorting. "I can stop anytime I want to! I just need something sometimes when things get bad and I can't keep from remembering..." His voice trailed off, and then he looked grim again.

"That's enough out of you, Melissa!" he snarled as he jumped to his feet. "You came out here and tried to take Rob away from me. You blinded him with your body, and you'd never stop if I didn't do something about you!"

"I blinded you, too, didn't I, Micah?" Melissa said, trying a desperate tack. "You liked kissing me yesterday, didn't you? Didn't you, Micah?" she demanded fiercely.

"I did not!" he yelled, but there was such self-defensiveness in his tone that Melissa knew he lied... and that lie gave her hope for his eventual cure...that is, if she survived long enough to see that he got the help he needed.

"I was just showing Rob what you're really like and making sure you didn't suspect how I really felt about you!" Micah went on, still yelling, still defending himself with a desperation Melissa knew sprang from his self-disgust that he had let a female bother him in the way she had during that kiss yesterday. "And it worked, too!" He then changed to gloating. "He was disgusted with you, Melissa, and he's going to stay disgusted after you're dead!"

He pulled something from his pocket then and started walking toward Fred, his laughter sounding hideous to Melissa. The moonlight glinted off what he held, and Melissa thought it looked like a syringe, though she couldn't be sure. And she didn't have time to wonder as she tried to divert Micah, now that he was apparently ready to stop talking and act.

"I didn't disgust you, Micah," she called out to him, trying to sound seductive, which was hard when her voice trembled with fear. "If you'll let me go from here, I'll show you why Rob likes me so much. I'll make you like me too, Micah," she yelled.

But Micah wasn't listening anymore. He was tying Fred's reins securely to a tree, and then he plunged whatever he held into Fred's flank, making Fred whinny in distress and pull his head back, straining against his reins.

Melissa didn't know what Micah was doing, but her fear was growing by leaps and bounds. Her heart came up into her throat when Micah started back to her, his face set and determined. He reached down and untied her hands, but before Melissa could try to get away from him, he had jerked her to her feet, and when she felt the enormous strength in his grip, she knew it would take a miracle to break his hold on her. Either he was on something that increased his strength out of all proportion to his size or his mania was affecting it.

"Rob's going to hate himself for a while because he let you ride Fred again," Micah said as he marched her to a clear space outside the trees. "But he'll get over it. I'll help him get over it."

He wasn't even breathing hard from his efforts to keep her subdued, and Melissa was struggling with every bit of her strength. She twisted and turned in Micah's grip, but he forced her along without any trouble at all.

"Everybody knows old Fred can't be trusted," Micah went on as he jerked Melissa down on the ground and pulled a bandana from his pocket. "When they find you, they'll just think he went wild and trompled you to death."

He straddled her as he tied her ankles together around her boots, ignoring the frantic pummeling of Melissa's fists on his back and handling her as though her struggles were no more effective than an infant's. And when he had the knot tied, he simply moved away from her and left her where she was while he went back to where Fred was now beginning to plunge and buck and shudder. Whatever Micah had injected into him was making Fred go crazy, and as Melissa at last fully realized what Micah had in mind, she started to work with furious effort to get the bandana untied from her ankles so she could run.

Micah had Fred's reins in his hands now, but he was having a hard time controlling the horse as he tried to pull Fred toward where Melissa was working desperately to untie the bandana. But her fingers were still numb from having the circulation cut off for so long, and Micah had tied the knot so firmly that she was making no headway at all. Her fear was making her clumsy as well, and Melissa was sobbing as she realized she might not be able to get the bandana undone in time.

Fred was rearing and bucking and fighting Micah's grip on the reins, but Micah was jockeying the horse closer and closer to Melissa. At last Fred's hooves were pounding the ground only inches from where Melissa sat hunched over, struggling with her bond, and she stopped what she was doing in order to roll away as far as she could get. Her sobs mingled with the neighing screams issuing from Fred while Micah was laughing in the grip of a sort of crazy mania. He was swiping at Fred with a coiled rope to get Fred closer to Melissa, and each time he did so, those pounding hooves came closer to her.

Melissa rolled until she came up against a fallen log

and there was nowhere else to go. She was certain it would all be over within seconds, and she spent those seconds praying and crying and calling Rob's name. She expected at any moment to feel the crushing blow of one of Fred's hooves against her skull or body or both. Fred was rearing so close to her, she could feel the ground shake when his hooves landed and the air of their passage whistled against her skin.

Gradually, however, when it dawned on her that Micah was becoming increasingly infuriated with Fred, she realized Fred was purposely avoiding her, and she felt a surge of hope. She wouldn't have believed the bond between herself and the horse had become so strong that he would try to protect her even though the drug in his system must be driving him wild, but now she did, and she began to call to Fred, trying to soothe him, though her voice was cracked and broken by sobs.

Her interference and Fred's lack of cooperation seemed to drive Micah over the brink into an unthinking rage. He hit Fred a terrific blow with the coiled rope and again tried to position the horse where he couldn't avoid striking Melissa, but Fred swerved away suddenly and began to fight Micah's domination with a fury of his own. Melissa lay where she was, watching the macabre scene being played out in the dim moonlight and praying that Fred would be the victor.

Fred fought to pull the reins from Micah's grip, and Micah held on with almost inhuman strength as Fred dragged him hither and yon. But then Micah tripped and lost his grip on the reins, and Fred reared in a mighty display of power. One of his hooves came slashing down against Micah's head, and Micah made a sound that Melissa would never afterward forget before he collapsed onto the ground and lay still. Fred screamed a horse's scream and then went pounding off into the night, the drug in his system negating the injury to his leg so that he ran like the wind.

Melissa lay trembling and sobbing where she was for a few more moments before she felt able to sit up and again try to remove the bandana from her ankles. The knot continued to defeat her, however, and at last she crawled as best she could to Micah's side. When she reached him and looked down at the smear of blood on the side of his head and the way he lay as still as death, she felt nauseated and dizzy, and then for the second time in her life she fainted, collapsing by Micah's side into a huddled lump of nonsensate exhaustion.

Chapter Sixteen

Melissa woke, screaming to the touch of someone's hands on her, and began thrashing and twisting her body to get away. It took several moments before she realized the voice shushing and soothing her and the arms holding her were Rob's. She stopped struggling and stared up into the grim expression on his beloved face before she collapsed into a heap in his arms, her whole body shuddering with reaction.

"It's all right, baby," he soothed with such tenderness that Melissa began to cry in great heaving gulps. Rob rocked her in his arms and continued to murmur assurances to her. "You're safe now, sweetheart," he crooned. "I've got you. You're going to be all right."

He reassured her over and over until Melissa had cried it all out and was lying limply in his arms. She became aware of movement and voices around them then, and as she remembered in detail what had happened, she raised her head and looked around her fearfully.

"Micah?" she asked, her voice shaking and barely audible.

"He's alive," Rob told her, and Melissa shuddered at the grimness in his tone. "Are you badly hurt, darling?" he then asked, and began to run his hands over her to inspect for damages.

Melissa shook her head. "No," she choked out. "Just bruised."

Rob started to move away from her, but Melissa clutched at him and wouldn't let him go. "Don't leave me, Rob!" she cried out, and he immediately closed her into a warm embrace again.

"I'm not going anywhere without you, dearest," he soothed her. "I'm just getting up so I can carry you to the van. We need to get you and Micah home."

Melissa loosened her grip on him and Rob stood, then reached down to help her up before swinging her into his arms. "Parker," he said over his shoulder as he started walking toward the dark shape of the van, "you drive. One of the others can sit in the back and watch over Micah. I'm going to hold Melissa."

"Yeah, boss," Parker's voice echoed behind them, but Melissa barely registered it because she was concentrating on clinging to Rob as though he were her link to life. She was filled with grateful love that he understood what she needed most of all right then, and she knew if he hadn't offered to hold her on the drive back to the ranch, he would have had a fight on his hands to get her to release him.

He cuddled her in his lap all the way back to the ranch house. When Parker stopped the van at the door, Rob instructed him to take Micah into Missoula to a hospital and to call his parents. Then, as Parker drove on, Rob carried Melissa inside the house.

Mrs. Price waited at the front door, a drawn look on her face. Rob passed her by as he carried Melissa toward the stairs. "Get some hot water and towels, Mrs. Price," he instructed the woman calmly.

Melissa was vaguely aware that all the girls were outside their rooms as Rob carried her past them and that their faces all looked as white and drawn as Mrs. Price's had, but she couldn't concentrate on anything but how safe and warm she felt in Rob's arms, and when he put her on her bed, she wouldn't release her hold on his neck.

"Sweetheart, I'm not going to leave you," Rob assured her gently as he sat down beside her. "But we need to look at you and make sure you're not hurt worse than you think you are."

Melissa nodded shakily, her eyes huge in her face, and then her eyes closed as Rob gave a groan and his mouth closed gently over hers. It was the best kiss she'd ever received in her life, and her heart sighed its contentment as Rob raised his head slightly to stare down at her, a tortured look on his handsome face.

"Oh, my darling," he whispered shakily. "When we found you, I was afraid you were dead. And when I realized you were alive, I decided then and there I wasn't going to let you out of my sight again, ever."

Melissa smiled with shaky contentment at that sentiment and Rob's returning smile was beautiful to her eyes. "Agreed?" he asked in a deep tone of emotion.

"Agreed," Melissa sighed, her voice a bare whisper. But it was loud enough for Rob to hear, and it was fervent enough to make him smile at her in a way that washed away the last of Melissa's fear and shock.

He was about to kiss her again when Mrs. Price entered the room bearing a basin of warm water, some soap, and a towel. Her expression changed from worry to one of surprise when Rob took the things from her.

"I'll take care of Melissa, Mrs. Price," he said in a possessive tone. "You go get her some coffee and something to eat."

Mrs. Price hesitated, and then she seemed to understand, for her dark eyes developed a definite warmth and her smile was satisfied as she departed the room again.

Rob undressed Melissa with tender care and then he began to wash her, inspecting her with his blue eyes as he did so. As he came across each new bruise, his eyes expressed clearly the depth of his love until Melissa began to feel guilty at causing him such distress.

"I'm not really hurt, Rob," she assured him. "I'm only bruised."

His jaw tightened, and his expression became grim. "I want to know everything that happened, Melissa, but not now. I want you to get some sleep after you've eaten while I call about Micah. We'll talk tomorrow."

Rob's tone when he mentioned Micah made Melissa wince. It was clear that Rob didn't understand about Micah, and Melissa wanted him to.

"Rob, Micah's sick," she said gently. "I don't think he can be held responsible for what he did. After his body heals, he's going to need a different kind of doctor . . . possibly for a long time to come."

"I'm aware of that," Rob said harshly. "But don't expect me to feel any sympathy for him right now, while I'm looking at what he did to you. Eventually maybe I'll be able to understand, but for the present I'd like to tear him limb from limb."

Melissa sighed, feeling tired to the extent that it was a terrible effort merely to speak. "I'll explain tomorrow, Rob," she said sleepily. "I can't right now."

"I know, darling," Rob said, his tone changing to one of concern. "You don't have to talk right now."

Melissa was barely able to sip down a cup of luke-warm, highly sugared coffee when Mrs. Price brought it, and she was unable to eat a bite. When she'd finished the coffee, Rob took the cup from her hands and settled her back against the pillow on her bed.

"Go to sleep, Melissa," he murmured quietly. "You're safe now and you're going to stay that way. I'll see to it."

He stroked her cheek lovingly until Melissa drifted into a peaceful slumber that departed slightly when Rob kissed her mouth with gentle lips that caressed and soothed her further, and then, still clinging to his hand, she sank into a quiet land unpeopled by violence.

The next morning she woke gradually to the aches of

a newly battered body, and she wondered with a sigh if she was ever going to be able to live on the Rocking R without feeling constantly like someone had pounded her with a mallet. And then she remembered fully what had happened the night before, and her eyes opened wide on a new day.

Rob was asleep in a rocking chair he'd brought up to her room. His face in repose looked drawn and tired and so utterly dear to Melissa that tears came into her eyes. He must have sensed that she was watching him, because his eyes opened suddenly, softened, and then a weary smile tugged at his lips as he sat up.

He ran a hand over his face and hair as he got to his feet and crossed the short distance to the bed. He sat down beside her and stroked her tousled hair away from her face as he looked her over to see how she was.

"Good morning, darling," he murmured. "Are you feeling better?"

"I feel stiff, but otherwise I'm all right," Melissa smiled at him, lifting a hand to stroke his face. "How are you? You look tired."

He shrugged one of those magnificent shoulders Melissa loved to touch. "I'm stiff, too," he said with a slight grin. "I'd rather have been sleeping with you than in that chair."

Melissa smiled back at him. "Soon," she whispered, and wanted it to be now. Rob nodded, his eyes beginning to soften again in anticipation of what she was promising.

And then Melissa remembered Micah, and her gaze turned anxious. "How...how is Micah, Rob?" she asked, almost dreading to hear his answer in case Micah's injuries had been more serious than had been thought.

Rob's expression became grim. "He has a concussion, but he'll be all right," he said shortly. "That's more than he deserves."

Melissa shook her head. "You don't understand, Rob," she said.

"I guess you're right about that," Rob replied, his voice harsh. And then it gentled as he added, "Do you feel up to explaining?"

Melissa nodded and raised herself to a sitting position. And then she very gently, very quietly, began to tell Rob everything he needed to know.

When she was done, Rob was looking at her oddly, which she knew was because of what she had told him about herself, her previous suspicions of him, and because she obviously bore no animosity toward Micah. She was grateful when he didn't go into the first two matters, but concentrated on the latter.

"I knew Micah was extremely fond of me," he admitted, shaking his head with disbelief. "But I didn't know it went any further than what a lot of the kids feel toward me after they've been here awhile. I just didn't think in those terms."

"That's not surprising," Melissa said gently. "One doesn't unless something like that has happened to them before."

"But you suspected," Rob said, frowning in concentration.

Melissa shrugged her shoulders. "I saw a lot of things during my years on the paper in D.C.," she explained. "That's why I finally went home to get away from all that. It got to be. . ." She groped for words with which to explain, but Rob seemed to understand without words.

"Yes," he agreed. "Sometimes I've gotten tired of hearing all the stories the kids tell me, and these kids don't have it as bad as a lot of youngsters do. It drains you after a while, and you long for peace."

Melissa looked at him in grateful surprise. "Is that one of the reasons you planned to stop doing this?" she asked.

Rob nodded. "For a while anyway," he agreed. "I need some recuperation time to recharge my batteries. Besides..." He paused, and looked at Melissa as though he wanted to say something but was uncertain of whether to do so.

Melissa raised her eyebrows at him to encourage him to go on, but when he did, his answer disappointed her. "Besides," he said as he got to his feet to cross to the small window and stare out. "As we've already discussed, I don't need the money now."

"Oh...that's right," Melissa said faintly, her guilt at having suspected Rob of obtaining that money in a corrupt way making her face flush a becoming pink.

"It was an inheritance," Rob went on, somewhat stiffly, it seemed to Melissa. "It had been tied up in court for several years, and was only recently settled. It's enough to allow me to hang on to this place for the rest of my life unless something disastrous happens."

"I'm glad," Melissa faltered, feeling miserable because she knew she'd hurt Rob badly by suspecting him of selling drugs to get money.

He turned and looked at her over his shoulder, his expression unrevealing. "Are you?" he said in a level tone, but it wasn't a question.

Melissa decided to change the subject. She was suddenly feeling very insecure about how Rob felt toward her after her revelations. She couldn't blame him if he was hurt and outraged over her deception and her suspicions of him. She only hoped time would heal that reaction and he would remember that he loved her and had promised he wasn't going to let her out of his sight again.

"Rob, how did Delilah get away from here after Micah beat her without anyone knowing she'd been hurt?" she asked in a puzzled tone.

He shrugged, and his face tightened again. "I don't know," he said curtly. "I was away at the time it happened. I'm going to ask the kids about it today. I suppose it's possible she wore concealing clothing or lied about her bruises, and I hope that's the case. I don't want to learn that these kids knew what had happened and didn't tell me.''

"I doubt if they knew, Rob," Melissa said. "If she wore jeans and a long-sleeved shirt, the only thing that would have shown was the bump on her temple, and she could have explained that away somehow. But you have to understand that Micah had the ability to frighten people. He didn't show that side of himself to you, but I can assure you, he had an aura of danger that made everyone else sit up and take notice."

Rob turned, and he looked truly formidable as Melissa's words made him remember what she'd told him about Micah's drug dealing.

"Not to mention the fact that he had a hold over them because they'd bought drugs from him," he said in a voice that was full of self-condemnation because he hadn't known what was going on.

"But he also said they stopped taking them after they'd been here for a while," she hastened to remind him. "That says a lot about your influence on them, Rob."

His expression didn't change, however, except to grow even grimmer. "Even Margo?" he inquired, the words a harsh rasp. "There wasn't a damned thing wrong with her when her parents put her in my care, and I'm sending them home a potential addict, for God's sake!"

"Rob, that could have happened anywhere," Melissa said, sitting up straighter and speaking sharply. "And now that we know, we can make sure it doesn't go any further. I'm sure she'll be all right."

"Are you?" Rob said flatly. "I wish I could be."

"Just give it time, Rob," Melissa suggested, empathizing with the way he must feel.

She had already apologized to Rob for her suspicions about him, but she did so again now, hurting for him as she saw what he was going through.

"Rob, I really am sorry I ever suspected you of doing anything wrong," she said, her eyes imploring him to forgive her. "It's just that I've seen so much...become so cynical, I guess...that it's hard for me to trust anymore. Although...."

"Although?" Rob probed, his gaze as he watched her piercingly alert.

"I'm afraid my journalistic ethics went out the window where you were concerned most of the time," Melissa confessed softly. "I had a hard time trying to be objective because I was so attracted to you. And I never could really believe that you were guilty of anything."

Melissa had looked away as she made her confession, but when Rob remained silent, she had to look at him to see how he was reacting to what she'd said. She felt a dart of despair when she saw that his face was closed up in a manner that didn't tell her anything. Melissa began to be very much afraid that her confession had killed what had been between them and that she was never again going to see Rob look at her with the unreserved love she'd seen on his face the night before.

A knock on the door interrupted the dreadful moment, and Mrs. Price entered the room, scanning Melissa's face with her dark eyes anxiously.

"Melissa, a Mr. Malcolm Keller has been calling here every few hours since yesterday morning," she said. "He just phoned again, and he said he was your boss...."

She looked at Melissa uncertainly, as though inquiring if that were the truth, and Melissa nodded. "He is my boss, Mrs. Price. I'm afraid I've been staying here under false pretenses. I'm a reporter, and Mr. Keller owns the newspaper where I work."

A gleam of satisfaction appeared in Mrs. Price's dark

eyes, and she nodded, as though that information answered some questions for her.

"I knew about it, Mrs. Price," Rob inserted dryly then. "In fact, I'm the one who insisted Melissa act as though she were one of the kids." He shrugged, his eyes running over Melissa's face with remote appraisal. "You have to admit she doesn't look old enough to be a reporter, and I was afraid her questions and all the attention would interfere with what we're trying to do here."

Mrs. Price nodded. "That makes sense," she agreed. "Some of these kids could be real publicity hounds if they got the chance." She turned back to Melissa then. "Well, I'm glad to know the truth," she said, a mischievous twinkle appearing in her eyes. "I have to admit, I didn't react to you the same way I do to the others. There was something about you that made me respond to you as one adult to another."

Melissa shot a look at Rob and saw a faint smile appear on his mouth. No doubt he was thinking of how *he* had reacted to her, and Melissa felt a wave of despair envelop her at the thought that she might have killed any chance of his reacting that way again.

"Well, I told this Mr. Keller that I'd give you his message," Mrs. Price went on. "I guess you'll be calling him later, then?"

"Yes, thank you, Mrs. Price," Melissa said, nodding. "I'll do it after I've had a bath and gotten dressed."

"You'd better have something to eat first as well," Mrs. Price suggested as she started to leave the room. "Oh, and by the way, Rob," she added before she went out the door. "You had a call, too. Sheriff Baker apparently heard something and wants to know what went on here yesterday."

Rob strode to the door upon hearing that. "Yes, I'd better call him and explain," he said, pausing before he left the room. He looked at Melissa steadily. "I imagine he'll want to talk to you later, Melissa. Shall I tell him to come out here?''

Melissa nodded. "All right," she said listlessly, certain from Rob's attitude that he was extremely upset with her.

"Call downstairs if you need any help," he said, his tone gruff. "One of us will hear you."

He disappeared out the door, followed by Mrs. Price, and Melissa was not at all certain that he hadn't just disappeared out of her life as well. She felt like death warmed over at the prospect as she climbed from the bed and donned a robe, then gathered up clean clothing to take downstairs to the bathroom.

She felt a bit better after bathing and washing her hair, and when she was dressed, she made her way to the dining room for some coffee.

Mrs. Price came in from the kitchen as she was pouring herself a cup, and the older woman looked at Melissa's woebegone face with sharp concern.

"Honey, are you all right?" Mrs. Price inquired with soft motherliness. "You look like you feel terrible."

"I'm all right, Mrs. Price," Melissa answered, smiling faintly. "Is there anything to eat?" she said to change the subject quickly.

"Certainly, dear," Mrs. Price said as she bustled back to the kitchen to prepare something.

Melissa sat at the table drinking coffee and feeling miserable until Mrs. Price served her breakfast, which she somehow got down her tightly constricted throat. Afterward she went to the study to call Malcolm Keller, and smiled at the relief in his voice when he heard it was she on the other end of the line.

After they'd exchanged greetings and Melissa had told her boss what had happened, he sounded even more relieved that she had come through the situation relatively unscathed.

"I tried to warn you, Melissa," he informed her in a

cross tone that Melissa knew was the result of his concern. "Delilah finally broke down when I mentioned Micah's name to her and told us everything. That kid must be something else," he said curtly. "He sure had Delilah scared. But of course you know that, don't you? He scared you the same way."

"Yes, I was pretty scared," Melissa agreed sadly, thinking that she was even more scared now. Micah had threatened her life...but Rob was threatening her happiness.

"Well, when are you coming home?" he demanded in his customary irascible tones. "Things are picking up around here, and I need you."

"In a few days, I suppose," Melissa said, unconsciously letting her reluctance come through in her voice.

"Well, you don't sound very happy about it," Mr. Keller replied grumpily. "Do you need some time to recuperate?"

Melissa seized at the idea, hoping against hope that once Rob got over his anger at her deception—and more importantly, her suspicions about him—he might be willing to take up where they had left off.

"Yes, I do need some time, Mr. Keller," she replied firmly. "I...need to get my head together."

"Well, don't stay away too long," he ordered gruffly. "It's been dull as dishwater around here since you left."

Melissa smiled, wondering when it *wasn't* dull as dishwater in Rockport, Maryland. And then her smile faded as she realized how much duller it was going to seem if she had to return there permanently.

She and Mr. Keller finished their conversation, and Melissa set the receiver down and looked up to see that Rob was standing just inside the doorway to the study. He had another man with him who wore the badge and gun of an officer of the law.

"Melissa, this is Sheriff Baker," Rob introduced the man who stood beside him. "If you feel up to it, he'd like to ask you some questions."

Melissa squared her shoulders, unable to tell anything from Rob's attitude. "Fine," she said, though nothing was really fine at all.

Chapter Seventeen

It was early evening by the time Melissa had finished talking to the sheriff and then to the kids. It wasn't easy to confess to them who she really was and how she'd lied to them, but after she'd finished her explanations and quietly apologized for her lies, she was gratified by their reaction. Not one of them showed by so much as a word or a glance that they held anything against her, and she was happy to learn in her turn that none of them had known about Delilah's beating. Apparently it had happened on the night before the trip into Missoula, from where Delilah had left for home, and she had taken pains to conceal her injuries. Melissa hoped that Rob would feel better when that worry was off his mind, but he wasn't there when she had her discussion with the kids, so that would have to wait.

After that Melissa slipped away to the barn to visit Fred. She knew he had been found, but she wanted to see for herself that his leg was all right and to express her love and appreciation to him for his protection the preceding night.

She discovered Parker and Rob outside Fred's stall, and since they didn't hear her behind them, she was soon bristling at the content of their conversation.

"The sheriff says maybe we ought to destroy old Fred," Parker was saying to Rob. "You gonna go along with that?"

Melissa didn't hear Rob's soft reply. She was too stunned at the idea of anyone harming her beloved Fred, and she was a spitting ball of fury as she stomped up to the two men.

"No one's going to touch Fred!" she raged, taking Parker and Rob by surprise as she brushed by them to go to Fred's head and hug his neck protectively. She had seen that his leg was wrapped in a bandage, so she was certain there was no physical reason to destroy her beloved friend.

She glared with hostility at Rob, who was watching her with a thoughtful expression on his rugged face. "If you don't want him anymore, sell him to me!" she demanded. "I'll take him home to Maryland with me, and then just let anyone try to hurt him!"

At that a rather dangerous light began to glow in Rob's eyes, but Melissa was too overwrought to take as much notice as she should have.

Rob didn't answer her. Instead he turned to Parker. "What do you think, Parker? Should I let Melissa ride off into the sunset with Fred?"

Parker looked from one to the other of them, and a sly grin twisted his mouth. "You know what I think, boss," he chuckled. "Just don't blow it, will you? She's got a temper, and you don't want to screw things up at this late date."

Melissa frowned at the two men in puzzlement as Rob answered Parker while keeping his eyes firmly on Melissa in an expression she had seen before and that made her uneasily aware that Rob had a temper of his own.

"I don't intend to, Parker," Rob said in a quiet, dangerous tone. "I think Melissa's going to find out shortly that she's jumped to one too many conclusions about me."

Parker went off chuckling delightedly while Melissa prepared to fight Rob to the bitter end if he didn't intend to sell Fred to her. She might have to leave the real love of her life if he was going to let his stubborn pride stand between them, but she didn't intend to lose Fred as well.

"I intend to have Fred, Rob!" she declared as Rob started moving toward her in a purposeful fashion. "Even if I have to steal him, I intend to—"

"Don't tell me your intentions, you deceitful little liar," Rob interrupted her, speaking in a grim tone of authority. "I'll tell *you* a thing or two instead. This morning you were apologizing to me for thinking I didn't have the morals of a pig, yet this evening you're accusing me of being willing to have an animal of mine destroyed for no good reason!"

Melissa swallowed, only now realizing, to her shame, that that was exactly what she had been implying. She opened her mouth to apologize, but she didn't have a chance to before Rob stepped forward, got an arm around her knees, and tossed her over his shoulder like a sack of potatoes.

"What are you doing?" she cried as Rob started walking toward the house, bouncing her stomach against his shoulder painfully. "Put me down, Rob!" she begged to no effect, and then she heard Parker's delighted laughter and spotted him peering at them from the entrance to the tack room. "Parker, stop him!" she begged fearfully, knowing even as she did so that she was being ridiculous to beg for help from a man who was giving every indication that he supported his boss's actions wholeheartedly.

"Not me, missy," Parker gasped out over his laughter. "You got yourself into this one!"

Melissa sputtered every step of the way as Rob carried her to the house, slammed the front door behind them, and started up the stairs to Melissa's room without paying the slightest attention to her pleas or her struggles. Mrs. Price came running out of the kitchen, an anxious expression on her lined face, but when Melissa appealed to her for help, the look on Rob's face must have discouraged her because she shook her head and tried to hide a smile.

"I'm afraid not, Melissa," she called after Rob's retreating form. "I think you better tackle this one on your own."

Melissa groaned as Rob climbed those three flights of stairs without a hint of compassion for the fact that Melissa was being jounced at every step and her stomach felt as if someone had used it for a punching bag. When he got to her room, he slammed that door behind him just as he had the front door, then practically threw Melissa down onto her bed. She was trying to scramble to her feet when he landed beside her, grabbed her shoulders, and began to shake her with such violence that Melissa couldn't get a word out. She was unhurt, but ready to burst with indignation by the time he stopped.

"What was that for?" she yelled at him, itching to retaliate.

"For maligning my character and for lying to me since the moment you got here!" he yelled back. "I'm surprised you even told me your right name, you have such a taste for deception!"

"Well, if you weren't stuck out here in the boonies, you would have recognized the name Melissa McKee from the start," she snarled in return. "I never lied about that."

"Well, that's a relief," Rob said, the blue of his eyes sparking with anger. "At least when we get the marriage license I won't have to worry about finding out someday I don't even know my wife's name."

"Why, you . . ." Melissa sputtered impotently, clenching her fist against the desire to strike out at him. And then the implications of his last words penetrated her brain, and her sputters died immediately.

"Wha-what did you say?" She gulped, hoping she'd heard him right.

"You heard me," he said harshly as he reached for her and pulled her roughly onto his lap. "I'm mad as hell at you, but that doesn't mean I'm going to let you get away. I just needed to express a little of the anger and frustration I've had to deal with since our conversation this morning."

He kissed her then, and it was a brief, almost brutal kiss, which was hardly what Melissa had dreamed about as an adjunct to a proposal of marriage. When she winced, he raised his head, shook her again, and his glare was ferocious.

"Damn it, Melissa, I've been working my butt off trying to get things in order so we could spend some time together once you got that damned story written, and all this time you've been suspecting me of being a first-class bastard. Can you blame me for wanting to give you a good beating?"

Melissa felt torn between guilt over what she'd done, her empathy with how Rob must feel, and a healthy sense of self-preservation for her future should Rob think he was entitled to lay hands on her like this every time she angered him, and she acted to allay all three feelings.

"I'm sorry for what I did," she cried. "And I know how you must feel. And...and please don't shake me anymore," she finished in a pitiful tone.

She wrapped her arms around Rob's neck then and gave him a kiss that drained every vestige of anger from him in five seconds flat. When she finally stopped kissing him, there was a rather dazed look in his blue eyes, but there was also a healthy spark of shame there that Melissa viewed with the relieved expectation that she had effectively short-circuited Rob's tendency to want to express his anger physically.

"I accept your proposal, Rob," she murmured softly as she covered his face with kisses. "But do you love me?" She coaxed him to answer her with another deep kiss that left both of them breathless. "Do you love me, Rob?" she whispered seductively as she moved her lips to his ear. "I love you."

Rob's answer was another kiss, and by the time this one ended, they were somehow lying side by side upon the bed.

"Does that mean you do love me?" Melissa whispered breathlessly as Rob trailed his mouth down her neck to the V of her blouse.

"What do you think?" he growled huskily as he began to unbutton her blouse with impatient fingers.

"Rob, *say* it," Melissa begged, pulling his face up so that she could plead with her eyes as well as her words.

Rob smiled a slow smile, shifted her until she was lying on her back, and half-covered her body with his own. Melissa thought she had never felt anything so exquisite as having his long, lean body against her own eager warmth.

"I love you," he whispered against her lips. He moved his hand to continue unbuttoning her blouse as he sipped at her mouth lovingly. "And I hope you really have had your fill of the big city, because I'm not letting you go back there. We're getting married as soon as possible."

"Lovely," Melissa murmured, accepting his kisses with sweet submission. "We can spend the rest of our lives rehabilitating each other."

Rob chuckled as he pushed her blouse aside and quickly unfastened the front closure of her bra. Melissa gasped when his warm hand closed over her breast and began to stroke the silken skin with skillful, tantalizing precision. "What would you like to rehabilitate about me?" he inquired in silky tones that were beginning to roughen with his arousal. "Don't you like me the way I am?"

"I love the way you are," Melissa groaned, thrusting against him with her hips. "Except for the shakings," she added quickly, wanting her feelings on that score to be perfectly clear.

"You've already convinced me there's a better way to handle you," Rob agreed raggedly. "I don't think you have anything to worry about on that score."

Melissa smiled happily and took his head in her hands to kiss him before she pulled his mouth downward to her breast, eager to dispense with talk and begin their loving at last.

"Beautiful," Rob murmured before his mouth closed over the swollen tip Melissa offered him. She gasped as she felt the warmth and moisture of his tongue begin to stroke her in an erotic massage that spread a trail of heat from her breast to between her thighs.

Rob kept the promise he had made her that when they did make love, it would be something to remember... something not to be engaged in hastily, but savored with leisurely, heavenly delays.

He undressed her slowly, covering every inch of her with kisses that feathered her skin like silk and heated her pulse into a throbbing accompaniment to the beat of desire within her. He then allowed her to undress him, which she did with less expertise than he had shown, but with equal enthusiasm.

They gazed at one another's bodies with bemused wonder for a few moments before they started to explore what they saw with hands and mouths, pronouncing their satisfaction in smothered words of praise and groans of pleasure. Melissa felt a sense of wonder that she was at last discovering what making love was really all about. It was this overwhelming desire to give as much pleasure as she was getting. It was the rough, sweet magic of passionate fire in blue eyes that held her own while warm hands and lips dispensed sensations she had never suspected could be so intense. And finally it was the utter satisfaction of being possessed and filled with the maleness Rob flaunted unabashed and offered without reservation.

"Rob!" She gave a muffled cry when he was fully inside her and she thought she might die of the ecstasy he was giving so completely.

"Yes, sweetheart," he answered, a grating hoarseness almost obscuring the tender love underlying his passion. "This is what I've wanted to give you all along. Take it, darling. Take it and take me... forever...."

She cried out her love when Rob's rhythmic possession became the center of her existence... and then she cried out her pleasure when he took her past the point of no return and into the realm of ecstatic release. Then he followed her into that realm, and she held him with fierce possessiveness as he shuddered against her and filled her body with the proof that she could make this strong and virile man as helpless as a child when he was under the spell of his love for her.

Afterward they lay side by side in the single bed, glued together by the languor of spent passion and the need to hold and touch and glory in the fact that the emotions that had sparked their passion were still there after the passion had receded.

Melissa was kissing the strong column of Rob's neck while he ran a hand down the slender line of her body, smiling his satisfaction at her need to touch him still, when there came a knock on the door that startled both of them into hastily pulling a sheet over their nude bodies.

They had barely covered themselves before the knock came again, and Rob called out impatiently to ask who was there. Instead of answering, Mrs. Price pushed the door open a crack, peeked through it, and when she was satisfied that they were decent, she stepped through the opening as calmly as though she were accustomed to walking in on couples who had just made love so thoroughly. They were unable to move from the bed.

"Mrs. Price!" Rob spoke with annoyance and chagrin.

"Oh, don't be such a prude, Rob," the little woman answered, waving her hand dismissingly. "Don't you think I knew what you had in mind when you carried Melissa up here the way you did?"

Melissa's cheeks were red with embarrassment, and she was choking on something between a laugh and a wail.

"I just want to know when the wedding's going to be so I can get started on arrangements," Mrs. Price went on practically. "I know you aren't going to wait long enough to have it back in Maryland, so I need as much preparation time as possible."

"As soon as we can get a license and a preacher, Mrs. Price," Rob answered firmly.

"And as soon as my parents and grandmother can fly out here," Melissa added, eyeing Rob with a plea that he understood she wanted her family at her wedding.

He frowned. It was obvious he'd forgotten that there were other people to be considered and who might prove to be obstacles in his making Melissa his wife as soon as possible. And then he looked down into Melissa's widened eyes and relented.

"Can they be here by next Saturday?" he asked impatiently.

Melissa nodded vigorously. "If I have to charter a plane to get them here," she promised.

"The kids will want to be in on it, too," Mrs. Price pointed out, which provoked an exasperated sound from Rob, but which he stifled as he faced reality. Mrs. Price eyed him sternly. "I know what you want to do, Rob Redding," she said crisply. "You want to take Melissa away, marry her without an ounce of frills, and ignore the fact that other people have feelings to be considered too. But you're not going to get away with it. Melissa deserves a pretty wedding, and the rest of us deserve to see it."

Melissa hid a smile as Rob looked guiltily uncomfortable for a second before he gave in. "All right...all right!" he capitulated ungraciously. "But a week is all I'm willing to wait. If you can't get everything done by then, the wedding's going off anyway."

Mrs. Price smiled blandly, nodded regally, and started to leave. Then she turned back and eyed Melissa and Rob with fond sternness. "You realize you won't have much time for *that* until after the wedding?" she pointed out, her meaning clear as she nodded her head at the two of them on the bed. "And besides, you've been such a stickler with the kids, you're not setting a very good example, Rob." She ignored his thunderous glare and swept out the door without another word.

Melissa choked on her laughter. "Is she going to do that all the time?" she asked.

Rob smiled with lazy determination, gave Melissa a peck on the cheek, and got up from the bed. "Nope," he drawled with laconic Western succinctness as he began to get dressed. "Just until I get Angela out of her room and moved up here."

Melissa raised her eyebrows inquiringly as she sat up. "Why are you moving her?" she asked.

"Because she has my old room, and it has a double bed and a lock on the door," Rob pronounced with satisfaction.

Melissa giggled, then sobered somewhat. "But Mrs. Price has a point about our being a bad example for the kids," she faltered worriedly.

Rob laughed. In fact, he howled. "Oh, Melissa," he got out, shaking his head disbelievingly. "If I didn't know better, I'd think they were the adults, and you're the youngster. Don't you realize there's not a virgin among that group of sophisticates?"

Melissa shrugged. "Even so," she started to say, but Rob cut her off through the simple expedient of crossing to her, bending, and kissing her senseless. When he raised his head, he inspected the drowsy passion in her eyes with satisfaction.

"Nobody's keeping me out of your bed for the next week, Melissa," he whispered seductively. "Not even you."

She sighed her capitulation and nodded. "Whatever you say, Rob."

He grinned. "Now that's the way I like to hear my future wife talk," he said smugly. "It's nice to have a woman who knows her place."

That brought an immediate glare from Melissa, and Rob laughed and stroked her cheek. "Don't worry, sweetheart," he teased. "I don't plan to punish you very hard if you disobey me."

"You'd better not plan to punish me at all," Melissa retorted. "I learned a thing or two about self-defense when I had to cover pimps and prostitutes and. . . ."

Her voice died as Rob's expression turned to one of grave concern. "What's the matter?" she asked anxiously.

"I don't like to think of you in situations like that," he said, sitting down beside her to cup her innocent-looking face in his hands. "And I might as well tell you now that I couldn't stand to see you do anything like it again. Are you sure you can give up that sort of life, Melissa?"

Melissa looked at him in astonishment. "But I already did give it up, Rob," she told him indignantly. "I got sick of it before I ever met you and that's why I went home to Rockport—for a little peace and quiet."

Rob studied her seriously, as though trying to determine if she really meant what she said. Then he smiled ruefully. "Come to think of it," he said with a wince, "I guess you faced more danger out here than you ever did on the streets of Washington."

Melissa placed her hand on his broad chest and looked at him lovingly. "Don't blame yourself for that, Rob.

I came through it all right.'' And then her look turned sober. "Have you heard how Micah's doing?'' she asked.

Rob nodded. "I called the hospital a little while ago. Micah's going to be all right. . .physically.''

A sad look came into Melissa's lovely eyes before she firmed her mouth. "He's going to be all right otherwise, too, if I have anything to say about it,'' she stated. "It may take a long time, but now that we know the extent of his problems, he'll get the help he needs, and one day we'll be able to make peace with him.''

"I don't know if I could ever trust him around you again, Melissa,'' Rob demurred. "You're too precious to me.''

Melissa's smile was sweetly understanding. "We won't take any risks, Rob,'' she said softly. "But I think we may be an important part of Micah's recovery. And we have a responsibility to him. I don't want to shirk it, do you?''

Rob shrugged his broad shoulders. "My first responsibility is to you, honey. Everything else comes second to that.'' But when he saw her pleading look, he gave in slightly. "We'll see what happens,'' he assured her. And then his eyes focused on her mouth, and the blue in them darkened. He leaned forward for a lingering kiss, and by the time it was over, he was unbuttoning his shirt again.

Melissa leaned back in the bed and stretched her arms over her head, her smile a delightful invitation. The smile disappeared, however, when Rob got to his feet and crossed the room to the door.

"Where are you going?'' she demanded indignantly.

Rob's grin was wicked as he looked at her over his shoulder. "I'm going to prop something against this door,'' he explained. "Right now I'm not in the mood to wait until I can get Angela moved, and I don't want Mrs. Price walking in on us again, either.''

"Oh," Melissa agreed happily, her smile mischievous. "Good thinking."

Rob propped a chair under the doorknob, and as he came back to Melissa's side, he was shrugging his shoulders out of his shirt. "Oh, I have lots of good ideas," he murmured suggestively as he stopped by the side of the bed and started unzipping his jeans, his eyes roaming Melissa from head to foot.

"I'll bet you do," Melissa murmured, inspecting his beautiful physique lovingly. "Why don't you come down here and tell me some of them."

"I'm better at showing," Rob answered with mock seriousness. And then he stepped out of his jeans, came down on the bed with her, and began to demonstrate his meaning so explicitly that Melissa was soon turned into a willing guinea pig for any experiments his facile mind could think up.

Chapter Eighteen

"Who's taking care of your chickens, Gran?" Melissa asked, taking a sip of champagne while she watched the happy celebration of her wedding over the rim of her glass.

"Would you believe me if I said Malcolm Keller volunteered?" Grandma Kate drawled michievously.

Melissa choked on her champagne, and her expression revealed her disbelief. Then she realized her grandmother was teasing. "No, I wouldn't," she declared on a giggle.

"I always said you were a smart girl," Kate nodded, smiling, her clear eyes sweeping the ranch and the surrounding countryside speculatively. "Delia's doing it," she said, finally answering Melissa's original question, but her tone was absent.

"But Delia hates those chickens!" Melissa exclaimed.

"But she loves you," Grandma Kate countered. "And she'd do anything to see you married off at last."

Melissa looked indignant for a second, but then her expression cleared as she remembered someone who hadn't been anxious to see her married off. She had called her old boss in Washington, Thurman Wilcox, to invite him to the wedding and to advise him he'd better get a permanent replacement for her, and his reaction had been interesting to say the least. It had been worse than Malcolm Keller's, as a matter of fact, Melissa thought happily.

Rob caught her eye then and winked at her. He looked resplendent in a new blue suit, his hair and mustache neatly trimmed, and his eyes glittering with anticipation of his wedding night. Melissa was pleased that he was still looking forward to it, since he had already made the most of the week preceding the wedding. But then she was looking forward to it, too, she realized as she winked at Rob.

"Isn't he handsome?" She sighed contentedly.

Grandma Kate looked puzzled for a moment before she took Melissa's meaning. "Oh," she said absently. "Yes, he is, Melissa. You chose very wisely, I must say."

"I'm not sure I had any choice," Melissa said simply. "I was swept off my feet." Literally, she added to herself with an inner smile.

She looked over at her grandmother when Kate didn't reply and saw that she was still scanning the horizon with that speculative look in her eyes.

"I'm thinking this land would hold a lot of chickens," Kate declared dreamily, making Melissa's eyes widen into astonishment.

"But, Gran," she protested, "what about your house? And you've lived in Rockport all your life!"

Kate looked at her with a disapproving frown. "It's never too late to change, Melissa," she said sternly. "And it wouldn't be as though I were invading your privacy. You've already got enough people living here to populate a small town!"

Melissa shook her head in disbelief. "Are you serious, Gran?"

"Never more so," Kate declared emphatically. "I've been stagnating too long. I think it's about time I had a little adventure in my life."

Melissa saw that Parker was heading in their direction with a look in his brown eyes Melissa recognized, though it was somewhat disconcerting to see it in a man his age. She turned her head to look at her grandmother and was astonished to see that Kate was preening herself like a young girl about to be called on by her first date.

"Oh," Melissa breathed, beginning to understand her grandmother's sudden interest in pulling up roots and making a new start. "I see..." Trying her best to stifle her laughter, Melissa started to move away. "I think Rob wants me," she murmured, but she was certain her grandmother didn't hear a word she said. When she reached Rob's side, he caught her around the waist and bent to give her a thorough kiss, which Melissa accepted joyfully.

"Enjoying your wedding?" he whispered, his voice softly caressing.

"Enormously," Melissa sighed. "But I'd love to be alone with my husband," she added suggestively.

Rob raised an eyebrow and looked toward the house, but there were people streaming in and out of the door. "That might be a little hard to arrange for a while," he said, his tone frustrated.

"Then how about a walk?" Melissa suggested.

Rob put down his glass of champagne and swept her away. "Sounds great," he teased. "I seem to remember a certain willow tree that affords more privacy than our bedroom would right now."

Before they got to the willow tree, however, they detoured to the corral, where Fred and several other horses were milling about. Fred came to the railing to nuzzle Melissa, making her laugh, and she moaned as she saw that he had left a slobbering stain on the bosom of her beautiful new pale blue wedding dress.

"Serves you right," Rob laughed as he took out his handkerchief to try to repair the damage. "That horse always gets you in trouble."

"No, he doesn't," Melissa defended Fred stoutly, though she was glaring at her beloved horse herself for his atrocious manners. "He saved my life, remember?"

"I'll never forget," Rob said more seriously, turning Melissa into his arms and gazing down at her lovingly.

Melissa kissed him, then held his beloved face in her hands. "How soon do you think we can have our wedding night in peace?" she whispered.

"I'm beginning to think we're never going to have any peace with the number of people on this ranch," he grumbled. "I guess I'm going to have to take you away for a while after this bunch of kids graduates and before another one arrives in order to have you all to myself."

That settled something that had been on Melissa's mind, and her eyes lightened into an expression of relief. "You mean you've definitely decided to continue that sort of work?" she asked eagerly.

Rob shrugged. "I guess I'm hooked," he admitted, but then he frowned sternly. "But we're going to take time for ourselves as well, Melissa," he said, his tone an order. "It's easy to get burned out when you do this sort of thing without a break, as you ought to know. We'll take one bunch a year and the rest of the time belongs to us. I want some kids of my own and plenty of time with them and with you."

"Sounds wonderful," Melissa agreed happily. "You aren't going to get any arguments from me." But then she remembered her conversation with her grandmother, and she looked up at Rob teasingly. "But even if we don't have kids all year, I'm afraid we're not going to get much privacy." And then she explained about Kate and Parker. To her relief, Rob merely laughed, and it was clear he didn't mind in the least.

"Maybe I'd better put *two* locks on our bedroom door," he teased back as he turned her toward the willow tree and started walking her in that direction. "Otherwise, we're going to have to put a bed under this tree."

After they'd slipped inside the sheltering branches, Rob lost no time in pulling Melissa into his arms and kissing her with all the fervor she could hope for from a new husband, but when he'd released her mouth to run his lips caressingly down her neck, Melissa came out of her slumberous state of arousal momentarily, reacting to their surroundings as she remembered the last time they'd made love under this tree.

"Rob," she murmured, pulling back a little so that he had to raise his head. The look in his eyes was frustrated at having to stop what he was doing, but his tone was tender as he answered.

"What is it, sweetheart?"

"When we were out here that other time and Micah came calling for you and interrupted us, what was it he wanted?" she asked curiously.

Rob looked even more frustrated at having their pleasant interlude interrupted again in connection with Micah, but after a moment he answered, though his reply was disappointing.

"Micah had a stomachache that night, Melissa," he said impatiently. "All he wanted was some coddling. I gave him some antacid, talked to him a few moments, then rushed back here to find you gone."

Melissa felt disgruntled that the mystery had turned out to be so tame. "Is that all?" she asked disgustedly.

"That's all," Rob said firmly as he pulled her closer again. "Now, can we forget Micah for a while and concentrate on us?"

"In just a second, darling," Melissa answered absently, failing to note the growing exasperation in Rob's eyes. "Did Parker tell you that he had suspected for some time that Micah's feelings for you were...ah... unhealthy?"

"Yes, he told me," Rob gritted. "I just wish he'd told me a long time before he did. He left it a little late."

"Well, he wasn't sure," Melissa defended Parker gently, "and he hoped it wasn't true. You can't blame him for not wanting to bring something like that up if there was any chance he was mistaken, can you? I felt the same way when I began to suspect."

"I can blame anybody I want to, including you, when the end result was that I almost lost you," Rob said firmly. But then he relented as Melissa stared soulfully up at him. "But now that I've got you back, with my wedding ring on your finger and a little privacy for the first time all day, I'm willing to let bygones be by-gones...*if*"—he put a finger over Melissa's mouth as she started to say something—"you will forget about Micah for a few minutes and give your undivided attention to your husband."

Melissa's answering smile was brilliant as she wrapped her arms around Rob's neck. "Now, there's a bargain I can live with," she informed him mischievous-ly.

"That's not the only bargain you're getting out of this marriage, Mrs. Redding," Rob murmured seduc-tively, pleased by the way Melissa was snuggling up to him.

"Oh?" she inquired languidly between the kisses she was bestowing on his bronzed throat. "What else do I get?"

"A slightly used horse, a suitor for your grand-mother—not to mention space for all those chickens she wants to land on me," he added in a tone of mock suf-fering, "and the secret of my heart."

Melissa smiled into Rob's eyes, her own luminous with love. "And what is the secret of your heart?" she asked softly.

Rob's returning look was devilishly mischievous. "That from the first moment I saw you, I suspected you had more on your mind than writing some sappy little story about how wonderful I was and what I was accom-plishing out here."

Melissa drew back and eyed him suspiciously. "That can't be true, Rob!" she chided, suspecting him of putting her on. "If you'd known anything, you'd have tossed me out on my ear that first night."

Rob shook his head, his smile tender. "Honey, after one look at you and especially after I took you in my arms and kissed you that first time, I didn't give a damn what you wanted from me. I was ready to do anything to keep you around—permanently."

Melissa still regarded him with suspicion, and her tone was half pleased, half disgruntled when she answered. "You couldn't have proved it by me," she retorted amiably. "Most female reporters I know would have run for cover after being subjected to the fiendish tortures you devised. If I'd been asked, I'd have said you were trying to get rid of me, not keep me around."

"Ah, but that's the biggest secret of all," Rob teased solemnly. "I figured if you stuck to it, you were as hooked as I was. And you did...and you are. Aren't you?"

Melissa hesitated, but at the commanding look in Rob's eyes, she gave in with good grace. "I was...and I am, Mr. Redding," she admitted. And then she wriggled closer to him. "But I'm about to change my mind if you don't take your own advice to heart and stop talking about the past. We've got a lot of lost time to make up for, remember?"

"I remember, sweetheart," Rob said softly, bending his head to tease her mouth with his lips. "And I haven't got another word to say...except I love you, Mrs. Redding...with all my heart. There's no secret about that anymore."

Melissa smiled and nibbled his encroaching lips hungrily. "And I love you, Rob," she breathed unsteadily. "I want to shout it to the world."

"Not now, darling," Rob objected, softly firm. "Right now we've got better things to do with our mouths. Later you can put an ad in the paper if you want to."

"Titled 'Investigative Reporter Subverted by Montana Rancher'?" Melissa teased shakily, her control slipping as Rob's hands began doing a little investigating of their own.

"Make that *'seduced,'* honey," Rob said huskily against her throat. "If you're going to report, do it accurately."

But by then reporting was the last thing Melissa had on her mind. She was much too involved in living and loving to pay attention to semantics...or to be an impartial observer.

Harlequin Stationery Offer

Personalized Rainbow Memo Pads for you or a friend

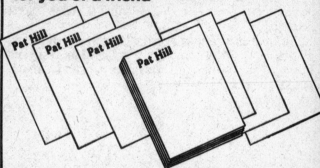

Picture your name in bold type at the top of these attractive rainbow memo pads. Each 4¼" x 5½" pad contains 150 rainbow sheets—yellow, pink, gold, blue, buff and white—enough to last you through months of memos. Handy to have at home or office.

Just clip out three proofs of purchase (coupon below) from an August or September release of Harlequin Romance, Harlequin Presents, Harlequin Superromance, Harlequin American Romance, Harlequin Temptation or Harlequin Intrigue and add $4.95 (includes shipping and handling), and we'll send you *two* of these attractive memo pads imprinted with your name.

WIN A CRUISE TO ROMANCE!
Enter the Harlequin Intrigue™ Sweepstakes.

Here's your chance to win a trip-for-two to the romantic Caribbean. A week of relaxing, sun-filled days and moonlit nights aboard the luxurious Cunard *Countess*.

And all you have to do is write in the name of the new Harlequin®* series in the top right-hand corner above. It's that easy! Be sure and send your entry before October 31, 1984.

No purchase necessary. Void where prohibited. Incomplete and incorrect entries still valid for drawing. See reverse for official rules.

SEND ENTRIES TO:

IN U.S.: Harlequin Cruise to Romance Sweepstakes, Suite 3395, 175 Fifth Avenue, New York, NY 10010

IN CANADA: Harlequin Cruise to Romance Sweepstakes, Suite 191, 238 Davenport Road, Toronto, Ontario M5R 1J6

NAME_____

ADDRESS_____

CITY_____STATE/PROV._____

ZIP/POSTAL CODE_____PHONE_____

INT-SW-2

Harlequin Cruise to Romance Sweepstakes
OFFICIAL RULES   NO PURCHASE NECESSARY

1. The Harlequin Cruise to Romance Sweepstakes is open to all residents of Canada (with the exception of the Province of Quebec) and the United States 18 years or older at the time of entry. Employees and their families of Harlequin Enterprises Limited, their affiliated companies, advertising/promotion agencies and RONALD SMILEY INC. also excluded.

2. To enter, complete the Official Entry form. It is not necessary to answer the questions on the entry to qualify. You may write the name of the new Harlequin series, Harlequin Intrigue, on a separate 3″ x 5″ piece of paper along with your full name and address, or on the entry form. Canadian residents mail each entry, one only to an envelope to: Harlequin Cruise to Romance Sweepstakes, Suite 191, 238 Davenport Road, Toronto, Ontario M5R 1J6. United States residents mail each entry, one to an envelope to: Harlequin Cruise to Romance Sweepstakes, Suite 3395, 175 Fifth Avenue, New York, NY 10010. All entries from Canada and the United States must be postmarked by the sweepstakes closing date of October 31, 1984, to be eligible. Not responsible for late, lost or misdirected mail.

3. Winners will be selected within 90 days after closing date in random drawings from among all valid Canadian and United States entries received by RONALD SMILEY INC., an independent judging organization whose decisions are final. Canadian residents whose entry may be randomly drawn must answer correctly a time-limited arithmetical skill-testing question in order to win the related prize. Major prize winner will be notified by registered mail and will be required to submit an Affidavit of Compliance within 14 days of notification. In the event of non-compliance or if any prize notifications are returned to Harlequin Enterprises Limited or Ronald Smiley Inc., alternate winner will be randomly selected and notified. Winner may be asked to use their name and photo at no additional compensation. Odds of winning depend on the number of all valid Canadian and United States entries received. No substitution, duplication or cash redemption of prizes. Any applicable taxes are the winner's responsibility. This offer will appear prior to closing date of October 31, 1984 in Harlequin Reader Service mailings, the August 1984 issues of *The Globe, People, National Examiner,* the September 1984 issues of *Good Housekeeping* and *Woman's Day,* and at participating retailers.

4. The following are the prizes to be awarded. One 7-day Cunard Caribbean Cruise for Two scheduled to depart and return to San Juan, Puerto Rico. Winner and guest will be provided round trip coach airline tickets from winner's nearest applicable airport to San Juan, Puerto Rico. Cruise prize includes 1 cabin for two and meals as served aboard. Cruise is scheduled to visit Tortola, Nevis, St. Kitts, Guadeloupe, St. Lucia, St. Maarten, St. Thomas and St. John. The cruise itinerary may be changed by cruise line. A cruise of same substance may be substituted by sponsor. Port taxes and any other expenses incurred by the winner and guest on the cruise boat or land is their responsibility. Cruise must be taken by June 30, 1985, subject to available dates. The approximate retail value of First Prize in United States dollars is $4,000/Canadian dollars is $4,900.00.

   100 Second Prizes will be awarded of a one-year subscription each to the Harlequin Reader Service for 24 Harlequin Intrigue publications. The approximate retail value of each Second Prize in United States dollars is $54.00/Canadian dollars is $60.00.

5. To receive a First Prize winner's list Canadian residents send a stamped, self-addressed envelope to: Harlequin Cruise to Romance Winner's List, Suite 323, 238 Davenport Road, Toronto, Ontario M5R 1J6. United States residents send a self-addressed, stamped envelope to: Harlequin Cruise to Romance Winner's List, Suite 3115, 175 Fifth Avenue, New York, NY 10010. Residents of Ohio only need not apply return postage. All requests must be postmarked by October 31, 1984, for response.

This sweepstakes offer in Canada is subject to all Federal, Provincial and Municipal laws and regulations and is void in the Province of Quebec and wherever prohibited by law. This offer in the United States is subject to all Federal, State and local laws and regulations and void wherever prohibited by law.

*Trademark of Harlequin Enterprises Limited.